BADLANDS

Book 2 of the *Savage Land* Trilogy

By Jacqui Murray

From the *Man vs. Nature* Series

Other Books by Jacqui Murray

Dawn of Humanity Trilogy
Born in a Treacherous Time (Book 1)
Laws of Nature (Book 2)
Natural Selection (Book 3)

Crossroads Trilogy
Survival of the Fittest (Book 1)
The Quest for Home (Book 2)
Against All Odds (Book 3)

The Savage Land Trilogy
Endangered Species (Book 1)
Badlands (This book)
Balance of Nature (Book 3)

Rowe-Delamagente Series
To Hunt a Sub
Twenty-four Days
Book 3 (forthcoming)

Non-fiction
Building a Midshipman: How to Crack the USNA Application

Praise for *Man vs. Nature*

The stakes are high, danger is ever present and struggle for survival is real. Yu'ung is a character that is easy to love. Her intentions and desires are honorable with the safety of her tribe first and foremost in her thoughts. She's strong and capable. But most of all, the powerful, compelling story itself drew me in and didn't let go. If you are up for an adventure that will have you holding your breath at times, this book is for you! —Amazon Reader

Once again, author and master of prehistoric fiction Jacqui Murray took me on a thrilling journey back in time with her recent book, Endangered Species. *Murray transports readers to 75,000 years ago, where Neanderthals (the People) and Homo Sapiens (the Tall Ones) face constant threats and survival challenges.* —Amazon Reader

Move over Jean Auel (author of Clan of the Cave Bear*) for Jacqui Murray. I went to bed right after dinner last night because I had to finish this book and would have stayed up all night to do it. What a fabulous read.* —Amazon Reader

I've traveled back through time with Murray's prehistoric fiction, starting 1.8 million years ago with her Dawn of Humanity trilogy, and then advancing to 850,000 years ago with her Crossroads trilogy. This book is the first in The Savage Land trilogy, bumping readers up to modern times, well almost modern—only 75,000 years ago! Murray's extensive research into the lives of the Neanderthals is evident in this book, which lays the groundwork for the rest of the trilogy. The research is fascinating, and something that I highly appreciate. The attention given to the daily lives of the People, including their challenges and ever-present dangers, does make this story a slow burn until near the end when the main plot literally "explodes" in the form of a volcano, forcing the People and Tall Ones to begin a perilous migration that, I expect, is the focus of the next two books. —Amazon Reader

What a treat to read a fiction work that goes so far back into prehistory. I enjoy reading prehistoric fiction in general, but this is a rare gem. The author successfully combines facts with imagination to create a believable story about our ancient ancestors. We peek into a distant mirror at a people who reflect our own hopes, emotions, and fears. —Amazon Reader

Born in a Treacherous Time *is a brilliantly researched book with an interesting and realistic story-line. I have read all Jean Auel's books and enjoyed them but I found the first book,* Clan of the Cave Bear, *to be the best by far. Why you ask? Because it was realistic. I appreciate that in a historical book of this nature. I loved this about* Born in a Treacherous Time. *The story and interaction between the various group members rang true to me. —Amazon* Reader

Thanks to Murray's book Born in a Treacherous Time, *I view the world and the creatures within it (including humans) with new eyes. —Amazon* Reader

I loved this book even more than the first in Jacqui Murray's Dawn of Humanity *trilogy. This new chapter in the story of Lucy and her eclectic little tribe picks up straight after the first left off and the reader is swept back to the prehistoric past where life is an ongoing set of challenges to be faced in the search for food and water, shelter, and safety. —Amazon* Reader

I have always been fascinated by what it was like to live in bygone eras. This book so satisfies this, as well as telling a good story. —Amazon Reader

I've waited I think a year for this book! I loved it so much and look forward to more of Lucy's adventures. —Amazon Reader

I'm always looking for books about primitive man. Loved the way she had the different species living together and interacting And of course, I fell in love with most of the characters. She writes very descriptive but has done her research. If you are interested in early man, this book is for you. Can't wait for book 3 ——Amazon Reader

Murray's novels are always filled with a plethora of facts about prehistoric man. What they ate. How they hunted, communicated, and survived. I can't begin to fathom the amount of time that goes into researching the worlds she creates. What strikes me the most about her stories is how people—and animals—from different cultures learn to live together. Come together. And form a pack. It's a wonderful lesson in today's tempestuous times. —Amazon Reader

Table of Contents

Characters

The People—Neanderthals

B'o—Yu'ung's hunt partner
Dhar—Yu'ung's father
Ese—B'o's pairmate
Jhat—female tribemember
Kriina (aka Aynoh)—Yu'ung's mother
Laak—future Lead warrior
Old One—revered tribal Elder; Aynoh's father
Ruk—Jhat's child
Yota—Elder, Old One's friend
Yu'ung—the People's Alpha

The Tall Ones (Chosen)—*Homo sapiens*

Bhidid—of Fierce's group
Braanroorv—of Fierce's group
Crevkukk—of Fierce's group
Eknilk—of Fierce's group
Fierce—Leader of Tall Ones
Grub—of Fierce's group
Qad—of Fierce's group and Grub's brother
Seer—a spiritual guide for Fierce's tribe, a proto-shaman

The Mountain People Clan—Denisovans

Ad
Naa

Neanderthals not of the People

Book 3

Ant—future Lead Scout
Dag and Jad—Ant's parents
Druyl—died trying to kill Kazeb before Book 3
Flint—survived the illness that claimed much of Kazeb's tribe
Gik— survived the illness that claimed much of Kazeb's tribe

Kazeb—co-Alpha with his brother Turk; aka Liis
Mook—a member of Kazeb's former tribe
Turk—co-Alpha with his brother Kazeb

The Ones—Mixed Tribe of *Homo sapiens* and Neanderthals

Asvulk—Kruutud's pairmate; mixed Tall One and the People
Gevol
Kruutud—band Leader—a Tall One
Vokar

The Kith Primitives—*Homo erectus*

Ak—Grg's pairmate
Dag—Grg's hunt partner
Grg—Leader
Toc—youngster
Zug—male child

The Canis Pack—proto-wolves

Blaze
Ocha
Ragged Ear
Urzp
White Streak

Others

Bruurv—Tall One Leader of the tribe that captured Yu'ung
Jvelk—mixed Tall One and People
Ronor—Jvelk's father; a Tall One
Shanadar—Neanderthal; aka Jun
Wik—Neanderthal
Xad—Neanderthal
Xhosa—spiritual advisor to Shanadar and Yu'ung

Glossary of Terms

Alpha	head of the Neanderthal tribe, what the Tall Ones call *Leader*
Angry Mountain	any volcanic eruption; in this case, Mt. Toba
Backtrail	path traveled to return to wherever the tribe or member came from
Big Rock	Gibraltar
Cudgel	a short, heavy stick; what the Tall Ones call a club
Dominant side	the right side; since many were right-handed, this was the dominant side
Extreme sight	when images and landmarks blurred to others appears clear
Forward path	path to a destination
Haft	glue a stone tip to a shaft to create a spear
Homebase	main Upright camp; where they sleep and eat after hunting and foraging
Lead Warrior	a Tall One term meaning the primary male skilled to defend the tribe
Leader	head of a Tall One band, what the People call *Alpha*
Mate	coupling; a casual activity, doesn't indicate a permanent relationship
Nest	where they sleep at night
Pack	the Canis tribe
Pairmate	lifelong partner
Predult	younger than a subadult
Primitive	Upright physiologically inferior to other species; often refers to Homo erectus in this trilogy
Shoreless sea	the Mediterranean; could also be the Pacific or Atlantic Ocean
Spirits	pre-cursor to gods, God; a supernatural entity
Strong side	the right side; since many were right-handed, this was the dominant side
Tall Ones	Homo sapiens; *Fierce's* band called themselves the Chosen
Upright	Any animal who walks on two legs. This included Primitives (Homo erectus), Neanderthals, Tall Ones (Homo sapiens).

| *Weak side* | *not the dominant side (they had no terms for "right" or "left")* |

Author's Non-fiction Introduction

Savage Land delves into a time when man almost became extinct. Scientists disagree why this happened, but DNA evidence confirms that if not for equal measures of luck and inexplicable circumstances, Nature would have beaten us. Drama, intrigue, mystery, heroes, and miracles saved us. We conquered fire, sewed clothes, applied chemistry to create glue and preserve food, and invented advanced weaponry. This was also a time when our ancestors demonstrated a reverence for the dead, belief in superior beings, and an appreciation of art, music, and self-adornment.

How Neanderthals endured the world's physical challenges is as exciting as most thrillers. The proof of their brilliance is that thirty percent of the Neanderthal genome lives on in us, not in one individual but throughout our species. That means their traits suit Nature's primary imperative—survival—even today. They reigned as the planet's apex predators until the arrival of *Homo sapiens*.

Enjoy this fictionalized account of your ancestors' existence. The proto-wolves Ump, White Streak, Ocha, and Ragged Ear are indeed spirits. I use them to introduce the seeds of spiritual belief. Their stories begin in earlier books.

The *Savage Land* trilogy is based on facts. Where evidence is unavailable, my conclusions are drawn from the opinions of scientists who studied Neanderthals. Check the *Bibliography* for names.

Each book in the *Savage Land* trilogy is a stand-alone story while building on prior events.

- *Endangered Species (Book 1)—the worst volcanic eruption man ever lived through forced the People to abandon their homes.*
- *Badland (Book 2)—the People and the Chosen leave the Altai Mountains to migrate beyond what we call the Mediterranean Sea.*
- *Balance of Nature (Book 3)— a tribe haunted by the past. Lies that threaten a new beginning. A reason to find the truth.*

Introduction

Nature warned them to leave, but they instead tore harder into her rich soil with their digging sticks. In the past, to stop the bad behavior of other life forms before these beings arrived, Nature released fire and magma into the sky, burned them as they fled and starved those who refused to leave. Nature felt no pity. The goal was to teach lessons they wouldn't forget. Always it worked.

But not with these who walked upright and trusted intuition over instinct. They didn't understand the balance of life, that plants, trees, rocks, animals, caves were all interconnected, part of a collective whole. To these who walked upright, nothing mattered except themselves and their needs. The longer they existed, the wider they spread and the more toxic they became to everything she valued. By the time Nature realized the depth of their travesties, their odd behaviors and messy habits had destroyed much of her beautiful land with no sign of slowing.

They must own the consequences. I will stop them in a way they understand.

Part 1

The Departure

Chapter 1

75,000 years ago
Modern day Altai Mountains, Siberia

Yu'ung's legs churned, arms pumped, throat straining to draw in air. Her red hair hung in damp sweaty ropes on her neck and shoulders. After narrowly escaping the cave-in and then Hyaena's attack, time had run out. B'o was supposed to leave with or without her when Sun reached a particular spot overhead. That point had passed and now, the maelstrom was upon them. She must get to her tribe.

Running never tired her, no matter how long or far. Today was different. Driven by desperation and worry for those who relied on her, she ran too hard and slammed up against her limit.

She stumbled to a stop and bent forward, chest heaving, sucking in one mouthful of air after another. The blue-eyed Canis–the massive Ump with his dark coat, the smaller White Streak with the light colored stripe cutting her black fur from one side of her forehead to the other, and the older Ragged Ear–circled back to her, huffing and prancing. Somehow, they knew time was short. Shanadar, who seemed to be their pack leader, wasn't even winded. He waited, patient but anxious.

She muttered, "The smoke–it's much worse."

Yu'ung had departed her homebase before Sun woke. She had gone there to tell the Tall One Fierce that the People would join him. The air tasted of ash then, but lightly. By the time she reached where Fierce and his Tall One band should have been, the small flakes had grown chokingly large. The Tall Ones–wisely–were gone, but her mother, Kriina, now Fierce's pairmate, left a message in the tunnel telling Yu'ung their destination and of a possible new homebase for the People.

It was there Yu'ung would lead the People.

"I'm ready, Shanadar," and she took off again.

She expected the Angry Mountain's destruction to clear closer to her homebase, but instead, cinders and smoke thickened and the air dimmed to a dingy gray. Uprooted trees blocked the usual passages forcing her to divert onto new, untried trails. Pockets of flames burned without pause on all sides. The grassland and forests that fed the People were almost wiped out.

It took longer than Yu'ung expected before she, Shanadar, and the Canis reached the outer boundaries of the People's camp.

As she skimmed the area for B'o, her hunt partner, Shanadar said, "They will ask."

They would. Shanadar was unusual. Yes, he displayed the People's stocky build, shorter limbs, and absent chin, but his body was bony in all the wrong places and his hair secured into an Equiis tail. Those were unusual but so was much about life anymore. What would catch their attention more than any of that was his face, striped in the way of Fierce's Tall Ones.

"I will explain how you saved my life, and that you will help us reach our destination."

That was easier to believe than the truth, that the Primitive Xhosa who visits my dreams sent Shanadar and his Canis to take the People where Nature can't kill us.

She took in the distant sea of frantic faces. She saw relief, at her arrival overshadowed by terror, and what should have been well-practiced preparation for an orderly migration—one so often performed that the People needed no guidance—was nothing short of bedlam.

What is wrong?

The mayhem was not caused by her late return. Whatever caused the chaos occurred after they loaded up their shoulder sacks, collected their spears and walking sticks, and foraged travel food.

They were prepared to leave. B'o told them to wait. What happened?

"B'o!" She shouted to an older male sprinting toward her. He waved and then slowed when his gaze found Shanadar.

He wonders about a stranger. She jerked her gaze over the clearing. *Where are the Canis?*

She clasped her hands over her stomach, telling him she would explain later, and shouted, "Where's Old One?"

"Coming!"

Despite her youth, the People, Yu'ung's tribe, selected her Alpha. Their trust in her leadership was based equally on her cleverness, B'o's reluctance to lead, and Old One's unwavering support. The tribe selected a leader only in trying times. Mountain's anger, the loss of their healer, and the search for a new homeland certainly qualified. All agreed that B'o and Old One's involvement would offset her inexperience.

"B'o. Mountain's anger is worse close to the Tall Ones' former camp. We must choose a different route."

B'o fidgeted, looking no more relieved than when she first arrived. *I'll reassure him.*

"But we can take the route Old One remembers from his youth. It is the same as what Shanadar suggests." She poked her lower lip toward the tall immobile male with the striped face and the Equiis tail. "And where the Tall Ones go."

Someone called B'o's name. He held a hand up and returned his attention to Yu'ung.

"According to Kriina and the message she left for me, we will find her and Fierce along our forward path."

B'o's face darkened. "Shanadar.... We don't know him...." B'o stared at Shanadar as he spoke, eyes probing, body quivering with nervous energy.

Ese called B'o which he didn't even acknowledge.

Yu'ung's gaze jumped from Ese to B'o. *Something is going on.*

She swiped a hand in the air, high enough for Ese to see. "Shanadar is a friend who can help us. I will explain later after *you* explain what happened since I left this morning."

B'o's shoulders dropped. His unequaled hunting successes should have given him confidence leading, but when Old One asked him to be Alpha, he deferred to the Elder. His reasoning was good. Old One served in the past, faultlessly guiding the group through treachery few tribes survived as well as the People. Even now, with his infirmities and inability to contribute to many of the tribe's tasks, he was well respected.

Old One suggested a better alternative. The new adult Yu'ung's unusual skills suited leadership well. One example was her skill with the Tall One weapon. Many hunters suffered their worst injuries closing on prey for a spear thrust. Yu'ung flung her Tall One lance from far away to avoid deadly hooves, fangs, and horns while still causing mortal damage to the prey. She was so successful in this way, she had never been injured on a hunt.

Next, she possessed what Old One called extreme sight. Images and landmarks a blur to most were clear to her. Where other hunters saw a herd grazing in the distance, she picked out the old and injured that the tribe should focus on.

The last, in the end, was the decisive factor. No one else wanted the job.

"What is going on, B'o? Sacks are packed, but no one is ready."

B'o smiled awkwardly. "This male you bring into our tribe like we should trust him. It isn't our way," but froze on whatever was at Yu'ung's side.

The Canis have shown up.

"This is Shanadar's pack—Ump, White Streak, Ragged Ear—"

She stopped. There was a new pawed-and-clawed creature, this one smaller, black with a tan muzzle, also blue-eyed.

Shanadar filled in. "That is Ocha."

Ocha's tail swayed, eyes on Yu'ung, snout open and panting.

"Ocha." It was more whisper than confirmation.

"B'o!" Ese again. "We're in trouble!"

This time, Yu'ung heard what Ese didn't say. A sharp spike went through her head and a shiver down her spine as she scanned the muddled consortium around Ese, the scattering of rocks, boulders, and dirt clods. Yu'ung's temple twitched and then exploded with what she didn't see.

"Where is Old One?"

Ocha bumped her leg and turned toward the edge as Shanadar poked his lips to the same spot. B'o's mouth opened and shut, finally said, "It's not Old One. Well, not just him."

B'o's pale face, the muscles creating tight ropes down the sides of his neck said the rest.

He wants to talk privately.

But there wasn't time for that. "Shanadar concerns you. Old One concerns me more."

B'o ran a hand down his face to clean off the ash. "There's more. Listen to me!"

He paced nervously then shifted from one foot to the other, glancing sideways at Shanadar.

"I am used to hunting prey and avoiding enemies. Is this one you call Shanadar our kind? Or one of the nob-less Uprights." He touched under his lip, the location of the Tall One's round bump, its purpose not even the Tall Ones could explain.

"He's like us." Yu'ung pointed to Shanadar's bulbous nose, wide torso, and powerful legs–all characteristic of the People.

"Why does he paint himself with Fierce's stripes and secure his hair in a cord?"

Shanadar fingered the nub behind his head. "Does One-called-Fierce wear a feather in it?"

Now B'o was confused. "No, well, I'm not sure. Does it matter?"

Shanadar shrugged. "No. To answer your question, I don't know why except we both feel it's right."

He looked at Yu'ung out of the corner of his eye, words unnecessary.

Xhosa.

Yu'ung gritted her teeth, choking on the taste of burnt blood from the carcasses that littered the landscape.

Shanadar faced B'o, unconcerned. "I've been told I am odd. We can discuss this later, in depth, but what's important now is what will soon demolish us. Do you not sense it?"

B'o's eyes darted over the area, his face stricken. Shouts grew behind him.

"B'o, if not Old One, what's wrong?"

"Before I tell you what only tribe members should know, Shanadar must convince me he is to be trusted." He crossed his arms over his chest and snarled, "Go ahead."

Yu'ung's head pounded. They didn't have time to waste, and then, almost against her will, she clamped her jaw shut and waited. If Xhosa sent Shanadar, he would know how to explain.

Shanadar plucked a short bone and a smooth pebble from his satchel and ran his thumbs over both.

"You haven't told him, Yu'ung, so I won't either."

B'o jerked. "Told me what?"

Yu'ung clenched her fists. "About Xhosa."

B'o growled. Ocha's hackles stiffened, but smoothed at Shanadar's touch.

B'o asked Yu'ung, "Who is this Xhosa? A Tall One?" He forced himself to calm and Yu'ung appreciated his effort.

Rather than discussing the vision, she replied simply, "No. A friend of Shanadar's and mine."

"A friend? You have no friends other than us." When Yu'ung didn't respond, B'o addressed Shanadar. "Why do you carry a bone?"

"It is a flute. I will play for you later."

He opened his other hand to reveal a round stone with a face etched onto its surface. "This is my talisman. Both are conversations for another day. Right now, you have something to do and then we must leave before we can't."

"B'o!" *Ese.* "They need help!"

If B'o intended to argue, his pairmate's voice stopped him. That's when Yu'ung knew.

She jerked side to side, searching. Smoke and ash shrouded everything in a dirty mist. "Where are the rest of the People?"

"In the cave."

Her stomach knotted as she spun around, but the cave was gone, in its place, a cloud of dust and dirt.

Chapter 2

"B'o!" Ese again, picking her way toward them with Jhat, another of the tribe's adult females.

Yu'ung looked at Jhat's red face and then B'o, gaze bouncing from Shanadar to the Canis, finally settling on Yu'ung.

"The cave collapsed? They're trapped?"

She started to snap, ask why those entombed didn't use the rear entrance, but B'o's mouth hung open and he crossed and recrossed his arms, as upset as she'd ever seen him.

This is why he didn't want to be Alpha.

The knots in her stomach tightened. "What happened?"

His gaze skittered over Shanadar and back to Yu'ung. "The first collapse we could have dealt with...."

A tingle passed through her body. "First?"

B'o's face paled. "Yes. The earth-shaking blocked the mouth. They were trapped inside. They said no injuries, but the back access, too, had collapsed so they couldn't escape. We started digging, not worried because the opening in the ceiling provided sufficient fresh air. We could also drop food and water in while we dug them out. Then...."

"Then?"

"Another earth-shake destroyed the vent and ignited a fire.... The cavern filled with smoke. We're trying to free them, but when you arrived ... I didn't know if ... Shanadar ... and the Canis ... were trouble … thought it best to not let you know, I mean, if they were enemies and saw our weakness….”

Yu'ung stopped listening. She'd heard everything important and now raced to the blocked entrance and the group of tribe members frantically digging with their hands, trying to move a mountain before everyone inside suffocated. From inside came wet coughs.

Yu'ung examined the rubble, mostly a dense pile of rocks that would take longer to move than those inside had air, but there was one rock—a huge inflexible boulder.

If we can move that….

“B'o! Shanadar! Help me!”

They immediately joined her as did Laak, a subadult anointed by Fierce to be the People's Lead Warrior, a position he took seriously. They finally dislodged the gargantuan rock and rolled it away. Dark clouds flooded the clearing.

Can anyone breathe in there?

She'd find out, and raced in. Her eyes watered, dowsing her cheeks, forcing her to squint. The hot, thick air made breathing almost impossible. She shielded her mouth with a hide, but it barely helped. A muffled scream erupted somewhere ahead. B'o and Laak elbowed past, but were soon stalled by debilitating hacks. Yu'ung crouched low to gulp in fresher air and waddled forward. In no time, tears blurred her vision and heat threatened to overwhelm her.

“Yu'ung!”

Shanadar's voice though all she saw behind her was a smudge of movement. She grunted, which he seemed to hear.

“Let the Canis by!”

Strong, furred bodies streaked past her and vanished in the smoke. Yu'ung tried to crawl, now also worried about the Canis, but was hobbled by the murk. She dipped her head and advanced by feel, then something pushed her aside. Ump–at least she thought it was him, the largest of the Canis–crawled the opposite direction toward the entrance, dragging a child by the arm in his soft mouth. White Streak, Ocha, and Ragged Ear followed his swaying tail, guiding other tribe members through the haze. A few females stumbled along with the Canis, retching. Someone tugged at Yu'ung's wrap.

“We got everyone,” B'o said, at least it sounded like him.

She crept out with him, finally gulping in sweet air, shocked to be alive. Lightning sparked in the billowing black clouds. It had started to rain while they'd been inside, transforming the wet ash into sludge. The ground trembled with such violence, anyone upright crumpled.

Yu'ung crawled toward the People. "Get away! Cross the clearing!"

A flood of the People scrambled as the cave imploded behind them. Dust clouds and shards of rock shot out leaving a rubble pile and the barest indication of the mouth. Luckily, supplies had been transferred in preparation for departure.

When the judders and rumbles stopped, B'o and Shanadar trudged to her side, using their spears as walking sticks, feet spread in case the quaking resumed.

She asked, voice not as steady as she wished, "Is anyone missing?"

"A child and an elder," B'o's voice gravelly and low.

Yu'ung's eyes drooped, body exhausted by the day's events. Her dark red hair, now grey with ash and soot, spilled over her shoulders in a tangled heap, but she didn't care, intent on rubbing her neck to arrest the ache taunting her head. She glanced around at those who called her Alpha, shaken but resolute.

She bobbed her head. "Old One?"

"Safe."

Yu'ung poked her lips toward a pile of limbs and wriggling fur. "Your Canis have new friends, Shanadar."

They lay intermingled with the tribe, the youngest giggling, the subadults smoothing the Canis' rough coats. None were frightened, despite having called these creatures dangerous predators this morning. What Yu'ung smelled, stronger than the smoke and ash, was relief. White Streak sneezed and toppled over, legs splayed, matched soon by Ocha amid howls of laughter.

Shanadar laughed. "They are yours now, too, at least for the journey."

B'o muttered, "I don't understand. They were almost killed and now, play like nothing happened."

The gangly stranger shrugged. "They work non-stop, quit only when completed, but what I've learned from them as much as anything else is how to relax."

Shanadar whispered to the one called Ump. He snorted and slapped paws the size of gourds on the ground.

Yu'ung said to B'o, "Shanadar and the Canis understand each other. He considers himself Canis and they Uprights."

B'o huffed, cautious but curious. "They saved your life, rescued many of the People, and offer to guide us to our new homebase. Why?"

The knots in her stomach unraveled. "I can't explain it."

That wasn't quite true. She could explain Xhosa, but doubted a mysterious vision she and Shanadar saw only in dreams would clarify anything for her hunt partner.

So she spoke a different truth. "He and his pack traveled from their homeland, driven by instinct, to help us. I will explain everything when we have time, but right now, it's more important to heal the injured and then leave this place before it kills us."

B'o perused the scattered tribe, his gaze stopping at his pairmate Ese salving a plethora of burns, bruises, gashes, and a possible broken arm. Her attention was split between the wounds she was healing and their conversation.

Yu'ung joined Ese, bent to help her, and B'o trotted up. "I'm glad Shanadar was there for you, when you needed help, but his timing goes beyond coincidental."

"I agree, but I can't explain it."

Again, she could, but a peek at Shanadar said he agreed—a discussion of Xhosa wouldn't clarify anything for B'o, at least not right now.

Shanadar interrupted before B'o could ask more. "You call her Kriina though her pairmate calls her Aynoh."

Yu'ung cast back to the day Kriina rejoined the People after healing a member of Fierce's band. She returned with a new name, stripes painted on her face, and a chain around her neck. Most surprising was she called the Tall Ones "Chosen."

Kriina "chose" them. When I see her again, I will call her Aynoh, as she prefers.

"That, too, is a longer conversation than we have time for." She switched her attention to Ese. "You do well as a healer."

When Kriina left the People to join her pairmate and Yu'ung was declared Alpha, the tribe lost both primary healers. Ese suggested herself as the next and Yu'ung agreed to train her.

Ese hid a smile. "Jhat's stew is ready."

Jhat was another tribe member who stepped up. Jhat could have pairmated a visiting tribe. Many offered, but she preferred her beleaguered cluster led by a too-young Alpha and novice healer. Here with the People, she could make a difference.

"I added plants for sore throats and coughs to it, for the smoke and hot air."

Ese and Yu'ung served it to those who asked, then prepared a dressing to be pressed atop cuts, bruises, and burns. Sun rested on the horizon by the time they finished. Ese rotated onto her heels, face damp with sweat, shoulders drooped with fatigue. The Canis plopped to the ground behind Yu'ung.

Shanadar said, "Not enough daylight remains to start our trip. Travel in the dark is risky, especially now. The earth's shaking cracked the land and boulders have been flung where they never were before."

B'o asked, "You have trekked where we go?"

He smiled. "No, but it is familiar, as it is to Yu'ung."

B'o scratched his ear. "The Canis confuse me."

Shanadar's lips spread in a smile. "Ump is the largest with the bushy black-tipped tail. White Streak, Ump's mate, is black and grey with a white streak across her forehead. Ragged Ear is brindle colored with black-tipped ears. Ocha is the smallish black one with the tan muzzle."

B'o cocked his head. "It's not that. It's their blue eyes."

"Yes."

Yu'ung understood why, but it was Shanadar's secret to share. He didn't.

Yu'ung touched her cheek. "You also stripe the Canis?"

"At times, but I have yet to find places they don't lick off. I hung collars around their necks, like mine, but they clawed them off."

"Why for either—the stripes or necklaces?"

"It tells strangers we are together. Attack one. Attack all. It worked well for us during our journey."

B'o picked meaty strips from a rib. "How long did the trek here from your former homeland take?"

Shanadar pulled a bone from his bag, its smooth surface marred with narrow gouges. "Each mark represents when Moon failed to appear in the night sky."

There were as many as Yu'ung's fingers. She blinked, once, again. "We have never migrated a farther distance than what it takes for Moon to cycle through the night sky. How did you journey so far without knowing where to go?"

Shanadar rubbed between Ump's ears. "They did. And Xhosa."

B'o slapped his thighs with his hands. "Her again! When will I meet her?"

Whatever Shanadar might have said was interrupted when a frenzied mother staggered toward them, her nameless child in her arms. The infant's unblinking eyes stared at nothing.

"I can't wake him, Yu'ung."

Her red eyes sparkled with unshed tears.

"Let me see," but it was no mystery. The rancid odor of death permeated his air.

Yu'ung gently took the infant as Ese tugged the mother aside, her distraught eyes never leaving the People's Alpha.

Yu'ung held the body. "Its time ended. That happens and there is nothing you or I can do."

The People buried the dead in crevices, far from the camp so the illnesses in lifeless bodies wouldn't infect the living, and deep enough that scavengers couldn't reach them.

Shanadar motioned, "We passed a depression coming here. It isn't far."

Yu'ung placed the body in the hollow, chubby legs curled against his stomach, arms at his sides. She was about to cover it when Old One tottered up, arms wrapped around Yota, one of the tribe's Elders and Old One's rare friend. Yu'ung brushed her hands down the side of her wrap to clean them as she took in the Elder who meant everything to her. She thought of asking what she already knew, but why?

Old One cuddled Yota in his arms. Bony spurs in her ears made hearing difficult, some said impossible. A bear swat to her head blinded one eye and caused a chronic shoulder injury. No one remembered how she lost her hand. Or cared. She worked as effectively with one as others did with both. All said that nothing could take the lives of Yota and Old One.

Now, the Mountain did.

We had too few Elders to lose one, but it wasn't our decision.

Old One huffed. "We talked about death. She understood this migration would not be as those in the past. She would be unable to keep up. I can't either, so I will soon seek her out."

Yu'ung looked at him, confused. What did he mean?

She backed up so he could see the hollow with the child's body. "We can inter her here, Old One."

Yu'ung and B'o sealed both with dirt and rubble. Scavengers might pick up the stench of rotted flesh, but never locate its source. Burials completed, the assemblage ate cat-tail root stew flavored by a tart white bulb native to most places the People migrated, augmented with scraps from bones and hides. Few had an appetite, but they ate when food was available.

Usually, afterward, all gathered around the fire to resharpen tools. Tonight, they slept, reserving their energy for tomorrow. Somewhere ahead was a place where the People could cobble together a future away from Mountain's fury.

Chapter 3

Yu'ung awoke to a shower of ash and cinder and hustled to the spot designated for departure. A sharp wind blew, chilling her skin, seeping through the holes in her wrap.

"Where's Old One?"

B'o growled. "He refuses to go. He says when the ground quiets, the Mountain People will come for him."

The People mated with the Mountain People, pairmated, and sometimes shared food and shelter. The last time together, their Leader—what the People called Alpha—offered to take Old One to live with them if he didn't feel able to keep up with the People's migration. The Elder declined. They never said they'd come back for him.

Yu'ung hung her head, hair streaming behind her in a dark red wave. "He intends this as his death place. He made that clear yesterday when Yota died."

"That is ridiculous. The route we will take is flatter than climbing into the mountains, less difficult—"

"It's not the difficulty. He's lost his will to live." Yu'ung added to herself, *It is up to me to change that.*

The People valued elders as much as they did children. They were the wise repository of how things were done in the past, where members went for advice, where predults and subadults were trained in adult skills. It was Old One who dexterously convinced everyone to select Yu'ung as Alpha.

B'o was lost in a frown when Shanadar padded up to them.

Once her hunt partner finished his annoyed consideration of what to do about the Elder, she asked, "You know something, Shanadar?"

"Old One sees a sign."

B'o glared. "You can't know that."

"Yet, I do. Let him abide by his instincts, us by ours."

Yu'ung thinned her lips. "I'll talk to him, B'o. You and Shanadar take the tribe. He knows the route. If we don't catch up soon, it means I couldn't change Old One's mind and will find you after delivering him to the Mountain People."

"But—"

Yu'ung's face hardened. "I won't leave him here to die."

B'o stomped. "I have been to the Mountain People's homebase. It is easier if I go. Besides, the People need an Alpha."

Yu'ung scowled. *He wants to see Naa one last time. She bore B'o's only child and he feels obligated.*

B'o stomped again. "It's not what you think. Naa means nothing to me anymore."

Shanadar tilted his head back and, as though it were an after-thought, said, "Naa took a pairmate. She is happy."

B'o's gaze flattened and the knuckles whitened around his spear. "How do you know?"

"You must have seen the male whose eyes never left her and her child."

Yu'ung didn't. She had allowed herself to be distracted by Mountain, by Old One, by her fatigue.

She growled silently to herself, but realized, truth or not, it didn't concern her or the People.

"I must be the one to deliver Old One or the Mountain People may not accept him. Our tribe has confidence in you, B'o. Old One and I will move as quickly as possible, but you may cross the path of Fierce and Aynoh before we reconnect. Look for Aynoh's messages to confirm what you already know through Shanadar and Old One."

Shanadar offered a calming smile. "Do not worry," and spread his lips to show his teeth. "I will sing every day when Sun hangs immediately above my head."

He lifted a hollow bone to his mouth and played a haunting song no bird ever sang. How could a bone emit such beautiful sounds?

B'o stiffened. "What is that tube?"

"It's a femur, similar to the whistle used to call tribe members, but with more holes and the ends whittled to shape the mouth. I spent daylights and firelights practicing after clothes were repaired and food processed. I press my fingertips to the round openings and shape my lips and tongue to coax different voices from the tube. I can mimic any sound—a bird beckoning a mate or a pig its pack. While traveling here from my homeland, I often fed myself by calling the animal to me. I can play other sounds, some unheard by any."

Haunting notes echoed in the air.

Yu'ung's mouth hung open as he rubbed along the bone's smooth surface. "I can't always control what it plays. Sometimes, I wait for the tube to release the song it desires to be heard."

B'o grumbled his impatience. "How will that help? Yu'ung could confuse it with a real creature."

"Close your eyes, B'o—and Yu'ung. Notice how the tones touch you inside where no bird ever did. When that happens, it is my song."

Yu'ung did as he suggested and he played again. To her surprise, something tingled through her chest, unusual prickles she never felt from birds or Aynoh's humming.

This is what he means.

She said, "How did you create this?"

"I didn't. Xhosa talked the right cave bear into giving this femur up. Somehow … Xhosa said I could call her with it if I needed her though I've yet to succeed."

B'o wasn't convinced. "The sound will bring predators, or strangers who mean us harm."

Shanadar smiled. "You forget Ump and White Streak, and Ragged Ear. The few predators still in this desolate expanse remember the Canis' supremacy."

Yu'ung took her partner's face in her hands. "Help Shanadar. He's never led before."

Shanadar dismissed the discussion as though nothing else needed to be said. "Yu'ung. Ocha will go with you."

The black Canis, Ocha, licked B'o's hand, nudged Shanadar, and padded to Yu'ung. Head tilted up, her tail swung side to side.

Yu'ung blinked. "But she is your pack."

"*Ours*. We are now one."

Yu'ung inhaled Ocha's feralness. It spoke of survival and dominance, of steady resolve, and her acceptance of the Upright. Ocha panted, blue eyes fixed on Yu'ung.

The tribe left, B'o in front with Shanadar and Ump, Laak on the backtrail with White Streak. Ragged Ear scouting. Ese trotted in the middle, a calm reminder to everyone of the People's strength.

Laak peered back once at Yu'ung, which she rewarded with a smile, and then he melted into the dusky smoke.

When the clatter and busyness subsided, Yu'ung easily found Old One. His many chronic injuries made him a noisy breather. She dismissed his displeasure at her presence and crouched beside him. Both picked at the shriveled dirt under their feet, comfortable in the silence. Without insect sounds, squirrels clacking and scurrying to their burrows, and Snake slithering through the grass searching for prey, an eeriness descended on the abandoned homebase. It would have unnerved Yu'ung if not for Old One.

"We can't leave until I repair my spear, Old One."

She paid no attention to his response. Doubtless, he ignored her, too.

She lit a fire with the cinder from her shoulder sack. Flames hot, she dropped stiff resin on a flat stone. Once softened, she poked the goo into the slit at the top of her spear's shaft. When dry, the connection became unbreakable, regardless how impenetrable the animal skin. When resin was unavailable, bitumen or bark would do, but changing them into glue was a protracted process. Yu'ung didn't want Old One's decision delayed long enough for that.

Repair finished, she wriggled to face him. "What are we waiting for, Old One?"

He smiled when footsteps thumped toward them, broken with heavy pants.

"That."

Yu'ung gripped her lance and placed herself between Old One and the threat.

He chuckled. "Laak is no threat to us, or anyone right now."

Ocha scrambled to her feet, hackles smooth, tail slapping her ribs, mouth panting her excitement.

Yu'ung snarled, "I will take care of that. By the time we return to you, he will make no sound when walking."

Laak raced to them, wheezing. "Old One, you promised to teach me how to cook glue. I smelled it from down the path and came to watch and learn."

Old One chuckled again. "And I will if necessary when next I see you."

Laak might believe the Elder, but Yu'ung heard the untruth. Not really a lie, rather the excuses Elders made when too old to keep up with the tribe's strenuous migrations.

Yu'ung said nothing to expose Old One's guile. "He taught me. I will do the same for you."

Laak hung his head. "The skill … is not why I'm here. I will travel with you, defend you while you take Old One where he must go."

Yu'ung placed her spears crossways on her lap. One was the People's thrusting weapon, rigorous and hefty, for up-close hunting. The other, the Tall Ones far-throwing lance, designed to kill from a distance. Ocha lay by Yu'ung and Old One, head between her paws. Yu'ung smoothed a hand through the Canis' rough fur.

She said, "With my weapons and the Canis, there is no worry. The tribe needs your warrior skills."

Old One waved a hand in front of himself. "Go. I've seen you practice with the far-throwing spear. You are almost as good as Yu'ung. The creatures who haven't fled are desperate which makes them dangerous. B'o can handle them, but better with your assistance."

That was high praise since Yu'ung's accuracy and power matched that of most Tall Ones.

Laak scowled. "If you insist, Old One, I go. You can depend upon me to be worthy of the title 'Lead Warrior'."

Before Yu'ung's mother, Aynoh, fairmated the Tall One Leader Fierce and the People called the Tall Ones friends, Laak attacked Fierce. He failed miserably, but his courage and willingness to defend convinced Fierce to suggest Laak as the People's first Lead Warrior, its primary defender and responsible for training other warriors. Fierce claimed that position would be important not only on the long migration but in their new homebase with strangers they knew nothing about. He had been there before so Yu'ung took him seriously.

Yu'ung fixed her gray gaze on the subadult. "Our People rely on you and B'o."

Fear flashed through his eyes, replaced by resolve. "I will."

Members always volunteered, were rarely conscripted. Injuries and pain from hunting, harvesting rocks for tools and shafts for lances, and physical stress from pushing their bodies too far, too fast were common, but never an excuse for failing to fulfill responsibilities. Predults grew into brave subadults who learned to be adults, as hard as the world around them and as durable. Mountain would have to try harder if it wished to destroy the People.

After Laak's departure, Old One huffed. "For the same reasons, the People can't do without you on this long migration. You are Alpha. You shouldn't come with me. If we run into problems and you don't get back to the People in time, well...."

Yu'ung eased to her feet. "I will, Old One. You will thrive with the Mountain People and I in our new homeland. We are both going where we must."

To her relief, his old knees popped into place and he grunted as he hooked his bag over a shoulder. Ocha yipped cheerfully and they took off.

Part 2

Yu'ung and Old One Journey into the Mountains

Chapter 4

They trekked throughout the day, always at Old One's pace. With the help of his stick, the elder never asked to rest and never complained. That didn't fool Yu'ung. The grunts and pants eloquently verbalized his discomfort. When it was clear to her he'd gone as far as he could, she suggested he wait for her while she scouted, to give him time to recover with dignity. She would return, discuss what she saw, ask his opinions, and they would continue.

If Old One was suspicious of her strategy, he hid it, probably accepted what must be. Before Angry Mountain transformed their lives, the more physical tasks like hunting and scouting were done by those younger. Old One occupied himself knapping tools, scraping hides, and teaching skills to predults and subadults. Migrations were as far as he ever walked. Those were completed well within a Moon. It had been many Moons since he walked longer than that. Now, he must and Yu'ung had no idea how that would work out.

Ocha split her time yipping at Old One and exploring the surroundings. Yu'ung welcomed the Canis' strong senses and positive attitude, evident with each tail wag and paw prance, snarling growl, and exposed fang. Yu'ung and Old One traveled as much as possible in open areas, avoiding spots where the few starving pawed-and-clawed predators might lie in wait for passing prey. How big a pack of enemies could Ocha and Yu'ung stop before *they* were stopped?

Day bled into night, though difficult to tell. Maybe the murkiness was more grey than black, but even at night the air felt hot and sticky, dense with ash and snowflake-sized shavings. She often breathed with a shirt pressed over her mouth and wished for rain.

Yu'ung spent much time searching in vain for the landmarks mentioned by B'o that led to the Mountain People, but the sizzling cinders and fire rivers caused by Mountain's anger transformed everything into an undistinguishable façade of ragged scars and androgynous scents buried under the rancid smell of rotting carcasses, decaying plants, and burnt life.

This caused her even more problems. Sun's absence meant Yu'ung couldn't use it to find directions. Usually, she relied on natural clues like termite mounds, their smooth sides built to face Sun's first rays. Now, though, they lay in crumpled heaps, crushed by stampedes or buried under ash. This was true also of the burrows for ground-dwelling animals. These always faced the morning breeze, but like the termite mounds, were destroyed. Other useful landmarks were buried in rubble and ash. She even wished for the annoying insect swarms that bit her skin and announced the imminence of water.

Luckily, the clan's high homeland was marked by towering white peaks glistening well above the devastation. They made the final destination easy to track.

The morning chill gave way to surprising heat. Sweat soaked Yu'ung's back, drenching her sides where the bag pressed.

How does Ocha tolerate heat with her fur coat? Most Canis pant faster. Not her.

And she never drank any of Yu'ung's proffered water.

In the past, the tribe didn't scavenge carcasses, but now, Yu'ung welcomed them. The problem was, the stink of Mountain's eruption permeated the air, blocking all other scents. If forage was out there, she would have to stumble on it.

Not Ocha, though. Today, she trotted up with a dead deer, lightly chewed and without the green color announcing the presence of poison. They ate their fill and Yu'ung stuffed the remnants—including the valuable leg bones—in her pack, the marrow for Old One.

She wiped her mouth on her shirt and muttered, "Bear."

Old One poked his lips. "It crosses our forward path, fresh, recent. It must know we are here."

Berry bushes filled the valley they crossed. Bears loved the sweet fruit, even dry and ashy as it was. In normal times, they assaulted Uprights to safeguard their cubs, not for food, but Bear almost certainly suffered the same hunger Yu'ung and Old One did.

"Its moving away from us, climbing to a forest at the hill's crest. We should be safe."

Still, Yu'ung and Old One squatted, waiting until Ocha's hackles smoothed. They didn't.

"Old One. Let's find a different route," but it was too late.

Bear exited the trees, steps ponderous, remaining high above them, but close enough to be a threat if motivated.

Does she have cubs up there?

It wagged its head, sniffing, and stopped, beady black eyes locked onto them.

It found us.

She and Old One sank further into the fronds.

She might miss us, or not identify us as perilous if she is without cubs.

That filtered through Yu'ung's mind as Bear lifted its—her—bulk to her hind legs and unleashed a roar that shook Yu'ung's entire body, the giant now nothing more than fangs and lips.

Swallowing my head whole would be no problem.

Her massive paws mauled the air, claws the length of Yu'ung's forearm, before she crashed to the ground and ambled away.

We have been warned.

Yu'ung crouched, eyes slit, waiting. Ocha moaned at her side, hackles as stiff as thorns. Bear would fight if threatened, but the behemoth seemed to have other worries on her mind. Yu'ung clutched her spears, glad to have both the far-throwing and the thrusting, and backed away. They skirted what she considered Bear's hunting grounds, making their way roundabout back to the original forward path, when Old One's pants grew too loud to be considered natural. Normally, she sought shelter when Sun dropped within a hand of the horizon. Today, without Sun to guide that decision, she had planned to walk until the gray air blackened, but changed her mind.

They spent the night in a cave. If none had been available, an overhang or cliff wall would suffice, or—with few dangerous threats remaining—an open site with Ocha as guard. Tonight, because she didn't know Bear's whereabouts, the rock wall's protection felt right.

Yu'ung lit the hearth with an ember from the People's last fire. Sometimes, they burned out if the day's migration took too long so she carried a fire stone for backup. Using that was a tedious process, so luckily, the cinder sparked and a hare soon cooked fragrantly on the flames. She mixed the tender meat with various stems, nuts, and roots dug from the ash. All were acceptable raw, but cooking made chewing easier for Old One's weak teeth.

Food consumed, Old One slept while Yu'ung patched a hole in her wrap and resharpened her spear point for the next day. That done, she had originally intended to string pebbles, eagle talons, animal fangs, and small bones she'd collected on cordage for herself and Old One, to mark themselves as tribe. She'd asked Ocha if she wanted one, but couldn't tell if her heavy pants indicated yes or no, and then remembered what Shanadar told her.

But after Bear's appearance forced them to deviate from the original route, she needed instead to confirm they still headed the right direction. Normally, she'd do that by checking their position against the flow of stars overhead. The sparkling lights were always there, but rarely in the same place. Yu'ung had tried greeting them, but they never responded with anything other than a wink. Old One considered them friendly creatures who watched over the People. He said they steered his childhood tribe reliably to many homebases and Shanadar said they appeared wherever he was regardless the location. No land-based marker did that.

But last night and again tonight, there were no stars. In a day of frustrations, this barely bothered her, at least, not yet.

"Ocha will know where to go," and lay prone by the Canis, contemplating Shanadar. The gangly, loose-limbed interloper fit Xhosa's description of who would assist her to escape Mountain's anger and he shared her goal to get her People to safety. What made no sense was why her safety meant anything to him.

She mouthed to herself, "Have my People escaped Mountain yet? Will I ever again see them?" Her head throbbed. "I will be satisfied if they are safe."

She returned to the cave, threw kindling onto the fire, and curled against Old One. It didn't take long before her mind drifted away.

Days ticked by in the sunless gloom. Eruptions persisted. Boulders, cinder, ash, decayed carcasses, and the charred ruins of those who failed to escape littered the land. The distant white summit oriented her, a lodestar to the Mountain People's home.

Yu'ung talked with Ocha a lot, sharing strategies and concerns. The Canis always listened and once Yu'ung learned to interpret the responses, offered ideas that made Yu'ung reflect on her own. Stiff hackles, tweaked ears, a twitchy nose, how much of her fangs were bared, the brightness in her eyes, mixed huffs or groans—Yu'ung originally thought Canis communication was limited to howls, growls, and a few barks. Now, she heard as many variations as in the People's words.

The group plodded onward, Yu'ung's pace measured, Old One's labored but without protest. They rarely saw Uprights or herds which gave Yu'ung time to think. Today it was how to locate the People after delivering Old One to his new home.

"Old One. Kriina scarcely knows the Tall Ones. Will they fulfill their promise?"

"You've spied on them more than anyone I know. Rely on your instincts and intuition."

He was right, about her spying on them, watching them hunt while training herself in the use of the far-throwing spear.

She switched to Ocha. "The Tall Ones had just departed when you and Shanadar arrived at their camp. Did you smell anything suspicious?"

Ocha yipped.

"I agree. The People have done well despite our lack of males. That's not why I'm curious about the Tall Ones," though adding this large group of burly warriors to the tribe was tempting.

A protracted yowl came from Ocha.

"No one would care if additional males were Tall Ones or Mountain People–" Another yip and Yu'ung grinned. "Or Canis. Let's find shelter for the night."

Old One jutted his lips out. "A cave is ahead," but when they reached it, a mountain lion family greeted them with snarls so they moved on. The next one, too, was occupied, the pawed tenants similarly unwilling to share their space. The group settled for an overhang, deep enough into a cliff to ward off the chill. Without an airhole, Yu'ung built the hearth toward the front, where the breeze would draw the smoke out. While Yu'ung gathered tinder, Ocha hunted, returning with a ground squirrel snatched before it could dive into its den, and a bird, wings too stiff with ash to fly. The unrelenting problem of water persisted. Slag-covered sludge now coated the preponderance of creeks and ponds, but in the rear of the overhang, the clear, fresh liquid trickled down the face. Yu'ung and Old One drank their fill and restocked the organ sacks.

As Old One dozed, Yu'ung worked on the necklaces and talked to Ocha.

"Black fur is unusual for a Canis. Many of our kind rejected Kriina and me for our red hair and pale skin. To the Tall Ones, those traits mark Kriina as special. Do you think that's true of all Fierce's kind—the Chosen—or just his band?"

She waited for Ocha's response, but the Canis was fully engaged licking her paw.

Old One murmured, "That might be why she hasn't committed to going with him."

"As pairmates, of course she'll go!"

Yu'ung dropped the pebbles she'd been stringing, gathered them up, but fumbled them again, so rolled back on her heels and concentrated.

Does he know something?

Red veins etched Old One's tired eyes, but they retained the clarity and intelligence she so often relied on.

"Be happy for your mother, Yu'ung. After a lifetime of being shunned for her hair color, used for her talents, and ignored by a pairmate, she found her place. The Tall Ones respect her and Fierce reveres her. I suspect if she refuses to go with him, he will stay here."

Yu'ung's thoughts folded inward as Old One's insights ran through the complex web of her thoughts, his words wiser with each rethinking.

"Fierce's discontent where he formerly lived is no secret, Yu'ung. He has told Kriina and me it is one reason he agreed to this journey of exploration. Think about it. Why return to such a place when he has the opposite here?"

"Because he is bound by duty. If she goes with him, I can't unless the People no longer need me as Alpha. How will I manage without her?" *Without both of you?*

Old One smiled. "You have always known you two would separate. What is there to fear? Embrace the start of a new journey that will recreate you into who you are intended to be. Let it happen. Then, decide what future to follow."

Yu'ung crouched. "Xhosa said the same."

When he closed his eyes, his broken but functioning body wrapped in a snug fur, Yu'ung picked at the dirt until her eyes drooped.

The farther they went, the clearer the air, but the absence of Sun, Moon, and stars persisted. Had Mountain taken them? And what about the birds?

"Ocha. Where are the songs that announce the start and end of each day?"

One woof and a tail wag cheered Yu'ung. "Of course. The birds escaped."

The availability of food declined with each day. They dug in the ash, hoping for seedlings, roots, or animal burrows, but everything was dead or rotting. No new sprouts poked out of the distressed ground. Wet slag coated the desiccated earth and tainted water, often dried to a tough crust.

Old One slowed more the farther they went. Unaccustomed to constant walking, his soles tore and bled with blisters under his foot covers. Yu'ung suggested carrying him or dragging him on a travois. He refused both. At night, she wrapped his sores in salves, but the relief never lasted.

The morning arrived when he refused to continue. "When Mountain's anger ends, I'll find the Mountain People."

"What will you do when the cave bear who owns this den reclaims it?"

"Bear knows the food is gone."

Yu'ung squatted at his side, elbows on her knees, lips a thin line to keep herself from arguing. He'd chosen death. That was his right. Elders must one day make such choices, but Yu'ung wouldn't allow Old One to do so unaccompanied.

She huffed a sigh, echoed by Ocha. "I too wouldn't mind a break."

With that, she waddled over to the firepit and began knapping. Old One joined her, both working in amiable silence. He sharpened a variety of cutting and chopping tools until he toppled over, asleep.

Yu'ung delayed as long as patience allowed for Old One to awaken. When he snored on, lost in some peaceful world of dreams and dark, she pushed upright and spoke to his motionless form, "Ocha and I will find what passes as food here. Stay behind the bramble barrier."

Old One was awake on their return. He'd stoked the fire and was sharpening stone tools.

"No problems?"

He shook his head. "You?"

"Ocha caught a ground squirrel," and set about to cooking it. The Canis always shared with her pack.

Daylight remained, but Yu'ung wanted to let Old One's feet and spirit heal for a few days.

"I'll scout tomorrow. I'm sure the Mountain People are nearer than we think."

She doubted her words, but the haze and unfamiliar landscape made it impossible to tell. He mumbled something and then his head sagged.

The meat sizzled, but only Yu'ung ate. Ocha guarded, body flat at the entrance, paws on either side of her head, peering through the twigs. Once in a while, her ears tweaked to sounds, nose twitched to scents.

Then, she thrust upright, hackles stiff. A faint annoyed sound rolled from her throat.

Shadows separated from the dark, growing the nearer they came. The skin on Yu'ung's neck prickled.

"Old One." She poked him with the point of her lance. "Wake up. We have company."

Chapter 5

Shanadar and the People

Shanadar marched forward, flute in one hand, spear in the other, Wise Stone nestled at the top of the bag hooked over his bony shoulder. For handfuls of Moons, before arriving in Yu'ung's homeland, only the Canis and Wise Stone were there to listen to his ideas and offer suggestions. Now, he led a large assemblage of Uprights. Even Yu'ung's partner B'o's assistance, Wise Stone's whispered encouragement, and his Canis companions huffs could convince him he would not fail.

But Xhosa asked him to do it so he didn't quit. Couldn't.

Shanadar knew he was the wrong person. That didn't change with the first Moon, or the second. Tribe members whispered when they thought he didn't hear, called him the striped stranger who played music on a cave bear bone, talked to a palm-sized stone, and was as likely to be lost in his head as aware of the group. What they didn't realize, though, was that he wasn't oblivious. He was scared, harking back to those countless times in the past when his tribe judged him wanting, appraised him as a failure, and found disappointment even in his successes.

Xhosa promised that Yu'ung would be there, that he could rely on B'o, but neither was true. When a decision had to be made, all turned to him, the one anointed by Yu'ung. His options were always between bad choices and worse. He hoped Ese would step up, but her glares grew more withering each day, as though blaming him for Old One's refusal to join People and Yu'ung's absence. Many days, he hovered on the brink of panic, keeping it at bay one breath at a time.

Laak alone offered promise. The Tall One Fierce saw the promise of a Lead Warrior in the untested, high-strung subadult and tasked him to become one by the time the groups reunited. Luckily, skilled leaders surrounded Laak.

"Shanadar. Can White Streak, Ump, and Ragged Ear teach me to defend the tribe?"

"Ask them."

"I tried. They avoid me."

"Spend time with them. Show respect."

Shanadar wasted no time making sure Laak understood, simply left, trusting the Canis to take over Laak's instruction. He could feel Laak's eyes on his back as his long strides carried him far enough to avoid additional questions. Shanadar felt trapped by the tribe's expectations and bruised by his own self-recrimination. Most of what a leader should clarify, he couldn't. The exception was Laak's queries about the Canis. Shanadar knew those answers, but not how to explain, unravel, or advise.

Xhosa had seen this coming. In the time he spent preparing for this journey, she had offered leadership suggestions. One was to shut down his brain, let answers come.

That might help in theory, but not in the now. No one wants to wait.

He had asked what to do if her plan didn't work—suspecting it wouldn't—and she told him to let his mind go blank. Stop nagging. It would let him know when it solved the problem. He did that once. The blank part worked, but the solution never materialized.

He wanted to ask Xhosa what to do when neither strategy worked, but she didn't respond to his calls on the bone flute or visit his dreams as she had in the past. What did that mean? Surely she didn't think he could manage on his own.

He lay in his nest, eyes closed, and tried again.

Xhosa. Where are you? Yu'ung is not with me and B'o dislikes leading as much as I do.

White Streak joined him, furry body pressed against his thin wrap, tail swishing against his legs.

"Did Xhosa send you?"

A low moan and vigorous ear flaps.

"You suggest I pay less attention to managing the tribe and more to the landscape?" A moan.... "Yes, the surroundings are nothing like what I told her to expect, but she is clever. She will find us."

White Streak nipped his hand. Shanadar snapped his hand away. "I *am* marking the caves, leaving cairns, even scratching the tree bark."

The Canis snorted, eyebrows bunched.

"You're familiar with this route?"

A low howl and White Streak trotted away.

All of that changed one day.

Shanadar had been plodding forward, lost in his mind, comfortable in the route because the Canis laid it out, when the murky cloak hiding his future lifted. A craggy leviathan rose out of an endless expanse of pristine blue water.

A sea without shores. Is it our new home?

Was this what Xhosa meant—let his mind go and eventually it would reveal what he must know? Would it now assemble a plan to get him there? Or had been awaiting a quiet moment to reveal itself?

The vision faded as quickly as it arrived, but he was filled with serenity, as though fated to fulfill not only Xhosa's expectations and Yu'ung's requirements, but his destiny. When he and B'o huddled for their nighttime chat, B'o asked, as usual, for insights from the day's travels.

Tonight, for the first time in a while, he grinned. "Depend on me as Yu'ung asked you to. I will lead you away from Mountain's ire."

B'o straightened, eyes narrowed. "Did something happen today?"

"*I* happened, nothing more complicated. The journey tests us and we must be patient."

B'o wriggled.

Why doesn't he understand! "You want more clarity."

"Of course I do! Start with, how do you know this?"

Because Xhosa told me! But should he tell B'o about this visionary spirit when there might be a good reason Yu'ung hadn't? He never heard the People discuss such creatures.

He tugged his lip, an idea forming.

"Fierce told Kriina who told Yu'ung that both our kind and Tall Ones live where we go. He mixed with both, but not long enough to determine their goals. His warning to us, until we are acquainted, don't judge them friend or foe."

B'o scoffed. "You aren't a hunter or warrior. I am the former and becoming the latter. I will be prepared."

White Streak and Laak approached, the young male calling out when close enough, "I will, too. I have learned a lot from the Canis."

The Canis' ears pricked forward, gait stiff as usual during conversations about her pack.

Shanadar roughed up her back. "Is that true, White Streak?"

That earned a loud bark and vigorous tail wag.

Laak answered also. "The Canis are the best scouts and explorers I've ever seen—"

"And defenders, "added Shanadar, "Though I hope you never have to see that."

B'o cocked his head. "But, you can't grow Canis fangs and claws, so come to me for spear skills."

White Streak toppled onto her back, legs aerial, tongue hanging from her toothy maw.

"I will."

B'o and Shanadar continued their discussion, focusing on defense. Laak listened and White Streak snored, lips trembling. She could sleep in the most uncomfortable positions. Then, without warning, she righted herself and sprinted down the tribe's backtrail, Laak behind.

Still intimidating to Shanadar was Ese. In Yu'ung and Kriina's absence, everyone relied on her to tend sore feet, cuts, upset stomachs, scrapes, lesions, gashes, and illness, but she had no experience with major injuries such as snake bites or broken bones. He had treated those and more while traveling, with no one to rely on except himself. Ese began to ask him about salves, mulches, poultices, and everything related to healing serious wounds. She wanted to learn the arts of healing and Shanadar enjoyed the conversations.

At one point, well into the journey, she said, "Yu'ung asked me to minister to your chronic ailments, but didn't tell me what those were."

Shanadar smiled. "I have cared for them." He extended both hands, fingers spread. "For this many moons. Or more. I will tell you if one worsens."

The most daunting hurdle for Shanadar was children. The tribe's few avoided him at first, but finally asked about games he played as a child. He practically spit out the truth, that no one invited him to participate, until one game he enjoyed watching popped into his head.

"How about 'I spy'? You guess what I see."

Not much could be seen in the murky sky and smudgy shadows, but the exercise trained the senses. The game soon became a favorite.

Day after day, Shanadar followed the Canis' lead. Partly, this was because B'o had no suggestions, but the bigger reason was it aligned with Shanadar's vision. The routine became comfortable—Ragged Ear scouted afar, B'o and Ump nearby, White Streak on the backtrail with Laak, and Ump ... somewhere ... of his choosing. The tribe credited Shanadar with finding the right path. He credited the Canis. Everyone was content.

Food was increasingly scarce. As a result, if even the slightest sign of a buried root or tuber showed through the ash and decay, travel paused so the females and children could scrounge in the desiccated soil. While they did that, B'o and the Canis combed for animal trace. Surely, Boar or Pig would be interested in buried food and left trace of their passage.

That wasn't the only goal.

Earlier in the migration, B'o stumbled on many carcasses, burned or freshly dead, which he passed on. The People preferred freshly killed meat to recently dead, but the farther they traveled, the fewer the living animals. This, if managed properly, offered opportunity to B'o and Shanadar. The creatures remaining were hungrier and weaker each day they couldn't find food, more ready to risk their lives for food.

What B'o missed with his spear, the Canis killed with claws and fangs.

When those options played out, the People scavenged the discards of other predators.

While the females foraged and B'o hunted, Shanadar checked the tunnels for messages. He didn't expect one from Yu'ung–she would still be catching up–but Aynoh should be ahead. She would leave guidance of Fierce's destination which should be the same as the People's.

During one night's strategy session, B'o called Laak over. "Tell Shanadar your idea."

Laak squatted, elbows on his knees "Fierce told me Tall Ones view those without spears as easy targets. Among the People, only B'o and I carry weapons."

Shanadar bristled. "I do."

"But you're odd and skinny, oblivious to your surroundings as you talk to Canis and wave your hands in the air. No one considers you a threat."

B'o covered his mouth, but couldn't squelch a smirk.

Shanadar smiled to himself. *Is this how they think of me? I suppose it's true.*

Ese shuffled over. "What is your idea, Laak?" Her voice calm, to offset B'o's titters.

Laak flushed so B'o answered, "The females should carry sticks as we do spears. From a distance, Uprights will see a well-equipped assemblage and leave us alone."

Shanadar sucked in his lips. "It's clever."

Laak stood, shoulders back. "As Lead Warrior, I will teach everyone to shape a branch to look like a lance and then wield it as fighters do."

Without another word, he left to get started, muttering about tree limbs and cutting tools. Ese rose to follow, but B'o stopped her.

"You can help with this next," and switched his attention to Shanadar. "The People are hungry. Is there anything your tribe did that could help us?"

Shanadar rotated his head, touching one ear to his shoulder then the other. "We often lacked food and learned to stretch what we had."

Ese asked, "How?"

"One idea is to render fat from bones. The result is a filling stew from resources that would otherwise be tossed."

Ese squeezed her knees with her hands. "How?" Again.

"Splinter the ends and boil the fragments."

"We start tomorrow."

Chapter 6

Aynoh (Kriina) and the Tall Ones

Far from Shanadar and Yu'ung's People, Fierce and the Tall Ones pursued a route that veered progressively away from the tribe, but was a necessary diversion on an expedition that now lasted longer than Fierce had fingers and toes to tick off the Moon's waxing and waning.

It started in their homeland, when the band's healer, Seer, tasked Fierce and others to locate a new homebase safe from Mountain's anger. The logical location was across shoreless sea, but the farther they trekked from the water, the more angry Mountain became, worse by magnitudes than in the band's homeland.

They gave up this part of the quest and focused on the final task. This one, they accomplished beyond their wildest expectations when they not only managed to make contact with the red-haired healer Seer had seen in a vision but persuade her to join them.

"What if I choose not to go with you, to the other side of the shoreless sea?" Aynoh didn't look at Fierce. She had no right to refuse. He was her pairmate.

He shrugged. "You are my pairmate. That makes it your choice."

"What?" *Did I hear right?*

"I don't own you."

"Own?" She muttered so softly he didn't hear, but the meaning of that word in this context escaped her.

A lot about the Chosen—what Aynoh's People called Tall Ones—was odd to Aynoh. For instance, how did their oversized heads balance on such slender necks? And why did they have a bump below their mouths which they called a "chin"?

They probably envy my prominent brow ridge which keeps rain from my eyes during storms and the blazing sun from blinding me.

It didn't take long to acclimate to each other's customs. Both were explorers which made differences more curiosities than challenges.

Tall Ones hunt better with their far-throwing spears, but my People see farther with greater detail, especially at night.

Aynoh also knew where to harvest fiber for cordage, sap for glue, and the hardest wood for shafts. This was invaluable knowledge to Fierce and his band, strangers to the area.

Fierce continued talking, as his kind was wont to do. They showed little respect for the power of silence.

"Your Tall One name "Aynoh" means "spirit," beings we as the Chosen rely on in the absence of others to do the impossible. How else can you explain your miraculous healing skills?"

"Not with the assistance of spirits because I am not one," but she couldn't explain the source of her unusual treatment ideas. They just made sense.

As for spirits, it was Yu'ung who dreamt about a female named Xhosa. Xhosa called their meetings "visions," the same term Seer used.

But Aynoh said none of that.

Other than the first days of fleeing fires, explosions, and overwhelming destruction, travel passed pleasantly. Migration was not unusual to the People. They rarely inhabited a spot long enough for Moon to come and go. They harvested available plants and meat, never picked a region clean, and always left adequate resources for the next tribe. If chasing a herd or mining the hard stones critical for spear tips and fire-making took them too far from their homebase, they didn't return, simply moved on. This was no problem as they carried most of their possessions with them. What they left behind was easily reproduced. It made for a convenient, simple lifestyle.

The day finally came when Aynoh inhaled air without burning her lungs. It felt so normal, tears came to her eyes.
If only Sun, Moon, and the stars would return.
Though absent in the past for short periods, it was never this long.

Aynoh considered herself no better or worse than other females of her kind with the exception of her healing skills. Fierce and his Tall One band disagreed. To celebrate her exceptionalism, Fierce painted her face with the prominent stripes of a healer and bestowed upon her the necklace of the Chosen. It was he who suggested Aynoh place it where Yu'ung would find it when the Chosen had to flee the last camp. It would serve as a message of their intent and a talisman for her.

If Fierce considered her remarkable, to her, he was a piece of herself that finally popped into place, there to repair what had broken, a beam of sunshine in a rainstorm, a smile in the midst of bedlam. How that was possible, she didn't know, but there it was. Truth.

Fierce's closest friend among the band was Grub. They grew up together, shared similar experiences and memories, and became adults devoted to each other. Grub's limbs bulged with strength, the hard muscular layer across his chest scarred with his victories, thickened from steady use, as durable as any animal's. Fierce was leaner, but with equal strength, just arranged differently. In contests, one might win, but the other beat him the next time.

No surprise Grub shared Fierce's admiration for Aynoh's cleverness, strength, and wisdom, how connected she was to her instinct, how what she called intuition—what Fierce and Grub agreed was spirits working through her—guided her steps. Grub hoped when the Chosen merged with her tribe, one of her People would mate or pairmate with him.

The entire band committed to the secondary goal save one—Qad, Grub's sibling. Grub had feared if he left Qad behind while he joined Fierce in this journey of exploration, Qad would be slain by any of a myriad of Chosen who hated him for good reason. Fierce agreed to take him, in hopes that Grub could teach Qad to be an adult. So far, he failed. Qad respected few of his kind and no Primitives, least of all Aynoh-who-might-be-a-spirit. He'd assaulted her once. When Grub threatened to send him back to the homeland if ever he did that again, he whined incessantly.

When the band ran out of meat and paused to hunt, one male always stayed in the temporary camp to protect Aynoh. The concern wasn't predators. It was their own kind, Tall Ones who knew Aynoh's importance to Seer, her spiritual connections, and would want to use them.

Grub always offered to stay.

Aynoh awoke, Fierce's odor overlaid by Grub's fresh sweat and Qad's mild stink. Today was a stay-in-place day, so the band could find the passage to the final task, based on an Upright Fierce had happened across long ago who knew someone who'd been there once. Something in the curves ahead and the placement of forests and hills fit the Upright's descriptions. He had warned it was nondescript, would blend into the dismal landscape, and if missed, they wouldn't find another passage for over a Moon.

Fierce took everyone to search for it except Grub and Quad who remained with Aynoh. Neither of them were good trackers anyway. Qad, in fact, had yet to find anything he excelled at.

Aynoh kept herself busy all day pounding roots, stems, and a few seeds for a stew to feed the males on their return. That done and with nothing else to occupy her thoughts, she rose, body stiff, eyes darting through the clearing.

Where is he?

Which was when he trotted up, sweat streaming down his sides, face red with exertion. A smile broke his lips as soon as he caught sight of her.

She handed him the cooked leg of a hare she'd brought down with stones. "Did you find it?"

He ate the entire leg in one bite and wiped the grease from his mouth with the back of his hand. "We did."

"How long will this task take? If we don't link up with Yu'ung and the People on the trail, they will worry."

She didn't ask what the task was because the band would go where Fierce led regardless of his answer to her. He glanced over at the rest, hungrily filling gourds with Aynoh's stew.

"I don't know. The Upright I talked to didn't offer many details beyond how to identify the egress point. He did say that what we need is far down the path, beyond a steep hill on the shores of a sparkling lake. More than a day of travel he thought. We will do what we must as quickly as possible and then return directly to the shoreless sea. From there, all we do is cross to the opposite side and make our way home."

"How do we find our way without landmarks?"

"That thankfully is not a concern. Once we reach the foothills, we keep Sun's sleeping nest on our dominant side the entire way."

"But Sun no longer shows itself."

"There are clues. Don't worry."

She thinned her lips. *If Fierce doesn't worry, neither will I,* and let herself be distracted by the other males, now gulping down the stew. Crevkukk was grinning, telling whoever would listen that Aynoh could cook like no one else. Bhidid mumbled something she didn't understand through a mouthful of stems and thick liquid. The others nodded agreement, with the focus of males accustomed to eating as much as possible when available.

Aynoh chuckled to herself. *They are more appreciative than this food deserves.*

She'd found only roots, soggy stems, a few nuts, and a handful of grubs from beneath the bark of a fallen tree, then flavored the water with herbs to hide the taste of mildew.

Crevkukk will make someone a good pairmate.

"This shoreless sea, can we cross by foot?" she asked as Eknilk shoveled a grub into his mouth and swallowed without chewing.

Aynoh often crossed waterways on foot. If the water was too fast, the tribe strung a vine from one shore to the other to hang onto while shuffling across. If the waterway was too wide for wading, they built a raft.

"No. We stowed our boat in a protected cove when we came over. We will sail it to your former tribe's new homebase."

"Where you originally landed?"

"Yes, a narrow channel that connects the shoreless sea to another much larger, also without shores and no obvious islands. No one sails on it. Why would they without land to head for?"

He squatted, stuffed a crunchy root into his mouth and chewed. "Well, some tried, carried gourds of water and lances to spear fish, but if they found a new homeland or died, no one knew.

"On the opposite side of the channel from our homeland is a towering rock filled with grottos, surrounded by fields and woods. Herds graze there. Birds flock to its shores. Others of your kind live there. We have met them. This would be a good homeland for Yu'ung's People, your former tribe. Once they settle there, we continue the journey to our homeland."

He peered at her out of the corner of his eye. She clenched her jaw. *They. Not "you."*

He jerked, misunderstanding whatever he saw in her face. "No, don't worry. Traversing the channel is rough, but our vessel handled it well on the original voyage. We will land on the shore opposite the towering rock and walk inland. It will take most of a Moon to arrive at our home."

Our.

"But it all hinges on this passage. The Upright we talked to was sure it led to what we need, but was dangerous with little food."

He pushed upright, pointed to Grub with his chin who then stood and motioned to the rest.

"We must hunt what meat we can before starting." He touched his cudgel, confirming its placement on his back. "Grub is my best hunter so Bhidid will stay with you because he is still healing. Qad and Crevkukk also."

Aynoh bristled, but tamped it down as she always did when he underestimated her abilities. He would change with time.

"It will give me time to harvest what I need for Bhidid's wound."

"Take your spear."

They went in opposite directions. After a brief search, she found the plant, right where she expected, and bent to tug it from the ground. Pain exploded at the base of her skull and the world went dark.

Chapter 7

Yu'ung and Old One

"Stay back, Old One. I'll deal with whoever is arriving."

"I have my walking stick," and he shuffled into the shadows.

Yu'ung grunted. In the dark, if they didn't look carefully, it could be a spear.

With Old One invisible in the gloom outside the hearth's light, she waited at Ocha's side. The Canis' blue eyes stared forward, paws spread, ears perked, fangs exposed, but hackles softer than when she faced off with Bear.

Old One and Xhosa taught Yu'ung to be prepared. Tonight, she gripped both the heavy thrusting weapon her kind preferred and the Tall Ones' thinner one. Each served a particular purpose. Across her back was a fire-hardened cudgel, a tool to stop those too close for a spear. In her shoulder sack were throwing stones, perfect for ground squirrels and birds, or a desperate last stand. Her greatest defense, though, was Ocha. Forced into a skirmish, Shanadar assured her countless would perish before Yu'ung or Ocha did.

Being Alpha had taught her more than weapons brought power to her leadership. Of the many circumstances that tested her authority, often it was good decisions that balanced strength and awareness.

These newcomers may not be troublemakers.

They emerged from the dark shadows of impending dusk into the fire's circle of light. The cool night air chilled their bodies, seeping beneath rough clothes, stitched together too loosely to sufficiently snug their skin in the way the People's—and the Tall One's—did.

Primitives … a kith or a family.

Some held lances, the sharp stone tips hafted to the shaft with cordage. Others gripped wood clubs. Most wore small necksacks sized to carry travel food, throwing stones, tools, and modest amounts of other supplies. When they saw her, they stopped, wary but not afraid. Yu'ung could come up with no events that frightened Primitives, including some that should.

Some instinct told Yu'ung these strangers knew the tribe in front of them was small. *They scouted us.*

They kept their spears lowered, but prepared to defend if necessary. They seemed familiar with this cave.

Have they dwelt here before?

She resisted the urge to reveal Old One's presence by asking for advice, instead, strode toward the strangers, head high, Ocha beside her. A square-faced Primitive, skin heavily lined with experience, scars across his neck and arms, his sturdy hirsute body smelling of mud and sweat, stepped forward. His alert eyes bounced from Ocha to Yu'ung, more curious than cautious. The Canis emitted a low growl, not to warn, more a reminder to be vigilant. Yu'ung extended her hand, level to the ground, fingers together, *Silence,* to give the impression others gathered in the shadows.

She barked, "What do you want?"

Feet spread, she gripped the shaft as a hunter would. The Primitives recognized her intent if not her words. They scuffled in place, uncertain what to do. Their foot covers were tattered, wraps unmended. Yu'ung guessed they had come far without stopping, anticipating a shelter not destroyed by Mountain's rage.

I will become a friend before they realize we are only a crippled elder, a new adult, and a powerful Canis who will die defending her pack.

She knew of Primitives because Kriina lived with them when they provided her sanctuary from a storm, when the male Lud saved her life.

Around the time Yu'ung was born.

"Come," she said, changing her tone from aggressive to relaxed, hoping that communicated her peaceable intent.

She scanned the group to see who responded as Old One hobbled to her side. His stick tapped in front of him, the sound muted by the cavern's thick layer of dirt. The Primitives tracked him with their eyes. Old One was right to expose himself. They would see him anyway since she invited them inside. She checked for others in the dark beyond this kith—what her People called a tribe and the Tall Ones called a band—but found none. One shouted gibberish at Old One and Yu'ung, then pawed the ground with his foot. Impatience? To her surprise, Old One prattled the same gibberish.

"How do you speak to them, Old One?"

"Your mother."

"What did you tell them?"

"Our necklaces concern them." He touched the one Yu'ung gave him. "They are similar to the Tall Ones. I am about to describe why we wear them and how we are a blend of many."

"I can't wait for you to explain Ocha."

When Old One finished, One-who-might-be-Leader jabbered to the confused faces around him. Yu'ung listened, connecting sounds to distill meaning as she always did, another skill she possessed few did. Yu'ung soon decrypted the Primitive's words, hand motions, and body movements.

Male-who-must-be-Leader described his kith. "Your kind deems us inferior because of our clothes, our spears, but we–"

"Aren't." From Yu'ung.

Her eyes flashed and then emptied of emotion. "Ocha, our kin, has never needed more than fangs and claws. I was born with your kind. My mother and I spent much time with a kith far from here before being forced to leave when a stampede trompled her mate."

Male-who-must-be-Leader scrubbed his face with his hands.

Old One smiled. "Why are you here?"

"We live at the mountain's base where we benefit from the rich vegetation and the specialized pebbles for tools. The wealth of stalks, roots, tubers, worms, grubs, and so many other foods in the fields provides ample sustenance in the absence of herds."

He sighed. "Not long ago, many kiths roamed these hills and canyons. We traded mates and stalked Mammoth together. When Mountain blew up, my tribe was tracking red-skinned deer we intended to share with others. We killed what we could carry, sheltered for the night, prepared the carcasses for transport the next day, and then slept.

"When we woke, the air was dense with smoke. Mountain has exploded in the past, but none this devastating. We raced to our homebase, passed many fleeing the area. We asked about our homebase. They confirmed it had collapsed and none escaped. Dag and I recalled this place from earlier trips and hoped because it was far from the usual homeland, it avoided the rock slides and cave-ins."

Old One asked, "Is this why your kith is small, because Angry Mountain killed the rest?"

Male-who-must-be-Leader squinted, his hands shaking. "That's part of it, but since then, sickness has claimed many, including our healer."

Yu'ung smelled the reek of disease that gripped those in front of her.

She approached Male-who-must-be-Leader, her voice low so he could hear but not the rest. "I am a healer. I will help if you'd like."

He fixed his tired eyes on her for the first time. They dampened and he forced a smile.

"I am Grg, Leader." With a wave behind himself, indicated, "My pairmate Ak, my hunt partner Dag, the child Zug, and our kin Toc. We were waiting for you to pass, but instead you entered our cave."

Yu'ung said, "This is Old One. I am Alpha of our tribe. Ocha is a tribe member, or pack member. We too almost perished in a cave-in."

Grg sighed. "Where are you going? There are none of your kind beyond this point."

"We go to the Mountain People. They offered sanctuary until the devastation ends." Yu'ung skipped the complicated nuances.

Grg pawed one foot then the other. "The mountains are a good refuge, but your Old One struggles to walk. How will he climb? The way up is filled with gorges, many deep waterways. Our healthy Elders can't manage the trails–"

Old One interrupted, "I can."

No one believed that, but didn't argue. Old One was an Elder.

Yu'ung said, "We will leave, go to another cave."

"The others have collapsed."

Old One met his gaze. "Ocha will find one for us."

Ak touched her ear and spoke to her pairmate. "Rest will help him," and nudged her lips toward Old One.

Yu'ung dipped her head. "She is right. We are tired and would benefit from a respite."

Grg understood. "How do you both speak like us?"

"As I said, I lived with a kith as a youngster, long enough to learn your communication."

She didn't explain about her innate ability to mimic languages and any skill after hearing or seeing them only once. Back then, she assumed all of her kind were similarly skilled, just not Primitives, didn't realize she was wrong until she and Kriina reunited with the People.

"When we left and rejoined the People, Old One's tribe, Mother and I used your speech for private communications. Because of that, we never forgot it."

Grg and Ak responded with surprised stares. Before they could ask more, Yu'ung changed the topic.

"Do you have as much difficulty pursuing prey as we do?"

Grg fixed his pale eyes on Yu'ung's grey ones. "There are few herds and less sign of them. Dag and I tracked one for a long distance, but by the time we caught up, other predators had beaten us there. When they finished, nothing but bones remained."

Yu'ung studied the assemblage in front of her, their hair brittle, wraps shiny with fur loss. The adults were haggard though alert, the youngster little more than bones wrapped in an insatiable curiosity that glowed in his eyes.

They have a good Leader. He keeps them optimistic despite adversity, first Mountain, now a well-fed, well-tooled tribe.

They were worth saving.

"We can help. Ocha and I rarely return without meat if it can be found." She brandished her spears. "Take us to your best guess of where herds are. We will do the rest."

Dag said, "I have heard stories of a female hunter." Yu'ung made no response so he asked, "The rest accept you?"

Yu'ung answered absently, picking bits of squashed bugs from her wrap. "Not at first, but when I out-performed them, what choice did they have? Now, I partner with B'o, my tribe's premiere hunter. The People rely on us."

Yu'ung beckoned Ak and Zug to her. Blood traced the boy's skin where he clawed long and hard.

"Ak. Has Zug suffered this itching for a while?"

She crossed her arms and hugged her chest. "Our salves no longer work."

"The blood attracts bugs which lay eggs in his cuts and make it worse. I have a poultice I will apply if you allow it."

After a rushed head bob from Ak, Yu'ung chewed a root into a mulch and then mixed in a sap.

"Zug!" The boy had been sitting with Ocha, but now hurried to Yu'ung, clawing his chest and neck. "Rub this where you itch. Press moss against the worst welts and tie it in place, to suck the poison from them. By tomorrow, it will stop."

With a nod of approval from Ak, Zug spread the dressing on his skin and left to gather brush for kindling and to block the entrance. Ocha gamboled along with him, drawn to the poultice's scent. When they returned, sticks piled in place by the hearth and the bramble barrier blocking the cave's opening, Zug dropped to his knees and wrestled with Ocha. Ak lifted a hand in warning, but the boy was too busy giggling to notice.

Ak's eyes dampened, face flushed. "He hasn't laughed or played like that since the destruction of our homebase." She rubbed her eyes. "That is a similar mulch to what our healer would have given Zug, but couldn't find it."

"I have a supply because of my healing duties, but I haven't seen any since leaving our homebase. It may be there, but buried in ash."

"The moss is a new addition. I will remember that." She indicated the hearth and scrunched her face. "Why store meat in the flames? Do you have so much you can waste?"

Yu'ung explained how heating flesh on hot flat stones made it more supple. "Elders with teeth problems appreciate it."

Ak pointed. "You put Deer's stomach in the flames also?"

"We fill it with water, scraps of flesh, roots, flavorings, and then heat it in the fire. When it bubbles, it's ready to eat. I'll fill a gourd for you."

As Ak slurped the stew, she poked her lips to another slab, this one with a depression that Yu'ung had filled with a mixture of damp lentils, nuts, roots, herbs, and stalks.

Yu'ung said, "We soaked them as we walked. I mashed in anything I could find along the way and heated it." She swiped a finger through the thick mixture. "Taste it."

Ak did, suspiciously. Her eyes popped open. "You must teach me," then indicated a bubbling gourd. "Is that food also?"

Yu'ung laughed. "No. It is sap, to repair spears."

"What?"

"Watch." Old One joined them and beckoned to the rest of Ak's kith. "They will want to see this."

Once everyone gathered, Yu'ung asked Grg, "Show me your spear? We attach our points differently."

Grg resisted at first, but curiosity won and he handed her his weapon. She rubbed her hand over where stone was hafted to shaft.

"You slipped the stone tip into a slot at the shaft's end and secured it with cordage. How often does it fall off on a hunt?"

Grg shrugged. "It's simple to rewrap."

"Glue means it almost never breaks."

"That can't be!"

Yu'ung extended her lance. "Try to break it."

Grg wrenched the tip, but failed to loosen it much less break it. Nor could Dag. They started to stick fingers into the bubbling sap, but Yu'ung batted their hands away.

"The fluid will stick to you and burn."

Grg asked, "Where do you get the sap-glue?"

"Watch."

Old One tossed a handful of rough bark into another gourd. Once melted, he stirred in beeswax. With a flat-tipped twig, he painted around a stone point atop a shaft. When cooled, he bound it in place with sinew.

Grg huffed. "What will you use in the mountains, when you are higher than where trees and bees live?"

"Glue can also be cooked from certain roots though the process is more complicated. We have never migrated anywhere without finding comparable ingredients."

Grg and Dag whispered together, concentrating. Yu'ung smoothed her hand along the shaft.

"We'll have a contest, see whose tip performs better."

Grg chuckled. "Neither of us has enough hunters."

"I have plenty," and nodded to Ocha.

Grg laughed. "That is your solution?"

Yu'ung rose. "I'll show you tomorrow. Now, Old One and I must sleep."

Dag stopped her. "Your spear is like the intruders'. Does your tribe include them, also?"

"You mean Tall Ones?" At his confusion, she explained, "The Uprights with high foreheads and narrow bodies who kill from afar with this far-throwing weapon?"

Grg's jaw tightened. "We avoid them, though there aren't any since Mountain's explosion."

Yu'ung ran her hand along the shaft. "It is superior to both yours and our thrusting weapons. I will show you tomorrow. It will change your attitudes about hunting."

Old One had fallen asleep against the cave wall. Yu'ung yawned, almost too tired to speak, but she had one more task to be sure they were safe.

"Grg, Ocha will stay in front of the cave, to stop any who try to enter. You and I, and the youngster Zug, can tend the fire."

Ak clamped her fingers together. "Zug and I will. From your looks, we are more rested."

Yu'ung yawned again, knowing she should disagree so Grg didn't see her as weak, but her lids never opened after a particularly slow blink. The last she remembered was Grg and Dag whispering about the upcoming hunt.

Chapter 8

Grg, Dag, Yu'ung, and Ocha gathered outside as the night sky lightened. Old One stayed behind with Ak, Toc, and Zug to show them how to make glue and prepare the hot stone and stew bag for cooking.

As Yu'ung left, Ak called after her, "The root mulch works. Zug improves."

Yu'ung's eyes clouded as she caught up with Grg. It felt good to help the boy, one thing she missed about being healer.

They set out, a mist covering the ground to just above her ankles. It hid the trace of other hunters, but Yu'ung doubted there were any.

She caught up to Grg. "Ocha will alert us when she finds prey. You and Dag do your usual. Ignore us. At the end, we see who brings in more carcasses."

Grg's jaw twitched. "The Canis will frighten the prey."

As he spoke, Ocha took off. Yu'ung watched her and dismissed Grg. "Except Ocha is smart enough to stay downwind," and raced after the Canis.

Yu'ung's head swiveled over the barren landscape as she ran. No worrisome trace, in fact, no life signs at all, just cold gray emptiness. She lost Ocha once, but the Canis beckoned with a low woof. Grg shouted from the opposite side of the field, "What–"

Yu'ung hissed to silence him. *No wonder he never gets prey!*

She finally picked up the scent Ocha tracked. Not deer. Pig? Then she heard a snort too loud and high to be Pig.

Grg appeared at her side, startling her. *What's he doing here?*

"It's not a herd. It's Giant Boar. We have tried often to bring it down, but it is smart. This is a waste of time."

They had traveled far from the cave with Old One. Yu'ung figured out why. "This is your old hunting terrain."

He grunted. "This Boar is alone. We thought it an easy kill, but the elder reached its dotage by being clever. It employs the same trick every time we chase it." He pointed to two close-set hills. "There's a passage between those hills that curves through the foothills. There is room for just one of us at a time to chase, in a column. Giant Boar knows this and sabotages us around the bends, attacking one of us at a time. Its tusk versus our spear. We never win!"

Even her far-throwing spear wouldn't work, not around bends.

"Instead of doing what always fails, Ocha will sneak upwind. Boar will smell Canis and flee toward you. Charge and funnel it to me. I'll attack with the Tall One spear. If I don't kill it, Ocha will."

Grg slapped his leg. "Let's go."

As expected, Giant Boar fled Ocha's scent toward Grg who flailed his arms to increase his size. Boar pivoted away and galloped close to Yu'ung. She cocked her far-throwing spear, waited for Boar to get just a bit closer, to give her a kill shot.

Dag destroyed her plan.

He didn't believe Yu'ung could kill Boar from such a distance so rushed Boar. It pivoted away from Yu'ung and rushed Dag, the new threat. Yu'ung hurried her throw and it hit Boar's back muscle instead of its throat, painful but nowhere close to lethal. Dag cocked his arm as he fearlessly ran full-speed and thrust with the power of youth, but the tip collapsed against the tough hide and Boar slammed into him, one horn catching his side. He flew into the air as though straw in a storm and would have been trampled except Yu'ung howled. The unexpected noise distracted Boar long enough for her to reach the creature and bayonet its neck with her thrusting spear. Boar tried to shake the spike loose which gave Ocha time to leap and rip into its throat. It bled out by the time Grg arrived.

Yu'ung left Boar to Grg and Ocha and rushed over to Dag.

"The puncture is deep but not fatal if you take care of it."

She packed the hole with mulch she always carried, sealed it with sap, and wrapped his shoulder in a soft skin. By the time she finished, Grg had cut Giant Boar into portable pieces. All of the group, including Dag, were in high spirits, despite that neither of Yu'ung's tips broke and Dag's did.

That evening, Yu'ung called Ak over. "Watch me clean Dag's injury."

Done, she motioned Ak into her position next to Dag. "Get me if the red fingers appear."

That would indicate poison entered his body. Yu'ung joined Old One by the hearth to replace and resharpen her tips, glancing occasionally at Ak.

She will do well as kith healer. She takes her task seriously.

Zug tended the fire and Ocha again curled up in the cave's entrance. No surprise to Yu'ung, Ocha didn't sleep, dozed at best, always listening for danger.

Yu'ung called to Ak the next morning, "Come while I check Zug and Dag."

"I did. They're both fine."

"They should stay here today with you, to check their treatments. Ocha, Grg, and I will hunt."

Zug growled. Dag grunted. No one liked to be incapacitated. Ocha quickly found the tracks of another Giant Boar, but they were old and Yu'ung and Grg never caught up with it. Ocha ranged far, searching for meat, but rejoined them as daylight ran out. No fresh kill so the group ate what remained of Boar, supplemented with the many tubers, roots, and worms harvested by Ak and Old One.

A gale blew off the range the next day, the burning rains keeping Yu'ung's head tilted forward and her eyes narrowed to slits as she released her early water. Inside, the fire crackled and smoke filtered outside through the vent. The storm continued all day and into the next. The group finished the last of Giant Boar and cooked the bones.

Yu'ung announced, "We have no more kindling," and left to collect it.

The land was soaked, but there were always dry places if you knew where to look. Yu'ung passed many scattered sodden logs before stopping at one buried under others. The harsh cold buffeted her as she muscled the stout log free and then chopped away the bark. As she worked, she ate her fill of the grubs who made their homes tucked against the interior wood and stuffed more in her satchel for Old One and the others. Finally, inside exposed, she chipped out piles of dry wood the rain hadn't reached and hurried back to the cave. The downpour worsened as she raced inside and dumped the tinder by the fire.

"This should last the night," and she squatted to warm her hands. Cold drained her energy.

Without discussing it, Yu'ung and Old One both recognized the time had come to resume their journey. She couldn't hear Grg and Dag's quiet discussions, but their bodies said they had arrived at the same conclusion. That evening, while eating the last of the marrow stew and a few rats Ocha snagged, Grg verbalized what was on everyone's minds.

"Food has run out here. We will follow one of the old herd trails. It will eventually lead to meat. You are welcome to join us."

Yu'ung glanced at Old One as she slurped the Boar-flavored gruel and chewed slivers of a rat.

"I appreciate your offer, but we will continue to the Mountain People. Old One will be able to rest and heal there while I follow the path my mother described that leads to the shoreless sea. Old One understands I may never come back but it is the best my People can do."

Scuffles and murmurs woke Yu'ung as the Primitives prepared to leave. The rain had stopped. Ash crusted the surface of everything that lived—plants, birds, burrows, trees, and waterways. Fat, gray clouds floated overhead. The tang in the air behind the soot must be snow.

Grg shambled up to her. "Dag found the freshest of the herd trails. It goes downhill, toward Sun's nest," the opposite of where Yu'ung and Old One headed.

She was Alpha. With that came responsibilities, but she didn't need to tell him.

She scratched her stomach and flicked a bug away that had been feasting on her blood. "The Mountain People await us. If Old One and I don't hurry, they will think we died, maybe move to a location I'm not familiar with."

Grg fixed his gaze on the white glistening peak that rose high above the devastation around them.

"There is an animal trail up the mountain's flank that wasn't blocked the last time we passed. It may lead to the Mountain People's likely home. Keep the woods with the highest canopies to your strong side, the valleys connected by earthen bridges to your weak side."

Yu'ung had swathed Old One's feet in hides as soon as she awoke, hoping they were healed enough to complete the journey. She had refilled her travel food and water the prior night, and stowed away the treatment herbs she and Ak collected, close to the ember that would light their evening fire if it didn't burn out as they traveled. She felt ready to leave, eager to finish this part of the trip and then make her way back to the People.

"Before we leave, I'll check Dag's wound."

Ak held a hand up. "No need. It is done."

She sounded confident, sure of herself and her new healing tasks.

"If poison enters the body, Ak, give him the fungus I left with you."

Ak held Yu'ung's hand, her damp gaze latching onto Yu'ung's. "I will not forget you or your lessons."

Face flushed, Ak pivoted and marched away. Yu'ung said nothing, just watched as Ak and her kith melted away like snow from a fire.

This is how Kriina must have felt parting from the Primitives long ago.

Then, she and Old One went uphill, slowly, at Old One's pace. His stooped posture and shambling steps were slower than Yu'ung would have hoped, but thanks to the extended rest, steady.

Ocha scrutinized Yu'ung and Old One, her blocky head bobbing from one to the other, and slapped her hand-sized paws against the ground. Yu'ung figured it out.

"Why not?"

She looped the strap of Old One's bag around Ocha's neck. The Canis wagged her tail, and bolted to do her scouting duty, no slower with the additional weight. Old One walked faster without the sack's weight, but she could see the strain it placed on his mind, that he didn't feel he was doing his part.

If we don't reach the Mountain People soon, we will be too weak to finish. Worse, if the snow arrives while I deliver him, I will not be able to leave.

She didn't want to be away from B'o, Shanadar, Kriina, and the rest of the People during the cold air time. Getting to the shoreless sea alone wasn't the problem. Them leaving before she did was. How would she find them then?

"Old One. We must go faster. It's time I carry you."

"No, that—"

Ocha snapped at Yu'ung and then at Old One.

"I think she wants my satchel. Me carrying you won't be much heavier than the bag."

"It's not—"

Yu'ung wasn't listening. All she wanted was to travel faster. She tilted her head. "I could hook them together and sling them across Ocha's back, one on either side."

Woof!

"Let's try it. If it fails, I'll take mine back."

Ignoring Old One's halfhearted arguments, she hoisted him onto her back, wrapped his arms around her neck, secured him with cordage, and started forward again. They ran when possible, otherwise, maintained whatever pace she could.

"You're lighter than my satchel, Old One. This is easier for me."

Additionally, the many migrations under the hot sun, a mark of the People's nomadic lifestyle, had strengthened her. It didn't matter how tired her muscles, how sore her feet, how hungry her stomach, or how exhausted her brain, she kept on, one foot in front of the other, as she did today.

Before leaving, B'o had provided detailed directions with landmarks to the Mountain People's highland home based on his one-time visit to Naa. For the People, it took no more than that to remember a route forever.

As they hiked, Yu'ung sang the Mountain People's danger call. If they heard it, they would come find Old One and Yu'ung.

They never did.

Later in the day, though difficult to tell how much later because Sun remained mostly invisible and the sky fuzzy, Yu'ung found water. It had become a challenge each day to find sufficient food and water, but eating worms, slugs, snails, spiders, ants, and smaller creatures proved sufficient for their needs. Similarly, finding instances of what she considered potable water had expanded significantly.

She panted to a halt by a muddy shoreline, deposited Old One among the reeds, dumped the bags off Ocha's back, and collapsed, too tired to drink. Her head hung, eyes slits. When her breath slowed, she sucked in enough water to fill her stomach. It was sludgy and gritty and glorious.

Old One lay prone on the shore, face immersed in the lukewarm pool. Ocha spun to her back, wriggling to scratch where her claws couldn't. Yu'ung massaged the kinks in her own muscles. Ocha's squirmy approach brought no relief so she ate a root bundle. Her supply of pain treatment plants was low, but not difficult to replace if she paid attention.

"Old One. Do you need this?" But he shook his head, stoic as always.

She stuffed it away. "Are you both ready?" Neither replied which Yu'ung took as assent and started again.

Is the day over?

She couldn't tell, without Sun to measure against the horizon, but she was exhausted. Her shoulders ached and arms cramped from pinning Old One in place. She tried to conceal her fatigue, but the growing futility made her legs heavy. Her feet barely lifted from the ground.

Old One hissed into her ear, "Let me walk."

"I'm fine. Mothers carry children. You are no heavier." She bounced Old One to her lower back, hoping a new spot would take the strain off her neck. "I will take more breaks." After a huff, she added, "Like now."

She slid him into the shade cast by the spreading branches of a tree. She clenched her jaw to keep from moaning as she forced her back straight, then shuffled in wandering circles until her breathing evened. Snake slithered over the cracked ground. It would be a good snack if she had the energy to catch it. The stale aroma of old dung revealed equally aged prints. Like Snake, if she weren't so tired, they would interest her.

Rejuvenated, she shucked Old One into place and continued, with as much vigor as she could muster. They came to a talus field skirting the flanks of what should be the final incline to the Mountain People's homeland. Yu'ung paused, staring up the cliff.

He said, "You can't climb with me on your back."

"I won't," and she stepped carefully through the loose pebbles, around boulders, and along a web of crevices that festooned the trajectory.

Too soon, she again slid Old One down and stretched. A solution to this problem existed. She just had to find it.

"You must stop. We can go no further," Old One grumbled.

That gave Yu'ung an idea.

Chapter 9

"A travois!"

It took no time to fashion one with the surfeit of logs littering the ground. Yu'ung would haul it by a strap around the end while Ocha carried the bags. They would trade duties as they journeyed. Old One objected. She ignored him.

"I've seen Mountain People trace." It wasn't true, but she wanted to give Old One hope.

Sweat soon soaked her wrap. It dripped over her pronounced brow ridge, stung her eyes, and plastered her hair to her back.

"A cave is ahead, Old One. We'll stop for the night."

It was early, but she could go no further. She dropped the travois and entered the space, ready to flee at the first sniff of menace. She inhaled aged dung and stale smoke, no recent habitation. She beckoned Old One. As he approached, she saw what she hadn't from his position on her back. His face was flushed, dimpled with sweat, and one of his injuries bled.

"I'll fix it." She exuded confidence as she smeared the re-opened wound with a mulched root.

Finished, he slept while she prepared a thin stew, more water than meat or vegetation, but it would be filling.

"Old One. Wake up. Eat."

"I'm tired, Yu'ung. Let me nap first."

Old One didn't wake the next day when Yu'ung did. His fever remained and his face still burned.

Ocha moaned, ears flat.

"I know, Ocha. We have to wait."

Ocha's head dropped between her paws, seemingly happy with the decision. Canis tended to hunt and live in a wide area, but they didn't migrate, not this far or long. She too must be tired.

Yu'ung drew herself up. *I'll hunt. There must be some critter that didn't escape. Food will raise our spirits.*

She debated taking Ocha and decided to leave her with Old One. Predators were few, but Old One's limited reserves of strength would never allow him to defend against an attacker. She positioned his walking stick-spear where he could reach it and left.

She hadn't gone far when porcupine tracks crossed her trail. Yu'ung hurried after the spiny creature. It smelled her and dove into a nearby burrow. It could hole up for days, but Yu'ung couldn't wait that long, not with Old One unable to defend himself. She could stab a burning stick down the passage if she had one.

If the tunnel is shallow, I can crawl in, lead with my lance, slay the porcupine when his escape runs out, and drag the carcass out.

Porcupine quills weren't as dangerous inside their lair so crawling after it was safer than chasing it in the open. The procedure became a repetitive routine—creep, stab, clear dirt, repeat. Bit by bit, Yu'ung advanced.

I hope there is no back exit.

I hope the roof doesn't collapse.

Heavy breathing and the scuffle of claws echoed through the narrow shaft.

You can dig, but I'm faster.

Her lance point hit the porcupine with a wet crunch. It hissed in anger—or pain—and she stabbed again. It squealed and she stuck again and again. When silence was the only answer, she thrust deeper, then twisted to hook her spear to the carcass, and crabbed backward, pulling the impaled animal with her. The creature gutted and slung over her shoulder, Yu'ung hurried back to the camp.

"I have food," she greeted Ocha and Old One and plopped the carcass by the fire.

Old One smiled. His eyes were clear, face visibly cooler than this morning.

"After I release my water, Yu'ung, I will help you."

He toddled outside as she cut the porcupine flesh into chunks, tossed some to Ocha, and laid the rest on flat surfaces to cook. A tantalizing aroma saturated the space as she resharpened her digging stick. The sky opened and a wall of hailstones crashed through the branches around their refuge.

Yu'ung jerked. "Where is Old One?" The weather had turned treacherous and now, Old One was out there, somewhere.

Ocha howled and sprinted away, Yu'ung behind. A fist-sized ball of hail hit Yu'ung in the middle of her shoulders and ice pummeled her arms, neck, and head. She dashed through the storm, attention fixed on a dark huddled shape curled farther down the cliff.

"Old One! Why are you here?" Her plea muted in the roaring storm.

"I am hot. I'll come back when I cool."

"You are soaked."

Without waiting for his response, she hoisted him up and raced for the cave, diving inside ahead of another barrage of ice.

"Dry yourself by the fire." He didn't argue.

Yu'ung tossed him her spare fur and rubbed her hands over her chilled arms. The small area was bright, the stone walls protecting them well from nature's chaotic assault. Old One slumbered and she ate, the juicy texture of Porcupine's meat filling her hollow stomach. Without planning to, darkness took her. The last Yu'ung heard was Ocha padding to the cave's entrance.

Old One was again flushed when Yu'ung awoke. She offered him the leftover flesh which he refused.

"Eat or be too weak to continue."

"I will," he said, and drifted away.

Yu'ung drooped. They could leave when the storm quit. A break would revive Old One.

But it continued. Ocha guarded. Old One slept. Yu'ung's cudgel had vanished somewhere on their journey, but she didn't notice because Old One rode where the club usually hung. This lull in their travels gave her time to replace it. She pulled out a short log collected along the trail, rounded one end and spun it through the flame. When the hiss of escaping steam ended, she tapered a handle and slammed the club on the ground.

It remained intact.

Old One awoke with his old energy. "I'll find food."

"We have porcupine."

He waddled out without acknowledging her.

It'll do him good to be independent, she thought, but expected nothing.

He surprised her, returning with a rabbit and a fish. He chopped them into pieces and placed the fragments in the fire. When the meat sizzled, she handed him a chunk, gave another to Ocha, and devoured the rest herself. Old One nibbled. She refused to let that bother her. He would eat when hungry. Besides, how much energy did he require to be carried?

As they huddled by the hearth, he tried again. "This is a good shelter, Yu'ung. It will shield me from the weather and enemies should there be any. I've demonstrated I can care for myself. I went to the river—"

"There's a river?" She thought the water in the air came from the storm.

"Ocha took me. It is stocked with fish like the one you just ate. It gives me everything I need."

Yu'ung didn't argue, rather picked a different approach. "If it is good for you, it is for me also. I am not leaving you."

He sighed, a heavy defeated exhale. "Then let's go."

Without further discussion, Yu'ung hoisted him onto the travois, shoulder sacks on Ocha.

The day was damp and raw. A wet mist blew over the hills and immediately covered their clothes and hair with fine droplets of moisture. The loose scree and increased grade forced her to pause often. Each time she stopped, she acted as though it was to drink. She did this slowly, allowing her overheated body to cool, checking the surroundings. Nothing she saw disturbed her. Most life fled Mountain's fury. Any they might face, she felt confident she and Ocha could handle.

"This river must be the Mountain People's water source. We will see them soon."

When they began again, the travois disintegrated with one tug.

Her shoulders slumped. "I'm surprised it lasted this long with all the scree fields and crevices we have crossed. I'll build another, Old One...."

"The same will happen. This ground is too rough."

Yu'ung forced a smile. "The Mountain People aren't far," and pointed as though at evidence of truth.

She hoisted him up, wrapped his legs around her waist, and marched onward. She followed a draw marked by tall sharp-needled trees mixed with others not quite barren despite the chill. Their remaining leaves shook in the breeze creating a soothing rustle. She moved at a relentless and deliberate pace, not as fast as usual, but not slow either. Still, the steeper grade tired her. Sun continued to hide behind the dirty clouds, making it impossible to tell how long before night arrived, but it didn't matter. Yu'ung couldn't continue.

"There's an overhang, Old One, close to the stream. Let's stop there for the night. We may not find better shelter."

With a small fire, the enclosure heated nicely.

After a meal of fish, compliments of Ocha, Yu'ung lay by the dying blaze, Old One toward the back with their satchels. She should check on him and resharpen her stone weapons, but her body refused to cooperate. She would never say to Old One or admit to herself, but if they didn't meet up with the Mountain People soon, she and Old One would die. The strain had become too much, but abandoning Old One wasn't an option.

We will die together—here if necessary.

Death meant nothing to Yu'ung. When her time came, or Old One's, neither would avoid it. Why would they? No one ever returned to explain what came next, how to prepare for it or embrace it. Xhosa in Yu'ung's dreams must be either dead or a spirit—like Ocha—yet their conversations were always purposeful. Both seemed without regrets for whatever they'd found after death.

She saw Old One move out of the corner of her eye. A spider crawled through his hair and he swatted it away, scratched where his scalp tingled from the tickle of its legs, then rolled onto his side, his back to her which was good. She wanted to talk to Xhosa.

"Xhosa. I appreciate your guidance, but tell me, will Old One survive? Will I?"

For the first time the entire journey, Yu'ung questioned if she could deliver on the promises she'd made to Old One and the People.

Disappointing them bothered her more than fatigue or hunger or personal threats. Shanadar would never quit a task assigned by Xhosa. Nor would B'o give up.

I will not be the one who fails!

She fell into a restless sleep. From out of nowhere came a handful of words.

No. And yes.

At some point, Ocha pressed her furred body against Yu'ung's and enveloped her in a sense of peace and security. An animal approached, but scurried away. The Canis' rhythmic breaths and the occasional paw kick lulled Yu'ung into peaceful slumber.

When morning woke her, Old One was gone. She jerked around. Ocha was also missing. The tension drained.

They're together.

The fire sputtered, nothing more than cinders.

They are collecting kindling, but something nagged at the edge of her consciousness.

I heard No *and* Yes *last night. What did that mean?*

A tingle spread through her body.

Ocha didn't go with Old One or in search of him.

Now fully awake, she followed the clear tracks left by Ocha until somewhere ahead, the Canis whimpered.

"Ocha! I'm here!"

Normally, she acknowledged Yu'ung, but not today. Yu'ung sped up, deftly maneuvering the twists of a meandering path as it snaked through a small forest. It wasn't until she freed herself from the last branches that they came into view. Old One had dragged himself to the stream. He was thirsty but tired, and toppled face-first into the water. Smudged paw prints said Ocha tried, but couldn't awaken him so lay at his side, head buried in her paws, drooping eyes fixed on Yu'ung.

Yu'ung collapsed to her knees.

Chapter 10

Kriina (Aynoh) and the Tall Ones

Hot cinders burned Aynoh's face. She slapped them away.

Why does my head throb? And why am I lying down in daylight?

"Get up."

She recognized the voice through pain's red mist. Her eyes managed to open a slit, enough to see a blur and then the stench of poorly cleaned wraps assaulted her.

"Qad. What are you doing?"

"Killing you, to prove you are not a spirit. You lied to us—as did Seer! You are not special, just a Primitive."

Aynoh shook her head, *No, I will never allow that,* but stopped short of growling. *Let him believe I am weak. When he gives me the chance, he will find how wrong he is.*

Aynoh's physical strength exceeded every Tall One except Grub, but was offset by their far-throwing spear. Qad must not get his weapon.

She trundled to her knees and then struggled to stand, managing to remain upright albeit wobbly. A crumpled body lay a short stone's throw away, a spear through his neck.

She whimpered, pretending fear.

Qad rolled his shoulders back. At his side, another spear. "He is not so dead he can't take your life, well, after *I* slay him in a failed effort to save you."

The lifeless body belonged to the People's kind. His tribe would wonder what happened, wait for his return. They would never know a lowly Tall One slaughtered him for no reason.

"You took his life to blame him for my murder?"

"Brilliant, isn't it? Fierce will thank me for trying to save you. My brother, Grub, will respect me. Your death will solve my problems."

"What did I do to inspire such hate?"

Qad's face changed from ebony to bright red. His teeth bared. "What did you do? Fierce and I were like brothers. You changed that when you stole his affection. How could you—a Primitive! I assumed he would become bored with you, but now, you're pairmates and he wants to take you with him."

To his homeland? She started to smile, but pinched it away. It served no purpose to annoy Qad, though as engrossed as he was in his rant, he probably wouldn't notice.

"You're a travesty!" He screamed. "I reminded him he called Primitive children an abomination in our homeland. How could he now sire one! Grub—he hated you more than I did until you saved my life."

Qad chewed his lip in confusion. His concentration diverted, Aynoh crawled toward him. If she attacked from close enough, he'd have to stab her with his spear, an unfamiliar skill for him. Her strength and familiarity with thrusting gave her the advantage.

He returned to his tirade. "Why pairmate you when another awaits his return?"

Aynoh jerked, pretending it was pain from where he hit her. "He has another pairmate? Doesn't your kind—like mine—have just one?"

Qad lifted his head, disgusted with her stupidity. "She *assumed*. It is supposed to happen when Fierce returned. It can't if you live." Qad chortled. "With you dead, they can pairmate! Fierce will like that."

When his crazed eyes darted far to the side, Aynoh crept nearer. She needed a lance. Wherever he put hers after knocking her out, she couldn't see it. The dead male had one, but removing it from his throat would take time and be obvious. Qad's weapon was her only reasonable alternative. It was close enough to reach if he was sufficiently distracted.

His head whipped back to her. "Why did you embarrass me?" Saliva sprayed from his lips. "You invited me to mate and then screamed when I led you to an isolated spot."

Invited him to mate? "No—"

"Fierce and Grub sided with you—a Primitive! Neither would talk to me."

"You shouldn't force mating on me. I am pairmated."

Qad guffawed. "You're a Primitive! And every one of us wanted to. Fierce refused to allow it." He scoffed. "But they'll forgive me when you're dead and I explain what happened."

"Your hate taints your words."

"You're wrong. Not about me hating you, because I do. About them not believing me. They will. I made sure of that. This morning, I told Fierce one of your kind was skulking around. I offered to protect you since he had to join the hunters. He thanked me!"

I don't believe you. Fierce doesn't trust you.

She listened for any rustle of movement. Silence, then inhaled but found neither Fierce nor Grub's scent. How long was she unconscious? Her fingers ferreted out the gash on her head.

Damp and sticky.

"Where are we, Qad?"

He glared at her. "Not far from the camp. You were gathering herbs," and he jabbed at the dead body. "When he assaulted you. I heard your cries, but was too late to save you. How sad."

Aynoh would have laughed if the situation weren't so dire. Fierce would never believe any of that. Her kind didn't hurt each other. It was not their way. Nor could the noisy Qad sneak up on one of them, not with their superior senses.

She shook her head, as though dizzy. He had no concept of her strength. The last time he tried to harm her, Grub intervened before she had to reveal it.

"How will you take my life, Qad?"

"Umm ... I'm not sure."

Aynoh bit back a giggle. *I'll help him.* "Claim this one overpowered me while I bent over to forage."

He scratched his shoulder. "You're saying I thought he would hurt you? Which explains why I struck him?"

"Yes! Because I am important to Seer and your Leader. You did what you must for the good of your band."

She pressed the raw wound on her head, swayed, feigning dizziness, and squinted as though struggling to focus. She put her hand on her temple pretending to block the pain. "No. There's a problem. My kind never murders—"

Qad jerked upright. "But you said I should act as though he was going to!"

Aynoh furrowed her brow and rubbed her head. "That's the snag. Fierce says you stayed with my kind when you first landed. You got to know them and their ways. Surely, you and the rest of the ... Chosen ... recognized we aren't violent."

"You're right, Aynoh, so what made this different?"

She fidgeted closer to him, eyes wide as though excited. "I've got it. You thought he was preparing to steal me back. You had to stop him kidnapping me, despite the threat to yourself. You assaulted him to defend me—and Fierce, my pairmate. And Seer who asked for my help."

"That's good! What else?"

She leaned toward him, pretending to ponder his request. "How you end his life is important. We're in the woods, among trees. Your far-throwing spear is worthless," she said, hoping he'd toss it away.

He didn't.

She wobbled to the dead body, as though to see him. "What if he knew me, came to rescue me. I told him I was happy with the Tall Ones, but he wouldn't listen, didn't believe that possible. You heard us arguing, saw him grab me, and attacked."

"Yes! I snuck up, skewered him before he could use you as a shield."

Aynoh shook her head. "No. That's a problem. You struck from behind."

"To stop him from hurting you!"

"No. He would hear you. Our senses are better than yours."

Qad tugged on his lip. "They *are*.... Why would I frighten him away and then chase him?"

Crows gathered in the trees, cawing, and a carrion bird already circled overhead. All waited for the Uprights departure to begin their feast on the rotting body.

Fierce will see the swarm and be drawn to it. I need to delay Qad just a little longer.

The scar above Qad's brow pulsed as he warmed to the topic of making her death appear real.

She interrupted his musing. "You must have chased him because the lethal stab comes from behind. We must explain why. If I was injured, you'd stay to treat my wounds, not chase him, so maybe I wasn't injured yet."

Qad glanced around, a dullness to his gaze not there before.
Something is wrong with him.

He smirked, poked his chest out, proud to come up with an answer she couldn't. "You angered him, enraged him, saying you'd prefer to stay with us—Tall Ones. He lost his temper and killed you. I could tell you were dead. I wanted revenge, justice."

He preened, but Aynoh shook her head, again.
Qad isn't thinking straight.

"That doesn't work either, Qad. My kind doesn't lose their temper and we don't react emotionally, not like your kind does."

Like you are doing, but she kept that to herself.

"No. He wouldn't kill me. Remember what I told you. My kind cherishes babies which means his tribe values mates. Fierce knows this. But I like the idea that he killed me. It makes more sense. Why else would he?"

"I made a mistake?" Qad asked, clearly unsure, but disliking the idea he must confess to a blunder to make the plan work. Aynoh grabbed onto it, a plan forming.

"Yes! A mistake. That is brilliant!" *For me. Not you.* "And that brought about my death! Everyone will feel sorry for you without blaming you. You must hit me, brutally enough that I pass out–again."

Qad drooled, anticipating being able to beat her again. "Hit you again?"

She secretly cheered. He now focused on the excitement of hitting her rather than the illogic of the kill. "I prefer to be unconscious when you stab me."

"Stab you?"

"By accident! Stay with me, Qad. You aimed for *him* to help *me* and missed! We are out of time."

Even to her, this sounded implausible, but he was too caught up in the excitement of beating her. She wasn't going to be able to use his spear so fumbled for the rock he assaulted her with. Even without it, she had no doubt she could beat him in a physical fight.

He lumbered nearer, spear gripped, eyes feverish with the thrill of what she asked of him, when someone yelled, "Aynoh!"

"Qad. You must do it now—quickly! I welcome it. The pain—" and she pressed her palm against her temple, "It is intolerable!" She swayed unsteadily while motioning him to her. "I think that's Grub. Look!"

He jerked toward the noise. Aynoh's hand closed on rock, as big as her hand and as round as a gourd. Before she could raise her arm to fling it, the ground trembled beneath her feet, at first mildly but then in waves. Her legs buckled. She plopped to her knees and spread her hands to steady herself. Qad toppled like a felled tree, hit his head on a stump and lay stunned. Above him, a boulder, precariously balanced, tilted.

"Qad! Move!"

All he managed was, "What?" before the huge rock crashed onto him. Aynoh screamed. The earth steadied. Grub called her name, the sound close and desperate. She ignored him and scrambled to Qad. If she didn't free him, the boulder's weight would crush the life out of his body.

"Aynoh!"

She barely heard the call. It might already be too late. She tucked her arms under the behemoth. With a howl, she flung the boulder, wider than her shoulders, away.

Qad's eyes fluttered open. "Aynoh. You're here. My legs.... Help me up...."

But she wouldn't be able to, not this time. Or ever.

Chapter 11

Qad's legs were squashed, but his chest and head remained untouched.

He murmured, "Thank you. I feel better. You saved me, Aynoh. Why?"

She bent over, eyes on his, face damp. "The boulder would … kill … you."

"But I tried to take your life."

"In the end, you hesitated," she lied. "I saw it, Qad. You wouldn't have, and you're important to Grub. He's my bandmate. It's that simple."

She forced him to focus on her, to keep his eyes off the red stain beneath his trunk. Death awaited him mere breaths away, but he needn't see it.

"Lie quietly. Once you have rested, I'll help you up."

Life would slip away before those few moments did.

"Nothing hurts, Aynoh, but I'm tired. Thank you... for...." He paused to gather energy to finish his thought.

Grub slid to a stop at his side. "Qad!"

Qad's eyes fluttered. He tried to smile. "Grub... Aynoh–she saved … my life...."

Grub whispered, "I saw her, Qad. What she did was impossible, and yet it happened."

Qad's torso rose and fell, rose, fell, and then didn't.

Aynoh wobbled to her feet. Blood sheeted down her forehead from some gash she didn't remember. Her head throbbed.

"But I couldn't save his life."

She jerked at the thought of another life she'd failed to save.

"Bhidid! His injury! I lost the treatment when I passed out."

Fierce shushed her. "He found it. That's how he knew something was wrong and searched out Grub and me."

Aynoh choked back nausea, tried to piece together how she got to this dark place where Qad intended to murder her and she him except the boulder beat her to it.

Fierce guided her back to the camp where he cared for her gash. As he worked, the excited chatter of her band mates discussing her capture and escape washed over her.

"Did you see her lift the boulder. No one I know can do that—not even you, Grub!" From Crevkukk.

Many of the People lift boulders, including children. They must. Our tribes are small.

Bhidid scuffed up to her, face flushed as he stammered a rush of gibberish that wouldn't have made sense even if she wasn't exhausted and in pain.

She stopped him. "Bhidid! Your wound—are you alright?"

He tugged at his lower lip. "Yes. I found the plants and did as you explained I should. That cleared my thinking which was when I remembered Qad said someone stalked you—"

Fierce grabbed Bhidid by the shoulders, face red with fury. "Why did it take so long to get me?"

"I wasn't sure I remembered right, being sick and all. I went to find the footprints Qad told me about. All I saw were Aynoh's and Qad's. No stalker. He lied to me, Fierce! That's when I came for you and Grub."

As Bhidid talked, Grub's face paled. Then his eyes darted every direction. Tension leaked from him like a gourd with a hole in the bottom. When Bhidid fell silent, Grub mumbled how Fierce trusted him and he failed to protect Aynoh.

Aynoh's eyes blazed. Her voice was barely a whisper, but no one missed her words. "I required no protection, Grub. Stop what you're thinking."

Grub hung his head. "That's true, other times, but today, you did and I wasn't there!"

Head pounding, she fought back another wave of nausea long enough to bristle. "No. I didn't."

Grub had no response for that. If he hadn't known before, he knew now Aynoh would never be weak or needy.

Fierce asked, "After what he did to you, Aynoh, why try to save his life?"

"He's a group member! And Grub's brother. Wouldn't you do the same?"

Fierce thinned his lips and glanced at Grub. "Regardless of his travesties, Qad must be interred in customary fashion."

Grub roused himself from his dark mood and hoisted his brother onto his shoulder, carried him to a deep hole off to the side of the camp, and dropped him in. Everyone tossed dirt and scree on top until no sign of the body remained. Aynoh didn't ask why they buried him in his clothes and necklace when others could wear them. Many Tall One customs were odd to her.

Fierce asked Aynoh, "How do you want the one of your kind interred?"

His tribe would never know if he lived or died, nor would Aynoh's People if she failed to reunite with them.

"The same, but I'll keep his pelts." These she stuffed into her sack, knowing one of the People would use them.

That done, the band gathered their supplies and left. No one spoke of Qad after that, the attitude in this case the same as the People, that normalcy must supersede death.

Cinder and smoke darkened the sky day after day. Landmarks that might have guided their travel were invisible. The distant soaring mountains, the aroma of particular flowers, the hill with the lone sapling on top–dirty air hid them all. The worst part was this began to feel normal.

That night, settled into the camp, Aynoh softened cordage by the fire, running the vine through the web between her thumb and finger, over and over, wondering if she like the land would ever be who she had been with the People? She had debated taking a life to save her own, something she never before considered. Fierce's kind commonly executed those deemed a threat, even before they caused trouble. The band accepted this to maintain safety. Would she slay an Upright who threatened her or her tribe? When Fierce first explained how such drastic measures kept order in their groups, Aynoh had disagreed, but did she now? Her head spun trying to make sense of recent events.

Am I becoming like the Tall Ones?

Fierce crouched at her side and asked, "How did you react so calmly to Qad?"

She chuckled. "Because I was. He considered me weak, saw what he expected, never me." She paused to study Fierce's face, then asked, "Are Tall One females frail?"

He squirmed. "They rarely do as you did."

"Why not?"

Fierce scanned the assemblage, but all looked away, some snickered, happy to leave this discussion to him.

"They deem men more skilled at tasks requiring aggression and females at others. Wouldn't you agree, Aynoh, the females of your kind consider themselves more and less capable depending upon the duty? For example, Yu'ung is the first to be Alpha. Why hasn't a female held that position in the past?"

It was a good question. "I suppose we agree with you in a way. Our females are physically strong, but males more so. Body strength has been considered fundamental to succeeding as an Alpha. Now that you have me thinking about it, I don't know why, especially since Alphas strategize and plan more than fight. Yu'ung has already proven her superiority as a hunter so the tribe was more willing to accept she could succeed as an Alpha. Other jobs—foraging, knapping tools, scouting, tracking, cooking, healing—males and females perform equally."

"But not healing. You and Yu'ung are the healers."

"True. That task has been filled by males and females in the past, but it is Yu'ung and I who save more lives than any healer in the past for reasons neither of us understand. This is probably the case of your Seer, too."

Her words were freighted with meaning, likely confusing to him, but she didn't bother explaining any further.

Fierce tugged his lip. "Why not B'o? For Alpha? Surely, he's competent enough and respected as a leader."

Aynoh hooked a loose rope of hair behind her ear. "He was selected, but refused."

Fierce scratched his cheek. "Alpha is temporary among the People. What will Yu'ung do when it ends?"

"The answer is more complicated than the question. It is best she answer that, but let me ask you. Why choose the bowed spear when you have a far-throwing one?"

Fierce chortled. "You've been watching. Bowed spears are new to us. We discovered them just before leaving on this journey, through another band. We brought them, hoping to practice, have done so only enough to consider it a better weapon than the traditional spear for particular situations."

"Like…"

"The obvious is once I throw the latter, it's gone. Arrows—the spear part of the bowed spear—are lightweight and as deadly as a lance. I shoot one. Another is ready."

"Like my throwing stones."

"But more lethal."

She never considered "What if one didn't solve the problem?" How had she missed that?

"Show me."

He studied her face for a breath, must have decided she was serious, and pulled materials from his bag. "The bowed spear is narrower than our throwing spear. We attach cordage to notches in the ends. This one broke. You can watch as I repair it."

Aynoh wrinkled her brow. "The cord is shorter than the bowed spear."

"On purpose. I slip the looped cords into the cuts. The special wood bends without breaking. Now, the arrows."

One at a time, Fierce smoothed the branches with sand and oiled them with fat.

When finished, he beckoned the rest of the band. "Come. Aynoh wishes a demonstration of the bowed spear."

They trotted to a field adjacent to the camp. At the far end was a haphazard pile of logs strewn by the storms. Each male shot one arrow after another until the logs looked like porcupine quills. All were embedded deep enough to be lethal.

"You see the difference with the spear. My spear is as accurate and mortal, but once thrown, I have no more. With the bowed spear, I have many arrows."

Aynoh made a muffled squeak. "I must master both."

Aynoh wiped her brow. They had been marching all day. Angry Mountain blackened the land everywhere. Dead branches lay naked against the landscape. Dry broken grass reminded her to be happy for her shredded and worn foot shields.

She was harvesting an herb to salve muscle pain when Fierce trotted up. "I found a cave."

She straightened and rubbed her back. "I will check for a message from Yu'ung."

"If there isn't one, she's probably behind us. Tell her not to follow our tracks if they haven't been erased, to keep Sun's nest to her dominant side, that we have a task to finish before rejoining her."

On overcast days, when Sun was invisible, the tribe used moss and lichen growth to identify direction, but here as everywhere, the fire had burnt or suffocated it. Mountain's anger, though, couldn't modify the wind. Yu'ung would see which direction the wind blew the trees and use that to guide her.

"Will Yu'ung reach the shoreless sea before us?"

"Children and elders will make her progress more sluggish than ours. Even falling behind as we must, I have no doubt we'll catch up."

Aynoh scratched her chest and behind her ears. She and Fierce hadn't groomed each other in a while because nightly duties kept both of them busy. The tiny critters feasting on their skin and dry sweat had become painful.

Her face clouded. "Without us as guide, you're sure the People won't miss the shoreless sea?"

"They can't. It fills the horizon."

He stared into the void, seeming to forget her presence.

Aynoh prodded. "If she is ahead and her tracks hidden, how will we find her in this vastness?"

He blinked and then again. "In your next message, tell her to light a fire each night. We'll look for it."

"What's so important about this side trip, Fierce?"

"Salt. We are almost out of what we mined at shoreless sea."

Aynoh wrinkled her brow. The People never lacked salt. When herds migrated in hot times, the tribe went to the animal's salt licks or harvested certain salt-filled leaves and roots. With those unavailable, she had been relying on Fierce, but it seemed his stock also was low.

"How do you separate salt from water?"

"I'll show you when we arrive. It is simpler than you think."

That night, while everyone worked, Aynoh shuffled into the cave's dark tunnels. Torch light splashed off the rough walls. There were no messages from Yu'ung so she stopped at an expansive unblemished surface and etched shapes and markings into the surface, placing a divided box adjacent to them.

The Tall Ones don't understand ours and have none of their own. How do they communicate with their kind?

By the time she finished and returned to the cavern, everyone was asleep.

Early the next day, they left the heavily trodden animal path they had been traveling and passed into flat, dry monotonous scrubland without landmarks or waterholes or any relief save the craggy, sharp-edged peaks that limned the distant horizon.

Will we climb those mountains?

Empty, lifeless quiet cloaked the landscape. Each day was colder than the prior. She donned both of her wraps and foot shields, and still the chill penetrated to her skin.

Well into another endless trekking day, eyes bleary from the nonstop emptiness, she froze in place.

"Fierce. Did you see that sparkle?"

He shook his head, eyes partially closed. "Probably a hearth fire."

"Maybe," but why did it blink on and off?

No, it isn't a firepit. Someone is watching us.

Chapter 12

Shanadar and the People

The rendered fat improved the People's diet. To this, they added vegetation, roots, and any other meat harvested by the Canis. With plant life more abundant farther from Mountain's eruption, hunger became less critical.

Most days started before night's darkness ended, like today. White Streak trotted at Shanadar's side through the high grass, stalks swaying to their steps as though from a gentle breeze. Ump and Ragged Ear, joined by Laak, bounded ahead to scout. Shanadar recognized the Canis' eagerness to get where they headed, but not why. White Streak stayed with the People, at a pace the females and subadults could maintain. He touched White Streak's soft pricked ears, asking why the rest of her pack moved so quickly, but the huffed response told him nothing. When the children tired, he told the females to carry them on their backs, that the group had to hurry.

B'o panted up to Shanadar's side, sweat dimpling his face. Shanadar thought he was going to suggest they slow down, but instead, B'o wheezed, "Tell us when you leave in the mornings. Otherwise, we waste time looking for you."

That confused Shanadar. "You saw me go, didn't you, with the Canis?"

He shrugged. "This time. Other times, you're just gone."

Shanadar thought back to other mornings when he left without seeing anyone, assuming they'd know he was gone and follow.

He could see B'o's point. "Of course. I should consider that."

They continued in companionable silence until B'o asked, "You freshened your stripes. Why?"

"The colors tell those who see the group that we are part of something bigger."

How is that not obvious?

B'o stretched his lips into the semblance of a smile. "Even with only you in the group painted?"

Shanadar sighed softly. "It's not uncommon."

B'o's awkward smile evaporated. He looked about to ask a question, but didn't. So much about B'o continued to annoy Shanadar. He massaged Wise Stone with his thumb, calmed by the smooth surface. The eyes often blinked and the red necklace sparkled. He kept it in his hand as often as possible during the day, in case it wished to speak to him. Nights, it held pride of place beside his head, where other males laid their spears.

B'o coughed, eyed Shanadar sideways, and asked, "Are you worried about Yu'ung?"

Do I act worried? "No." *What worries me is taking the wrong route, but B'o doesn't need to know that.*

Shanadar nimbly clambered over a pile of debris, hoping to leave B'o behind, but his fellow leader matched him step for step.

As though the quiet made him nervous, B'o asked. "How much farther?"

Shanadar responded by brandishing a stick from his satchel at B'o.

"That means nothing to me, Shanadar."

"On my outbound trip, I scored this stick each time Moon didn't appear. There are as many notches as you have fingers. The journey we now take will be shorter, so not as many no-Moons, but it will be long."

He'd never been to shoreless sea, but Xhosa told him it was closer.

B'o wiped a hand across his brow and flung the sweat aside. "Did you explain that to Old One? Is that why he refused to join us?"

"He didn't need my guidance. Old One knows things that can't be explained. His decision to remain behind and Yu'ung's to stay with him were right. His crippled legs and gimpy feet would have forced us to leave him somewhere along the way, in strange lands."

He peeked at B'o to see if the comment disturbed him, but his co-leader strode resolutely onward, spear clutched, brawny legs as energized as when the day started. Their kind–his and B'o's–did what must be done without complaint. Shanadar's duty was to lead the People to the shoreless sea, B'o's to support him.

With my stripes, B'o's menacing form, and the Canis, we appear commanding.

On his outbound trip, being alone, Shanadar had examined what would make him appear indomitable or vulnerable. A wide stride, raised head, puffed chest, and tensed muscles did the former while a curled-in body, furtive glances, and nervous steps announced easy prey to those watching. When he could find no Uprights to study, he analyzed the gait and stance of Canis. They always delivered the impression of lethal deadliness. He made these characteristics part of who he was until little was left of the carefree, distracted youth who once naively accepted the impossible task of rescuing Yu'ung. He purged his insecurities, his movements now efficient instead of unsure, his eyes the sharp focus of a predator.

"What frightens you, B'o?"

He glared sharply at Shanadar. "Nothing. Don't mistake worry for fear. They're not the same."

Shanadar didn't agree. "Worry that Yu'ung will not return is fear," but he didn't blame B'o.

Today, White Streak led, establishing an aggressive pace Shanadar could maintain but which might be a struggle for the females with subadults and children. B'o walked with Ese. Ump and Ragged Ear scouted while White Streak and Laak patrolled the backtrail. Each Canis announced themselves with short howls and woofs. At one point, Laak called with an almost perfect Canis voice.

He is learning.

A termite mound rose ahead, taller than Shanadar and as wide as a boulder. During good times, it was stuffed with enough of the white furless critters to feed the entire tribe. This one was dead and rotting.

Beyond it stood leafless saplings that smelled of soot and dirt. In better times, they provided sanctuary to squirrels and birds and all sort of tasty treats. Now, they were abandoned.

"Shanadar. Did you hear the Canis howl? Do we have a problem?"

"Not since the last."

Those "last" were a ragtag assembly who mistakenly assumed Uprights led by females and a skinny male who waved empty hands in the air would be easy prey. They fled, barely escaping the Canis.

Shanadar took note of B'o's hunched shoulders, the lines in his forehead, the parted lips, and decided encouragement was called for.

"How is Laak's plot to arm everyone?"

"Better than I expected. The females have no fear." B'o grunted. "Fierce was right. Laak possesses a warrior's attitude." He poked his lower lip ahead. "The occasional howls and yelps you hear–that's Ump teaching him."

B'o stopped talking, finished with what he had to say.

A pleasant change from the nervous babble of the journey's start.

Shanadar spent the quiet ruminating. Yu'ung's People trusted him despite his slender build, the knot in his hair adorned with a feather, and the stripes that colored his face. Trust was unusual to Shanadar, given his oddities, but Xhosa convinced him that normal in a changed world was a poor goal. She picked him for his intellectual fearlessness and willingness to do what others wouldn't. She convinced him to own his oddities and appreciate their purpose in this new world. Because of his skill calling meat with the bone flute and the Canis' hunting prowess, the tribe thrived.

Laak hurried up to them. "White Streak and I found a lake ahead. It's clear. I think we can all drink."

B'o waved. "Lead. We could use a break."

The tribe quenched their thirst, then fished, ate their fill and stuffed what remained of their catch into their satchels. While many harvested cat-tails to supplement later meals, B'o and Laak tracked Giant Pig prints Ragged Ear found. They had seen none of this animal since the migration began. The flesh would fill their stomachs and the fat protect their skin and smooth their weapons. Shanadar rested under a tree with Ump and tried to beckon Xhosa with his bone flute. Their last contact had been before departing the People's original camp.

A scream erupted. "Ruk! He was here and now he's nowhere!"

Ruk only recently acquired his name. Infants weren't assigned one until they proved capable of surviving the rigors of early life. Then, they became part of the tribe which included simple age-appropriate chores like delivering stones for knapping and bones for cooking to those who required them. Ruk always ran, chubby legs churning, eager to help.

Everyone scattered, searching. Shanadar called Ump and White Streak to him. The Canis had explored Ruk many times with their noses, curious about the tiny, clean-smelling Upright. They enjoyed his giggles and fearlessness. Each member gave off their own unique scent which the Canis imprinted into memory.

"Locate Ruk."

The Canis snuffled around where Ruk was last and galloped away. Yowls exploded somewhere out of sight, accompanied by wet snarls and a painful cry. Ruk's mother collapsed, but when silence followed, Shanadar relaxed.

Victory.

Ump trotted into sight, head up, blood on his fangs. Ruk straddled his back. White Streak nuzzled the giggling child to keep him in place. A bite festooned Ruk's leg and a scratch his arm, both easily treated by Ese's poultices. Coming up behind were B'o and Laak lugging a Giant Pig, its throat torn out.

It must be the one that left the tracks Ragged Ear found.

B'o tugged Shanadar aside. "Laak and I passed a cave. We can shelter there for the night."

Ese and Jhat started a fire in a pit set up by a previous inhabitant. They cut the carcass into pieces, some to cook immediately, the rest to dry. As everyone ate, the conversation centered on the usual topics.

"When will we see Yu'ung and Old One?"

"Tell us again about our new homebase...."

"Is Kriina safe with the Tall Ones?"

Shanadar rarely joined in, using the time to study the group or ruminate over his own thoughts. Tonight, he studied B'o. The male's haunted eyes, strained face, tense shoulders, and rough breathing reinforced what Shanadar felt earlier. Something bothered him. Ump too gazed at B'o, fringed tail waving.

You feel it too.

As though reacting to their interest, B'o spoke without looking at Shanadar. "I was happy Old One supported Yu'ung as Alpha. I'm not a problem-solver in the way she is or a sage like him. But I didn't consider what I would do in their absence."

"If those duties fell to you."

"I should have. We tell the youngest to look around, see what needs doing, yet I didn't."

"We are both learning." Shanadar was as frightened of leading as B'o.

B'o slapped his thighs. "Yu'ung will lead when she rejoins us, but you and I will do what we must until then."

Laak yelled from the cave's mouth. "The fake spears are ready!"

The group gathered and Laak presented the faux spears to the females and taller subadults, explained how to care for them as though real and carry them like a warrior. Those ready for more, Laak and B'o showed how to thrust with two hands, one for power, the other for direction. Laak repeated Fierce's caution–Tall Ones were not nice.

Shanadar observed, willing to help, but hoping he wouldn't be called on. B'o's mixed personality–tough and fearless when necessary, friendly when required–reminded Shanadar of the early days with his former tribe, how he tried to mimic those best at stalking prey and invariably failed, how his actions would have led to his ousting if not for his mother's intervention.

He poked a stiff twig into his teeth trying to loosen a piece of food lodged tightly where it shouldn't be, lost in the females' enthusiasm as they grew into their task as tribe defenders.

The next day, as Shanadar played a fast tempo on his bone flute, to keep everyone moving quickly, Laak joined him.

"How do you pick what to play on your flute?"

"Sometimes, I match birdsong, other times, tones inside my head."

That night, all gathered to practice with their pseudo spears while Shanadar slipped into the cave's tunnels. On a pristine rock, he chiseled triangles, circles, dots, lines, and shapes, coloring some but not all. Satisfied with the message, he stowed his paint kit. His firestick burned out and he hadn't brought a fresh one, but the passage went only one place. He shuffled along in the dark, hand guiding him, fingertips scratching the rough wall.

Chapter 13

Ragged Ear woke Shanadar. Hackles raised, after a soft moan, he sprinted away.

Something is wrong.

"B'o!" They chased after the Canis and found him stopped not far from the camp, legs spread, snout raised.

B'o squatted. "Upright prints," visually tracking where they headed. "Shanadar. Go back. Get the group started. We'll catch up when I see where these go."

He sprinted away, Ragged Ear in the lead.

Good. I am not the best tracker.

When Shanadar rejoined the People, White Streak moaned, head pivoting from Shanadar to his backtrail. Whatever she figured out made her yowl and spring after Ragged Ear and B'o.

Ese stared at Shanadar briefly, for the first time since they started, her gaze tinged with respect.

"Let's go, Ese."

Without question, she shucked her sack to her shoulder. "That's how it's going to be," and headed the opposite direction of B'o, motioning the rest to follow.

She is valuable.

Shanadar established a fast pace with his musical tones, never slowing, never stopping for a break, wondering how B'o and the Canis were doing. Laak stayed with Shanadar while Ump scouted just out of sight on a ridge where he would see threats before they saw the tribe.

B'o and Ragged Ear caught up before the People had gone what Shanadar guessed was both hands of Sun's overhead travel.

Face strained, eyes alert, B'o muttered, "It is Uprights. I'm not sure if it's our kind or Tall Ones. They travel adjacent to us." He nudged his lips to the strong side. "I couldn't tell if they were hostile, but they carry spears."

"I'm Lead Warrior. I'll follow them," and Laak darted off, Ragged Ear in tow.

B'o turned back to Shanadar. "They aren't trying to catch up or intercept us, just follow our route."

Shanadar spoke calmly, hand on Ump's head, "Then we have nothing to worry about. The Canis protect us."

B'o dipped his head. "Laak's scouting—"

"And warrior instinct."

B'o nodded. "Has improved. Spending time with White Streak and the other Canis has made his strategies more focused and movements less erratic."

"He mimics them."

"They are building him into what Fierce calls a Lead Warrior."

B'o prattled on, but to Shanadar, it was nothing more than the nervous blather of someone unsure what to do against armed strangers with unclear intentions. Shanadar stopped listening. If the Uprights' intent was evil, the Canis would take care of them. Somewhere ahead, Ragged Ear woofed and White Streak took off. Ump started to, but stayed, as though realizing that would leave Shanadar and the rest of his pack unprotected.

"Whoever hunts us is now the hunted."

That evening, after the People settled for the night, Ragged Ear limped into the camp and plopped at Shanadar's side. Mud caked his belly and legs, dirt and gravel rooted in his pads. A gash scored his head, fangs tinged crimson. His tail swayed side to side through the dirt, steady. White Streak pranced after him, bloody, but Shanadar saw no cuts or gashes on her body.

He lifted Ragged Ear's sore paw, extracted an embedded thorn and was rewarded with a happy pant.

Shanadar said to B'o, "No one threatens us anymore."

Daylight resumed without stalker prints. Shanadar played his flute faster than usual, wanting to put distance between themselves and this enemy, in case there were more of them. They found an alcove for the night just as what pretended to be sunlight faded. They ate, skipping the hearth, not wanting the sparkling light to reveal their position, and slept.

A day later, they had a new stalker.

"Where?" asked Shanadar.

B'o marched to the clearing's edge, White Streak with him, and indicated child size prints.

Shanadar eyed White Streak. "She recognizes the scent. This might be a member of the tribe that she and Ragged Ear rid us of earlier."

They followed the youngster's trail to where the tribe tossed spoiled and old food, far enough away that scavengers would not become a problem. The remnants from an old stew, discarded the prior night, had vanished.

From then on, the youngster shadowed the People, hiding his identity but not his presence. He—or she—had either made friends with White Streak or was too hungry to worry about the threat posed by a Canis.

B'o said, "He keeps a distance, but not too far. Anyone watching would consider him our scout."

Day after day, the child dogged them. Only when caves weren't around was he absent.

Mountain had stopped destroying the land, only sporadically thundering fiery cinders atop the travelers, but the rain when it fell seared their skin. Without leafy canopies, the air was cold. The tribe huddled in piles of arms and legs to share body heat. Shanadar wondered why the young stalker didn't freeze. All he had for protection was disheveled mounds of crumpled leaves or occasional dug-out tree roots with just enough space for a subadult.

I need to bring him in.

That night, Shanadar slipped away with a hare Ump caught. He placed it by the waste and then hid in a hollow trunk next to Spider and its web. He tried to remain alert, but the enclosure was cozy and movement would give his presence away. Soon, his eyes drooped and his head nodded.

If not for the stink—like rotten carrion—Shanadar would have missed the boy, clothed in a tattered shirt with more holes than hide. He crawled forward, eager to snatch the treat. A blood-crusted gash cut his brow and a puncture on his leg in the dim light looked to be a bite. Shanadar thought about the first tracks he and B'o discovered.

White Streak defended you from someone.

Shanadar rubbed hard under his nose. The child's stench was appalling. White Streak lifted her head, a short stone toss away, and snarled. The boy started to shake.

Part 3

Tribes Search for Each Other

Chapter 14

Yu'ung, alone

Yu'ung collapsed beside Ocha and stared damp-eyed at the dead elder. It was Old One who taught her the skills that must now guide her. He believed her capable of leading her People to unknown lands, what most would deem impossible. Did he envision her doing so alone, the sole companion a floppy-eared, fur-covered Canis?

"His passing served a purpose. He knew I would never desert him."

Ocha woofed.

"I saw no chasms in the cave, so we inter him here, by the stream."

Should I take the necklace I crafted for him, to match mine?

In the end, she placed it with him, in a narrow crevasse, covered with mud and dirt. What if he needed it wherever he ended up? Besides, if anyone discovered his skeleton, it would tell them this elder belonged to something larger than himself. Quivering cat-tails marked Snake's progress below the waterline. A shift in the dark shadows announced the presence of another creature rapidly absorbed by the gloom.

If a hungry animal digs him up, I won't begrudge him a meal. I consume green carcasses during starving times.

Ocha moaned.

"Not yet. I have a final task."

Back at their shelter, she heated pulverized bones and blended the oil with ground red ochre, charcoal, stone chips, and spit. After stirring the concoction with a flat stick, she tromped into the tunnels, stopping at the wall she identified on an earlier exploration, and painted pre-arranged lines, dots, and triangles by a peaked square, the symbol for a revered elder. The message announced to any who recognized the drawings the burial outside of someone important.

This was the People's way.

As she worked, Ocha lay on her back, paws aerial, head tipped to the side, sides rising and falling, nose mashed against the ground in a most uncomfortable-looking manner. Any intruder who thought her asleep or dead needed to pay better attention to her infinitesimal ear twitches and tiny shudders.

However, the snore might say otherwise.

"Ocha! Wake up!"

The Canis jerked upright, ears akimbo, and panted a happy grin.

Yu'ung stuffed the paint kit into her shoulder sack, next to the porcupine spines she expected to discover a use for with time, and scuffed up to the glowing fire pit.

"We're alone."

Ocha nudged her and licked a muddy leg, pausing once to snap at a bug with the temerity to crawl through her fur.

"Now, we must locate the People and Kriina."

Ocha snorted.

"Your query deserves an answer though it may not satisfy you. My faith in Shanadar is based on yours." She looked away, hoping the Canis didn't see the doubt in her eyes.

Yu'ung's only option had become relying on this strange Upright with Tall One facial stripes who wore his hair in a tail.

"He did save my life."

Ocha padded around the hearth to flop at her side, asking, "When do we depart?"

Yu'ung yawned. "Tomorrow. Wake me."

Ocha was already outside, waiting as Yu'ung plucked a dying ember from the fire, stuffed Old One's bag into hers, and marched out of the cave. Ocha snorted happily, gaze on Yu'ung, awaiting direction.

"Let's hope those cairns and landmarks are still there, Ocha."

B'o assured her he had placed them firmly. The question was whether they survived Mountain's anger.

Ocha yowled as they trotted which made Yu'ung chuckle. "Why do cairns mark an out-of-the-way trail? It's a good story, Ocha. When I was a new subadult, B'o offered his hunt expertise to assist the Mountain People. The hunt was so successful, he helped them carry massive amounts of Mammoth back to their home cave and then spent time with them discussing hunting strategies and weapons, cooking techniques, and how to preserve flesh for later consumption. B'o was a natural fit for the group, mated the Mountain People Naa often, and discussed pairmating with her. To make that happen, he must confirm his current pairmate Ese would join them and ensure his People would not suffer by their departure. The Mountain People Leader told B'o of a fast but challenging route to the People's homebase which B'o marked with cairns and in memory with landmarks, his intention to make the return trip easier. After rejoining the People, he gave no more thought to this trail.

"Until Yu'ung's journey with Old One."

The People never forgot a course whether traveled often or once or simply described by another who heard it through someone else. B'o declared this one too taxing for Old One, but good for Yu'ung after delivering the Elder where he would likely live out his life. Since Yu'ung wasn't where B'o expected her to be, she must cross the steep flanks to the intersection of B'o's shortcut and her path.

They picked their way across the slope, finally arriving at the soaring tree that leaned heavily to the side as B'o described, where the downhill trek began. There was a plethora of paths, depending upon where the traveler wanted to go, and none with a cairn. Well, one might have been there once, but Mountain's anger had destroyed it. Yu'ung crouched, rested her arms on her knees, and tossed pebbles downhill while studying the too-many choices.

One dropped off a ledge.

That's too steep.

Another curved out of sight.

That circles back to where we started.

The last had the most broken branches and scuffed scree. *It must lead to a waterhole.* She sniffed. Ocha stared ahead.

"Let's take the first, despite its sheer slope," and Yu'ung strode forward.

In no time, they were skidding on loose shale, slipping around huge chunks of dirt disgorged by Angry Mountain, leaping over cracks, and clawing for balance on the rubble-laden slope. Ocha's reassuring presence offset Yu'ung's disquiet.

To distract herself, she asked, "Do you migrate?"

Ocha's brows bunched, what Yu'ung took to be *No. Why leave a good area?*

"I see your point."

After several steep ravines and a few ledges—one skirted to avoid a snake nest—they landed at the bottom. The terrain here was rumpled land spotted liberally with dead shrubs, nothing like the fields of bright flowers B'o had described. The borders were bounded by what both Xhosa and B'o proclaimed to be a jagged string of smoking summits.

She was in the right place.

It was days before another cairn revealed itself. Though toppled over, its meaning was obvious.

"B'o wants Mountain on our dominant side. If we don't discover additional messages or the People's trail, we'll follow the instructions Kriina left in the Tall One's camp on how to travel to shoreless sea. If we don't find Kriina before, we will find her there as well as our tribe."

She glanced at Ocha, to see if she had any comment, but got only more bunched eyebrows.

"I agree. It's confusing. Let's rest."

The only shade was a spindly tree, but the trunk was stout and they leaned back to rest. Yu'ung nibbled an old root while Ocha licked her muzzle with slow sweeps of her long tongue. Angry Mountain's black craggy summit poked above the smoky haze. It was surrounded by other peaks in the range, most which had also replaced their majestic white crowns with similar dark crests, some with flat jagged plateaus atop sloped flanks.

Yu'ung asked, "What is a permanent homebase like, Ocha, that doesn't constantly change and isn't lived in by other tribes—or packs—passing through."

Ocha huffed.

"You don't migrate except in extreme circumstances. For us, it is normal."

The Canis moaned and a growl furrowed Yu'ung's brow. "We do encounter problems, trying to find safe shelters, more now that Tall Ones share our habitat. They are devious and dangerous. We must avoid them."

This time, Ocha barked a warning.

Yu'ung slipped behind the tree trunk and waited, a spear in each hand, her club strapped where Old One used to ride. That's when she picked up the hooved markings pressed into the mud.

Ocha drooled.

Yu'ung studied the shape, size, and depth, and smiled. "Boar!"

She didn't want to take time, but food was critical. She advanced in a crouch, body rounded, the bent stalks marking Boar's passage. The creature surprisingly skipped past plants it normally devoured with relish, the reason soon obvious.

It heads to a waterhole. If not Boar, we'll find another there.

Boar entered a small forest, typical of those near ponds or streams.

Yu'ung stopped at the shredded bark on one trunk. "Deer! And recent."

Yu'ung smeared her skin with dirt to mask her odor and soon caught up to the quarry. The famished creature hunched forward, ribs etched against its fur, one leg raised to help its muzzle clear away the ash atop the tender shoots.

It died from Yu'ung's spear before it hit the ground.

She didn't take time to build a fire, fed her starved stomach on the fresh flesh and rich blood, starting with the eyes and tongue. Ocha ate the hind quarters. Though engrossed in the first filling meal in too long, they remained alert for those drawn to the scent of blood.

Hunger reduced, Yu'ung chopped the carcass into portable pieces, shouldered what she could carry, and straddled the rest over Ocha. They continued to the waterhole, but the liquid was spoiled by ash.

Yu'ung scowled. "We aren't desperate enough."

Without warning, Ocha tore forward. Yu'ung sniffed, didn't smell whatever alerted Ocha, but abandoned a pile of inedible innards in case the scent was a scavenger drawn to her kill. Then, she too ran. The chunks of carcass bounced against her torso as she darted over a series of ridges and into a boulder bed, putting distance between themselves and the predators. Against one cliff was a cave. Since bulbous clouds packed the sky, Yu'ung considered this Ocha's goal until she passed it up, targeting instead squawking buzzards circling an elongated mound.

"Another carcass, Ocha? We can't carry more."

The Canis ignored her, discouraging the vultures with yips and barks, but something else kept them from landing.

It must be alive, wounded. I'll end its pain and preserve the meat for later.

As she advanced, cautious of horns or hooves or other weapons near-dead prey employed when desperate, the dark lump morphed from a lethally injured animal to a desperately pale child.

Who moved.

Chapter 15

"He's alive!"

Yu'ung raced forward, bellowing and waving her arms to frighten off the carrion birds hungry enough to brave Ocha's fangs and claws. When Yu'ung brushed the ash away, she uncovered a boy of her kind except without the stout trunk and muscular limbs of even the youngest among the People. He'd tucked his face against his chest, but suffered a panoply of gouges and slashes on other exposed areas. Yu'ung scanned for anyone racing to him, the only interest from the scavengers eager for his death. She scooped him up, ran to the cave she and Ocha had passed, and laid him at a fire pit built by earlier inhabitants. She ran her hands over his body. Nothing broken, just boundless scrapes, gashes, and abrasions. If he were conscious, he would be miserable.

Many of the lacerations crisscrossing his body appeared old, most healing, but a few were poisoned and must be treated immediately. His uncovered feet were the worst of his injuries, so bloody and gouged she didn't know how he walked on them.

"Maybe he couldn't anymore and lay on the ground to await his end. Gave up hope. But I don't allow that. Ocha, I have a lot to do. Besides injuries, he's dehydrated, hot, and must be hungry."

Yu'ung kindled a fire and tossed a slice of deer onto a flat stone. She dribbled the last of her water between his lips and applied poultices where needed. The prods and pokes should have been painful, but he never woke.

"More water will perk him up."

She found the creek the deer must have smelled before being distracted by the fresh sprouts, scraped away the sludge and filled a gourd.

Back in the cave, the boy hadn't moved despite Ocha vigorously licking his wounds so Yu'ung placed the water to his side, knowing he would smell it if thirsty. It wasn't until she'd almost finished a slab of deer meat that he flailed one-handed at Ocha's rough, damp tongue, a smile creasing his face.

Yu'ung crouched at his side. "Are you thirsty?"

His eyes fluttered open. "Yes, I think so," his whispered words hoarse, gaze bouncing between Ocha and Yu'ung.

She proffered the water. "Drink slowly."

His red eyes flat and sunken, said they saw more sadness than one his size deserved. He pressed his frail body against Ocha to sit up. If the Canis frightened him, he didn't show it.

Or what he left was worse.

Drool oozed from the corners of his mouth at the aroma of meat sizzling on the fire.

"Hungry?"

He wriggled to get comfortable on bones with no fat. "Not eating does that."

"Almost dead and you maintain your courage." *I like that,* and handed him a fragrant, dripping chunk. "Eat."

He devoured it in one bite and wiped the juice away with his hand.

As he studied his surroundings, she plopped another piece of the fragrant flesh by him, and asked, "Are you a threat?"

"I'm not. Are you?"

Good. He distrusts strangers.

"You mean me or Ocha?" Ocha's tail waved.

He giggled. "Ocha isn't. Have you seen my father?"

Yu'ung shook a *No*, senses alert. "We are passing through."

He tried to rise, but collapsed. "My father went in search of my mother. If he's not here, he must be in trouble."

Yu'ung steadied him. "Rest. Get your strength back." And then, almost an afterthought, she asked, "What are you called?"

"Jvelk. My father is Ronor."

"I am Yu'ung. You already met Ocha. If I can, I'll help you. How were you and your father separated, and why do you think your father is in trouble?"

It delayed locating the People, but she couldn't abandon the boy. His raw red eyes radiated intelligence and determination.

He rubbed a hand through Ocha's fur and answered plainly, "Because he wouldn't abandon me."

The shape of Jvelk's face tickled a memory. She tugged and the secret surfaced.

"You came for pairmating with my tribe, the People. I am their Alpha."

"Yes. I remember, though I went for a different reason. My skill with the far-throwing spear exceeds any in my tribe except my father. He heard of a female who hunted like a Tall One. I wanted advice, but was told she wasn't there." He scratched a bite on his leg, taking in the Tall One lance at Yu'ung's side. "You're her, aren't you?"

"Yes."

Yu'ung recalled the boy who lurked around the edges of the gathering and talked to Ese and then no one else. Ocha panted, relaxed. If Jvelk was lying, Ocha would tell her.

The boy's eyes softened. "I've always considered Canis hostile. I was wrong."

Yu'ung smiled. "Many are. Ocha is my tribe. I am her pack. If you present no threat, you have nothing to fear. "

"I'm not a risk to you." He picked at his shredded shirt, head dipped.

Yu'ung prodded. "Why isn't your father here with you?"

"It started when the Tall Ones attacked our camp."

A raspy call summoned the carrion birds away. Jvelk's cheeks dampened and his lips quivered, but Yu'ung didn't care if reliving the memory frightened him. She must know the answer. What endangered Jvelk's tribe might also jeopardize hers.

"Why, Jvelk? Why attack you?"

"They stormed into our camp, waving their spears and screaming about making us slaves, but then their Leader saw my father and stopped his warriors. They had lived together across the shoreless sea. Father called him Bruurv, told him our tribe neither wanted nor offered trouble."

Bruurv. Fierce's group included no one with that name. "Was anyone in the band called Bhidid, Grub, Eknilk, Braanroorv, Crevkukk, or Qad?"

Jvelk shook his head.

"They were friends, your father and this Bruurv?"

Jvelk hiccupped a yes. "Father told me Bruurv had always been dependable. Father left his homeland and hadn't seen Bruurv since. Apparently, he changed."

"What happened?"

"One-called-Bruurv was shocked to see my father. He said something about thinking he was dead and now, here he was living with Primitives. He wanted to know if we were Father's slaves. Before Father could answer, Mother came up and Bruurv realized they were pairmated. He exploded, called my father an animal and said he must learn a lesson."

Jvelk shook, face pale. "I have never seen Uprights assault another tribe. Who does that? As though we were prey!"

Yu'ung stiffened, hands clenched around her weapon, trying to stifle the anger welling within her.

Fierce warned us about Tall Ones other than his band who weren't friendly. She shuddered. "What did you do?"

"Father must have known something like this could happen because he had prepared me. We fought back, launched every spear thrown at us back at them. We were the only tribe members capable with far-throwing spears, but we slaughtered many. Bruurv finally withdrew and Father and I fled with those who survived. That's when the ground shaking started and the mountain exploded. Dense black steam poured down the flanks and rushed across the landscape. Sizzling hail burned the ground. The ash in the air made it difficult to breathe and everyone scattered, trying to find somewhere safe. When it finally ended, Father and I were alone."

"At that point, why not leave? Bruurv was still around and a threat, probably worse than before because you killed many of his band. Why not go to a safer area?"

"We planned to. Father had seen many mountains explode, though never this badly. The herds would instinctively know where safe was. We would follow them. Then Mother disappeared."

The tremor in Jvelk's voice immersed Yu'ung into her past, the cold night after she lost Old One.

"Father refused to abandon her. He pushed me up into the stout branches of one of the trees that survived, told me he would return when he found Mother. Then we would all leave or worst case, he and I would.

"The first time he returned was with a group of males. Father had talked about a Tall One who might help. It was dark, but I thought this might be him with his tribe—or they call it a band. I almost revealed myself when Father gave our *danger* sign, telling me to remain hidden. When they got near enough, I recognized Bruurv."

"Are you sure it was him?"

"He is memorable. Scars zigzag his forehead where someone or something sliced him once and again. Colors stripe his cheeks. His hair falls past his shoulders, straight and gray as an Elder's would, but he is not wise."

"They talked, but quietly. I couldn't hear them. Then, they left. Father didn't come back for a long time after that. I decided he must be in trouble so tried to find him, but slept in the tree at night in case he came for me. I discovered piles of dead, but not Father or Mother."

He twisted his fur with dirt-encrusted fingers. "I finally decided to seek out the male my father mentioned, named Fierce—"

"Fierce!" But she stopped herself from saying more. She didn't know this boy. "Tell the rest."

"Right before I left the tree for good, Father returned again. I could tell Bruurv considered him a captive. Father spoke loudly, as though to be sure I heard, and told Bruurv that the tribe had agreed to meet here, at this tree, in emergencies, that if any still lived, they would be here. Since none were, it meant all were dead. None of that was true, Yu'ung. He came to warn me away, tell me to escape, but his gaunt body, the bruises on his arms and legs, the attitude of these brutes toward him did the opposite. I know I'm only an inexperienced subadult, but I decided right then to do what I could, whatever that was.

"I waited for morning to follow, but I'm no good—yet—at tracking. I lost them quickly and decided instead to find One-called-Fierce. If Father trusted him, I could too. Father must think One-called-Fierce was in the area, but I never found him."

Yu'ung huffed. "You're in luck. He's also whom we seek."

Chapter 16

Yu'ung bit into a slice of deer and asked, around swallows, "What else did One-called-Bruurv say to your father? Maybe he gave a clue to his location."

Jvelk shook his head. "No. He didn't seem smart. The last time they stood under my tree, One-called-Bruurv yelled at Father for confusing him. He kept repeating how the ground shaking and Father's spear work took too many of his tribe and the Primitives must replace them as slaves. Not Father because he was Chosen. Just Primitives. When Father finally convinced him that everyone had been killed, either by the earth-shaking or Bruurv's warriors, he gave Father a choice. Join as a fighter or slave. Either was fine, but remaining free wasn't."

Bile rose in Yu'ung's throat. She gulped it down before asking, "They force Uprights to work for them?"

Jvelk nodded, and she asked, "What else?"

"Nothing. My plan as I've said was to find Bruurv or Fierce, but I ran out of food and water, and energy, and collapsed. I expected to wake up dead."

Anger sheeted through her with such intensity her face burned with heat. "And now, you led your enemy to us!"

Jvelk bristled. "Of course not. Father taught me to conceal my backtrail. Nothing leads to us."

His face was now bright red, his cheeks damp. Ocha leaned into the youngster. Yu'ung had hoped he'd give her reasons to leave him, continue on her journey, but he'd done just the opposite.

Fists clenched, she sucked in air, dug out a chunk of meat and a mulched poultice, and said the words she didn't want to. "I will help if you obey. If you disagree, take this meat and salve and go."

He sniffled, his nose running and tears dripping quietly. "I accept your aid, on any terms."

She rubbed her leg, as Old One had often done. Yu'ung at first did it reflexively, brought on by annoyance or concern, but now acknowledged it was something else. That movement, the distraction, gave him power over time. At his death, unintentionally, she adopted the trait.

She relaxed her shoulders and chose her next thoughts carefully. "What happened to your father and mother will not happen to you."

She figured out what about the boy caught her attention. His face had the high forehead, the small nose and pinched eyes, the minimized brow ridge. His build lanky was not stocky like the People. Children of the People who mated with Tall Ones showed those traits.

"My mother like yours is from the People. She pairmated a Primitive, your mother, a Tall One."

"Father described the horrors taking place in his land, how deceitful his kind had become, even to each other. He warned me to avoid them."

Yu'ung sighed. She had nothing to say about this. "Where is your shoulder sack?"

He curled forward. "I misplaced it."

She tossed him Old One's. "Take this."

He pawed through the supplies Old One always carried.

He swelled with pride. "An adult satchel. I will treat it with respect."

Yu'ung rested her forearms on her knees and yawned. "Jvelk. After I resharpen my tools, I must sleep. You tend the hearth. If you tire, wake me and I'll take over. Ocha will guard the entrance. Let her know if you require support. Be ready to leave when I wake."

When Yu'ung completed her tasks, she realized there was one more. She lit a torch and shuffled into the tunnels. It took the entire fire stick to convince herself no message had been left. Back in the cavern, Jvelk had covered the entrance with a bramble barricade leaving gaps for Ocha to peek through. Yu'ung joined Ocha. The Canis acknowledged her with a huff, hackles stiff, eyes bright and intense. Yu'ung understood immediately.

"Someone spies on us."

A warning vibrated from Ocha's trunk, ears flattened against her head, eyes on the brush by the entrance. Yu'ung hunkered down and scoured the shadows. Ocha dozed which Yu'ung took as permission to do the same.

For the first time in a long time, Xhosa appeared. She was frustrated. "You don't have time to help every Upright in trouble. Be cautious, and hurry."

Yu'ung started to argue she hadn't meant to delay, but the misty form had already dissolved into the dark.

Yu'ung rose before Sun to find Jvelk crouched by the hearth, spear in hand. She collected her lances, strapped the club to her back, verified her stone supply, and stomped over to Jvelk.

"Show me your feet." Her tone gave him no choice.

The bleeding had stopped, but the swelling and redness persisted.

"How did you gather tinder for the fire? And brambles for the barrier?"

"I ... had to."

She tossed him Old One's foot shields. "Wear these."

As he covered his feet, she pitched a chunk of the deer to him. "Carry that. If we get separated, you have food," and strode in Ocha's prints, the Canis almost out of sight.

Jvelk shouted, "Yu'ung! Wait! I can't go with you. My father risked his life to warn me. I can do no less for him." When she turned back, he hung his head. "Once I free him, we will join you. There is nothing for us here."

She scowled. "Do you know where I am going, young one?"

I feel like an Elder with him.

"To your People, who are not where my father is!"

"You said you didn't know his location."

"Well..." *Pant pant.* "How do *you*?"

"I don't. Ocha does."

She slowed to allow him to catch up and then increased her speed.

"You're too fast!"

She laughed. "Your legs are long for a reason. Use them."

He caught up again and this time, managed to stay with her by thrusting harder on his rear leg to propel forward and pumping his arms.

"It works!"

I'm sure your father is a good individual, but he never taught you to survive. Aloud, she said, "Jvelk. Our goals are the same. I must eradicate these rogue Tall Ones. Otherwise, my People are not safe."

He sucked in a breath. "So you'll help? With you and Ocha, we will succeed. Wait till my father sees this!"

Yu'ung stifled a harsh response and set a pace he would have to speed up to keep or be left behind.

He chose the former, gasping slightly but maintaining, and asked, "How do you and Ocha know the right direction? Usually, my father and I rely on Sun—"

"And clouds—how dark or light they are for how far away a storm. Those don't work anymore. We use other clues. For example, keep moss and lichen always in the same position on our dominant or weak side."

"Oh." *Pant.* He stumbled, righted himself, yelped when he stepped on a sharp stone, and wheezed. "I didn't know that."

"Don't talk. Watch. You'll learn a lot."

The methodical pace, the leaves rustling, her club's rhythmic slap against her back, memories of other journeys during better times, how they passed quickly with Kriina's humming. She missed that, missed so much about her mother.

Missed Old One.

But there was no time for memories or missing people or anything other than moving, not with an enemy near, a boy in need, and a warning to deliver. It was up to Yu'ung and Ocha. She scanned for shadows or fluctuations in shapes, for clues who chased them. She needed a better view.

"Jvelk! You lead!" She scrambled up a hill, flopped to the ground, and lay still.

The grasshoppers burred, their flight dry and scratchy through the dead stems. The scents of decay and old dung swirled around her. After waiting to be sure, she scrambled down the flank, back to Jvelk.

Whoever Ocha and I detected last night might have been checking the strangers in his territory. We are gone. He can forget us.

Jvelk was with Ocha in a boulder's shade, earnestly explaining his strategy to rescue Ronor. She squirmed in behind a bank of brush to listen.

"I will do anything to save my father. You and Yu'ung are the smartest creatures I have ever met."

He trailed off. Ocha slapped the ground with her paws. Jvelk's forehead crinkled.

"No. If my father was as smart as you or Yu'ung, the enemy wouldn't have captured him, but among my tribe, he was clever and brilliant."

Jvelk studied his spear, where the tip attached to the shaft.

"Yu'ung is magnificent! Oh, Ocha! I'm impressed with Yu'ung, but if I could grow up a Canis, I would want to be you."

Yu'ung fought a sneeze, and failed. When Jvelk snapped toward her, she pretended to just arrive.

Jvelk extended a round smooth pond stone. "I am knapping a point for my lance."

"That is too weak." She tossed him a shiny black one. "Use this instead."

Jvelk slapped his hands on his knees and huffed out a loud breath. "How lucky I am to have found you."

If he had Ocha's tail, he'd wag it.

Yu'ung snorted. "Come. You must be thirsty," and hurried away before Jvelk picked up the dampness in her eyes.

Jvelk murmured behind her, "I didn't see a waterhole."

She ignored him as they traipsed across the grassland to a cliff where a dark damp streak marred the face.

"Water!"

He says he's not good at tracking. I'll add scouting to that list.

They satisfied their stomachs, filled their gourds, and left. She surreptitiously eyed him while paying attention to the forward path, ever cautious for those who slaughtered his tribe and threatened hers. His face glistened with sweat. His legs shook from pushing beyond their capability and his skin, naturally darker than hers, was now ashen.

His injuries must be worse than he let on.

"Wait with Ocha. I'll see what I can find."

The boy leaned against the cliff, Ocha alongside him, muzzle on one paw, eyes slit, ears alert. Yu'ung shimmied upward, across the sheer face, to a ledge well scratched by the hooves of mountain sheep.

There, she clambered along, moving carefully, but confidently, tracking the route left on the rocks by the sure-footed sheep in their pursuit of water. She would kill one later. Other tasks came first.

Yu'ung summitted the peak and flattened herself. Within a breath, she saw the flicker of fire.

Who huddled around the flames? Was this Bruurv, Kriina's Tall Ones, the People, or a tribe of unknown Uprights? If it was either of her groups, she must warn them about Bruurv who took slaves and butchered Uprights. Fierce wouldn't be surprised, but her People might consider them friendly because of their experience with Fierce. She couldn't let that happen.

I start to understand the importance Fierce places on warriors.

She lay on the rough ground, the slight breeze caressing her body, and studied the shifting shadows–from the wind?–and the sensory clues. A curly-horned mountain sheep with its mate and kid hid by the gnarled trees that fringed the cliff's crest, colors blending into the background.

"Protect your young tonight, Mountain Sheep. Danger walks, though not me. Not this time."

The biggest concern, and increasing, was rain. She smelled it, light at first, but stronger the longer she remained up here. Ocha beckoned below, spread-legged in front of a dark shadow on the cliff. Yu'ung shivered, shoulders hunched against the first fat drops. The wind at this height blew fierce and cold. By the time Yu'ung caught up with the Canis, she was inside the cave with Jvelk. The boy stoked the hearth. He had gathered enough sticks to last the night and bramble bushes to block the mouth. Ocha plopped by the front for a nap.

Yu'ung processed the grouse the Canis had caught and placed the pieces in the fire.

"Good job, Jvelk and Ocha."

As they waited for the flesh to pinken, Jvelk sharpened tools and Yu'ung stitched a hole in her foot covers.

Food ready, they ate, silently.

Jvelk paused to scratch his cheek, rub Ocha, and check out the entrance. Something made him clench and unclench his jaw, then squint and brush a wet tear away.

Yu'ung didn't care what bothered him unless it impinged their search.

Does it?

"What bothers you?" Her voice curt, bordering on angry, softening by a touch of genuine curiosity. Which was what she wanted.

"My father trusts the Tall One you intend to meet—Fierce. Do you?"

Yu'ung bristled. "He, like your father, eschews the old lifestyle and respects not only my mother but my kind. They are together voluntarily as I'm sure your mother and father are. Fierce delayed going back to his homeland to help my tribe, the People."

"Where is this new place you hope to settle?"

"It is part of a huge, honeycombed colossus where shoreless sea meets another like it but larger."

Jvelk stabbed at the fire with his walking stick. "Tall Ones other than my father bring nothing but trouble. I don't want this Fierce to be one more like them."

"Jvelk. Why do you trust Ocha and me? You just met us and have never before called Canis friend."

He shrugged. "It feels right?"

Yu'ung tapped her stomach and answered with a quiet confidence, based on the lifetime of experience she'd gained in the few Moons since becoming her People's Alpha, "That's called instinct and is how I will judge your father, also a Tall One, when I meet him. Ocha and I must be convinced he is one of the good ones."

"I assure you—"

She ignored him, tiring of the conversation. "Your guarantee is meaningless. Ocha and I alone decide."

"How will you do that?"

She tossed a rock into the fire and waited for it to burst in the heat. "I can't tell you what I don't know."

Jvelk clenched his fists. "I understand."

Yu'ung had already cleaned the deer pelt and now cut it into a wrap. Enough remained for one foot protection.

"Yu'ung. My father always made the decisions, always good ones. He may not be here, but he is inside my head. I am not ready to let him go."

"Does he say seeking him out, planning a rescue is what you should do?"

Jvelk hung his head. "No.... but...." and fell silent.

She smiled. "I must do this because Bruurv and his band endanger my tribe. That is enough for me. There comes a time in every individual's life when they must trust themselves to choose their path. You may have reached that moment."

Yu'ung knelt on the hide-to-become-a-shirt and forced a slender bone with a sharp tip at one end and a string at the other through holes she'd poked in the hide.

As she finished up, she asked, "When we rescue your father, what will you do? Join others of your kind?"

Ocha popped up before he could answer and glared outside.

Jvelk bolted to his feet. "I heard that, too."

The Canis leaped over the bramble barrier and disappeared into the gloom. Yu'ung tore outside and scrambled up a cliff with the alacrity of the sheep she studied earlier. From the edge, she scanned the horizon, sparkling with rain drops.

Movement. I hope it's the Tall Ones. It will save time.

Moon arrived by the time Ocha sidled up to her, panting, feet caked in mud. Yu'ung brushed her hand along the Canis' body, the back, legs, arms, and joints.

"No injuries. That's good."

They returned to the cave where she and Jvelk groomed the thistles and twigs from Ocha's hair and dug the mud from her pads. Yu'ung dragged her fingernails through Ocha's thick fur to the skin below. Ocha moaned with pleasure.

"You ran far, Ocha. Rest."

Jvelk said, "I will guard the mouth while I feed the fire."

"Don't be tricked. Ocha seems to doze, but alerts to anything."

Sometime during the night, the storm started, sending water down the cliff in sheets, blocking the entrance to their cave in a waterfall. Thunder cracked and streaks of fire shot from the clouds, accompanied by fiery explosions as the land burned. Yu'ung shuffled to Ocha's side.

"We'll find them, I have no doubt."

When she awoke, the rain had stopped and Jvelk was gone.

Chapter 17

Yu'ung leaped to her feet and raced outside. Did last night's strangers abduct Jvelk? It didn't take long to uncover fresh prints, layered by Ocha's. Her stomach unknotted when Jvelk appeared, beaming ear to ear, hands dripping with honey. Behind him pranced Ocha, tongue lapping her muzzle.

"Did you hear it?"

Yu'ung froze in place, still unable to decide if she was angry or relieved, but now confused what he meant. "Hear what?"

"Honey-lover! The bird! It led me to a tree I saw yesterday with bees. The lightning last night burned it."

Yu'ung blurted, "Bees hate smoke."

"If the hive is on fire, they flee! I climbed the trunk, snatched as many combs as I could, and ran! I left enough for the bees which is why they didn't chase me."

He extended one hand to Ocha who licked it clean and offered Yu'ung the overflowing gourd. She swiped her fingers through the sweet treat, her heart no longer about to explode. It surprised her how worried she'd become about this young boy she barely knew.

When her hand stopped trembling, she asked, "And the birds?"

"I dribbled honey down the bark to keep them busy."

Yu'ung licked the remnants off her fingers and said, "Wrap the gourd in leaves. Let's go."

As they hurried away, the rain started again, soft at first and then heavy. Their shirts were soon drenched, hair dripping in rivulets down their backs. Yu'ung tied hers in a knot at her neck. Jvelk's hung loose. He opened his mouth to speak, but she shushed him and hustled into the shadows at the forest's edge.

"Tall Ones are here."

He sniffed. "I don't smell—or hear—them. How could you, through this rain?"

"Do you see Ocha's stiff hackles? Her curled lips? Do you feel their pounding steps beneath your feet?"

Jvelk clenched his fists and fear washed his face and neck. "What do we do?"

"Hide. There are too many."

She grabbed him by his arm, tightly to get his attention. "This is good, Jvelk. Stop worrying! It's our first clue. If you recognize this group, we track them, free your father and whoever else they hold as slaves." *Like the People.*

He cocked his head. "What if this is not Bruurv."

Yu'ung thinned her lips. "Did your father mention others to be wary of?"

"He said most Tall Ones."

"We will decide what to do once we see them."

"What if he's not with them, Yu'ung?"

She wanted to snap at him, but the horror on his panicked face and the white surrounding the black circles in his eyes made her bite back her response.

Through gritted teeth, she muttered, "He will be. Where would he go without you? And we will rescue him."

He rubbed his eyes and straightened his shoulders. The stubborn set to his jaw told her he dug deep for the courage he hadn't thought was there. Yu'ung felt both excited and edgy and forced her body to quiet. She crouched as they moved onward, keeping herself in front of Jvelk as a shield. She examined the damp greenery, hand tight around her spear. Jvelk proudly carried a Tall One far-throwing spear, deserted by one of the warriors killed during the attack on his tribe. Yu'ung took him at his word, that he could throw accurately and fast.

Ocha too crept, paws soundless on the muddy ground, patrolling farther ahead than usual. Yu'ung caught up. The Canis' hackles were stiff, fangs exposed.

They must be obscured by the thick-trunked trees or atop those low hills.

She felt her cudgel, the weight comforting on her back. By the time the smudged ball that was Sun touched the horizon, the rumble of steps beneath her feet had disappeared. Wherever the Tall Ones went was not close though she took nothing for granted. She and Jvelk sloshed through a shallow stream, the splash of their movement hidden by the relentless patter of rain. They bent their heads back and filled their mouths without slowing, clambered up the opposite bank, and pressed onward despite calf-high stubble and a copse of slender, tightly-packed saplings to their destination—an outcropping where they found a cave within the boulders.

Around the soaring flames, they squeezed the water from their wraps, but let them dry on their bodies in case they had to leave quickly. Yu'ung fluffed her hair and draped it in ropes while soaking bark in a hollowed-out gourd to separate the fibers. They ate, then did chores, in Yu'ung's case, wound the damp bark into cordage. Jvelk ran sand up and down his spear, over and over until the surface shone in its smoothness. The small fire popped each time a stone exploded, a pleasant background to her work, her senses unfettered.

Yu'ung said, "Tell me how you prepare the Tall One's weapon."

"I sluff the bark off, then smooth the shaft so it flies faster and straighter."

Jvelk paused, but instead of continuing, toppled over.

I'm surprised he didn't sleep sooner, with his injuries.

She joined Ocha on the drenched overwatch hill. Gigantic water-laden branches dripped onto the ground, the mellow sound complimented by the night insects chirring in the damp air.

The Canis huffed, eyes fixed on a flickering light where shadows dimmed and brightened. They lay there, dozing on and off, until Sun's dull rays poked above the horizon.

The flashing light was gone.

Time to go.

They maintained a steady pace, but slow enough for Jvelk and his damaged body. Yu'ung said nothing of the fire she and Ocha saw. He could offer no explanation and should focus on finding clues to his father's location. He did ask about the Tall Ones from yesterday.

"Do you feel their steps under your feet, Jvelk?"

"No."

"Are Ocha's hackles stiff and is she overly alert?"

"I don't think so."

"To me, that says they probably weren't looking for us, passing through, or they may be downwind, so we remain alert."

They stopped where Jvelk and Ronor usually met, but found no fresh tracks. Jvelk climbed the tree, hoping to see something, and yelled down to her.

"He's been here, Yu'ung, and left a mark!"

"Can you tell where he is going?"

"Our former camp."

They did too, but once there, Ocha galloped past without a glance, stopping at prints, not fresh but not old. Hand extended to quiet Jvelk, she crouched. They were easy to identify.

Ese and B'o.

A shiver ran through her chest and her throat tightened.

Why?

Jvelk bounced excitedly. "Those are my kind—"

"But these are my tribe, not yours."

Jvelk crossed his arms. "If it's your People, why aren't you happy?"

"I am one of the tribe's main hunters. In my absence, Laak would hunt with B'o, but these prints are too shallow for him. They look like one of the females, probably B'o's pairmate. They could be foraging together, but why? Do they know about this Tall One tribe, suspect them as enemies? Or is B'o simply cautious?"

Jvelk interrupted, "What if they are searching for you? Is this the time you would re-unite with them? They know you are alone."

Yu'ung caught Ocha's gaze. "Not alone. I have Ocha. Shanadar is of Ocha's pack and he travels with the People. Because of that, they know she is a better defender than any Upright."

Yu'ung reverted her attention to the tracks, following them through the brush, up and down hillocks with no sign of digging up plants.

"They are meandering, as though scouting. I think the Canis alerted to Tall Ones. They're searching for their trace to figure out what they are doing. My tribe is larger than those Tall Ones following you and me."

"Would the Canis defend them as Ocha does you? Are they all like that?"

She didn't know the other Canis like she knew Ocha, but had seen them attack the hyaena to protect her.

"I think so," but said no more.

Ocha led them to another spot with more of the People's trace, these mixed with Canis.

It looks like they are guarding the People.

Yu'ung ruffled Ocha's smooth hackles, padded over to fresher Tall One tracks not far from the People's Canis. They merged, either tracking each other or the same prey.

She shivered, excited. "The mix of Canis and Uprights doesn't make sense to the Tall Ones."

We are close. It is good to have this come to an end.

Jvelk slipped to her side. "Now that I see these clearly, the tracks match Bruurv. He may be chasing your tribe, Yu'ung."

"But he thinks the Canis stalk them and respects the Canis' superiority. Until something about that changes, he is no threat to my People."

Jvelk slowed. "Here the Tall Ones went their own way."

Yu'ung strode forward, anger clashing with duty. She wanted to pursue the trail of her People, but that wasn't the wise choice.

"Let's find your father."

That was her surest way to protect the People.

Chapter 18

Yu'ung, Jvelk, and Ocha hurried onward, fast and quiet. They tracked Bruurv's band and at some point, realized he was aware of their presence. Yu'ung didn't care. The sooner they confronted each other, the faster she stopped this menace to her People.

Old One told me to make great decisions in the moment, not before or after, to evaluate an adversary's strengths and weaknesses when they were on display. This is that time.

Yu'ung and Jvelk settled for the night into a small alcove, ate the food scavenged during the day, then repaired damaged tools and replaced supplies.

Jvelk mumbled through clenched jaws, "Did I?"

She separated a root into threads and twisted them into a cord. "No. You didn't lead them to us. I let them find us."

"But we were hiding."

"While providing enough clues even one as dense as Bruurv would notice. Ocha found the male he left to spy on our progress, but left him alone. I wanted to look like we were trying to be sneaky so he wouldn't suspect my plan."

"Plan?"

"Of course. Why does that surprise you?"

When he sputtered, she stopped him. "How else do I rescue your father and defend my People? You will understand when you grow more. Until then, do as I say because time is short!"

"What do I do?"

"You have killed Tall Ones before. Be prepared to again, but not until I give the signal."

"Have you?"

Yu'ung grunted. "Killed Uprights? I do what I must, Jvelk. I am the People's Alpha. Before attacking, be sure the Tall Ones are enemies, not my People or Fierce's."

Sweat beaded his forehead as he panted. "I will."

Yu'ung secreted herself inside the cave, back from the entrance to avoid being silhouetted by the fire, hidden from inquisitive eyes, but still with a clear view outside. Ocha would alert to anything Yu'ung's senses didn't pick up. Everyone hunkered down to wait, sure it wouldn't be long.

It's time.

She sensed it in the air, but in her urgency, she'd forgotten to check for messages. There should be one. If not, she'd leave her own. Either way, the task must be completed in case she didn't return to this cave.

"Stay with Ocha. I have something to do."

She lit a torch and shambled down the rear passageway. Soon, the light from the entry dissipated to darkness, as did the slight breeze. That was good. It meant no other exits—or entries. Not much further, she discovered Shanadar's message.

We are safe. The Canis are on edge. Beware.

She started to add a response—*They are here*—in case Fierce and his band passed through, but a gruff voice filtered through from the cavern. She didn't bother with the torch, just hurried to the front. Loud, angry voices yelled Tall One words. Ocha snarled. Yu'ung flew into the cavern in time to see huge Tall Ones shove spears at Jvelk and Ocha. Every one of them stood taller and wider than Fierce, as much Bear as Upright. In a boulder-lifting contest, these brutes would win.

One-who-must-be-Leader jolted toward her and leered, exposing broken yellowed tooth. His ripped shirt revealed a muddy torso liberally striped with scars.

He yanked Jvelk out of the way to better see Yu'ung.

"The female!" And offered a lascivious grin. "We've been waiting for you."

So my tribe remains undiscovered.

Jvelk yelped from the pain to his damaged arm and Ocha leaped at the snaggle-toothed brute. He slammed the Canis with a massive cudgel. His speed for someone so large shocked Yu'ung. Ocha bounced off the stone wall onto the ground in a flaccid heap.

Yu'ung's heart raced, her breath trapped in her body. Beads of sweat sprinkled her brow. She wiped them away and willed herself to calm.

A spirit can't die, can it?

The brute flung Jvelk aside to raucous cheers from his group. With a yowl, he strode toward Ocha.

"I'll finish off the mongrel. Don't let the female escape down the tunnels," he said with a head jerk at Yu'ung.

He cocked his spear and grinned, but as he threw, Jvelk leaped onto his back and bit into his neck. Snaggle-tooth bellowed and his weapon clattered off the wall beside Ocha. The Canis jerked upright, one paw elevated, head dipped.

"Ocha!" Yu'ung yelled. "Run! We will find you!"

The Canis did, though limping badly. Her backward glance held neither fear nor defeat.

As Snaggle-tooth lifted an arm to smash Jvelk to the ground, Yu'ung yelled, "Stop!"

Feet spread, hovering on the brink of panic but hiding it, her short time in leadership had already accustomed her to pretending strength under fire.

"What do you want, Bruurv?" She waved a dismissive hand. "We are trying to escape Mountain. We have no interest in challenging you for this area's limited resources."

Her words surprised the Leader. He squared his shoulders to her, eyes blazing, muscles rippling. He slung Jvelk aside and smirked at Yu'ung.

"How do you know my name?"

Jvelk described the wild mane, craggy face and dirty broken teeth, the welts scarring your forehead. You tried to shroud them in stripes. They commanded respect in your youth, but now, they peel. Your gray hair stands out. No one who's seen you more than once will be intimidated.

"Who doesn't know your power."

He puffed. "Angry Mountain took our females. You will live with us."

Yu'ung advanced one pace and sneered. "Then ask."

He howled. "You are in no position to make demands." He waved a hand at the armed warriors arrayed throughout the small area. "I am lenient. They are not."

He spit on Jvelk. "He is not your kind! He is—"

"My tribe. His died. I adopted him."

He studied her for a breath and another. "You are a Primitive. How do you speak in our way?"

She strutted forward, fixed on him. A tiny smile played on her lips. Kriina taught her how to occupy a stranger's attention.

"I am Yu'ung, the healer. I speak like all tribes."

She addressed Bruurv, prepared to explain the tracks left by the People if he asked, but he didn't.

He is as dense as Jvelk said, probably considers the prints from Jvelk and me! Doesn't even notice the difference in size. She ducked her head. *I won't change his mind,* and approached one of Bruurv's warriors. His face flushed hot. Sweat dimpled his forehead and hairline, and a crimson gash dug deep into his upper arm. She touched it and he winced.

"You will soon be poisoned and die." She poked her shaft into the festering laceration. "I can treat him, Leader, and erase the pain you suffer from your broken tooth, but not unless you stop threatening us."

He stared at her, his eyes now void of the predator-who-cornered-prey glint. Instead, they glittered with respect for a worthy opponent, excitement that he might soon control her.

He guffawed. "Big demands from a captive!" His gaze moved over her body. "You carry our lance as well as the clunky Primitive one. Who did you steal it from? And how?" Then strode from the cavern. "Explain later when we discuss your 'demands'. The subadult can be your helper."

Jvelk bristled at the insult. Yu'ung offered a tiny shake of her head. *Don't resist. Remember I have a plan.*

She wouldn't mount a getaway until sure the People—or Fierce, or Jvelk's father Ronor—were not enslaved by this Tall One. If they were, she must free them first.

She crossed her arms and made no move to follow. "How many wounded warriors? And injured captives? I will bring sufficient treatments for all."

Bruurv's eyes flattened. "You will know soon enough."

"I will heal no one if you harm Jvelk or myself. We will be slaves, but not abused."

She said no more. If Ocha was too injured to rescue them, she and Jvelk would manage.

Fierce is on the backtrail which means he will catch up. What a surprise he will present to this tawdry assemblage.

Bruurv beckoned. "Come. Leave your weapons. We will defend you and provide your food. You have other tasks."

Yu'ung glared. "I keep mine."

He shrugged. "Use them against us, we slay you and the small helper."

The trek to Bruurv's camp was short, to Yu'ung's relief because Jvelk hadn't regained his strength. She sniffed a light scent she recognized, mirroring their trail.

Ocha.

At the crest of a steep hill, the land flattened to an open bluff. The Tall Ones' site was backed up to a cliff but otherwise well separated from the area trees. Yu'ung at first thought their supplies and sleeping nests would be in a cave under the cliff, but then saw piles of food, wraps, spears, stone tools, and kindling in unkempt heaps. Bruurv shoved her toward the hearth which was, like everything else, poorly placed and hastily constructed.

He growled, "If the flames die, so do you."

She kindled the fire, slowly, giving herself time to glance discreetly around. What lay around the camp appeared to have been dropped carelessly or tossed without intent. There were no piles of foraged plants or partially eaten carcasses in preparation for future meals, no gourds of water.

They have no backup supplies. That is good.

Jvelk sidled up to her, arms stuffed with kindling he dropped by the fire. Leaning in to her, he whispered, "There are no other males here. Do you suppose the rest are hunting?"

As she pondered this, a tired group trudged in, a few with hares slung over their shoulders, one a small fawn.

Did they eat the rest, returned with this pittance for the band?

No, what made better sense was they could find nothing else.

She called after Bruurv, "Your fire tenders do a poor job, Leader. Who are they? I will teach them."

The newcomers glanced at her, muttering among themselves about a slave who addressed their leader so aggressively. Bruurv felt the confusion, walked up and slapped her, brutally. She didn't fight back, didn't budge. She wanted to touch the growing welt on her cheek, but resisted.

After a long uncomfortable silence, she whispered to him, "Don't ever touch me again, Bruurv, or it will be the last time."

He leaned in as though they shared a private secret, his rancid breath washing over her nose and mouth.

"What will you do, female, against so many males desperate to kill you?"

His forehead glistened in the firelight, his breathing ragged. The skirmish with Ocha and Jvelk and the hike up the steep slope had tired him. Not Yu'ung. She fought the impulse to knock him to the ground and break his neck. This time. That was not yet the plan.

"I may not kill all your motley crew, but you die first, before they get close enough to touch me."

He backed away, a flash of fear at what he saw in her eyes, heard in her voice, quickly squelched, and then howled. "You will be fun, maybe the first to survive training."

Let him believe that. The time will come to use his idiocy against him.

She lowered her eyes and rounded her shoulders as he crawled into a dirty foul pile of scrub that shimmered with crawling insects.

If these Tall Ones were representative of those in Fierce's land, Yu'ung understood Fierce's—and Ronor's—flight.

Jvelk crept to her side. "You allowed him to hit you?"

She didn't bother responding. The reasoning was too complicated.

Bruurv's eyes drooped, her signal. "Surely some captives live, to flush out prey for the hunters. Better they die from claws and horns than you. I can treat their wounds before I sleep."

He didn't open his eyes. "All died. No more talk!" and rolled away from her, wrapped in stinking pelts.

He baits me by pretending to nap.

She squatted to tend the fire, to any watching defeated by circumstances, making sure to block Bruurv's view of Jvelk. The guard assigned to watch them already slept.

Jvelk! She hissed. *Do you recognize any besides Bruurv?*
All of them. We are in the right place.

Without the snug stone walls, the chill night air seeped past her wraps to her skin. Yu'ung slapped her arms and chest to warm herself.

The site was small, but permanent. Tree trunks mixed with mammoth tusks had been embedded in a circle not abutting the cliff. Hides were draped over some, sporadically and not enough to keep the area inside warm. The hearth lay in a natural hollow surrounded by big stones with troughs dug into the ground to feed air to the flames. That made keeping the flames alive easier than what Yu'ung was accustomed to in the People's hearths.

We should do that. I'll ask Fierce to explain it.

The camp layout itself mimicked the People's with zones for knapping, pounding roots, preparing skins, and sleeping. Many sections included old bone chips, stone flakes, and rotting food. Soon, the only sounds were gurgling snores. If Bruurv planned to trick Yu'ung, fatigue defeated him.

Jvelk hissed at her, "Let's go!"

"I didn't allow him to capture us to then escape. This is how I locate your father and track my People. If you're tired, sleep. I will wake you if necessary."

"What will you do?"

"Wait for Ocha."

He blinked and shrugged. "I will spell you. I am stronger than I look."

"You saved Ocha's life. That means everything to her. And me."

"What can she do?"

"Save us."

"How?"

"You will see."

Jvelk dozed. The wheezes and snuffles of the enemy kept Yu'ung awake and her thoughts jumped from Ocha to her People to Fierce, and surprisingly, Old One.

Xhosa! Is Old One with you?

Xhosa didn't respond.

Chapter 19

Bruurv kicked Yu'ung, intending to wake her but to his shock, she yanked his foot and he fell on his bottom. Rather than anger, he chortled, as did others.

One shouted, "This slave is feisty."

Bruurv scratched his arms. "You said you're a healer. What can you do for my injured warriors?"

Yu'ung, eyes raw with sleeplessness, didn't see any males other than the original group.

Time to begin.

She muttered between yawns, "Nothing when I'm this tired. The snores of your … band … kept me awake."

She wanted to call them brutes, but restrained herself.

Without giving him a chance to respond, she continued, "While I rest, have your minions collect moss, vines, honey," and rattled off a long foraging list. None were essential, just to keep him off balance. "Then, I'll be ready when I awaken."

At his bewilderment, she snapped, "You ask me to treat injuries. How do I without supplies?"

"We are not here to scavenge for you!"

She rubbed her eyes. "I'll do it after I sleep," and started toward one of the nests, but stopped. "Where are the stalks that keep insects in abeyance?" The response didn't matter. She could tell there were none. The goal was to annoy him. He stared at her like she'd asked for a slab of Mammoth meat.

"If I lie on those, I'll end up scratching the way you and your band do." She pivoted and stomped away. "Come. Be sure I don't escape while I collect the grasses I need."

He raised his arm and Yu'ung brushed him away. "Don't come. I don't care. Why would I leave when you have food," and marched toward the brush.

Her attitude shocked Bruurv and he raced after her, doing her bidding as she gathered certain stalks, skipped others, rattling off the differences. "In case you succeed in killing me as you did the other females."

As she dug and yanked and shook root bundles, Yu'ung listened for Ocha. It surprised her not at all when Ocha howled. Bruurv squirmed behind her.

"Do you hear that, slave? Canis packs inhabit this area. If you try to get away, they will feast on your carcass!" He shrieked with laughter.

How little he grasps about his habitat. Why is he not dead?

But she played along. "They won't enter the camp, will they?"

"They never have before, but they may want a taste of you!" and he guffawed.

From then on, he kept close to her, in the flawed thinking the Canis would attack her first, but Yu'ung made that as miserable as possible, cutting pathways through the stiffest brush, waist height or more. She pushed it aside and let it snap back on him. He yowled and she giggled to herself, then apologized and took "easier paths," these even more difficult to discourage him from joining future harvesting.

Finished, they clumped into the site, Bruurv bleeding from scratches and gouges, Yu'ung carrying all the grass.

She ignored his scowls and grunts, and said simply, "You will thank me tonight."

He asked, "Can you treat the itchiness or must we wait?"

Yu'ung tossed a handful of the stalks to any who asked, keeping enough for herself and Jvelk.

"Rub your body." Though she doubted it would help. The rotting skins were the biggest cause of their misery.

She squatted by Jvelk, scraping a skin, tedious work the others happily assigned to him.

One yelled, "Don't bother him!" and prepared to yank her away.

She resisted the urge to throw the Tall One to the ground, instead, cowered. "He doesn't know how to make clothes out of skins. I will teach him." Before the Tall One warrior could refuse, she added, "What can a mere female and a subadult do against you and the other powerful fighters?"

He froze, then preened, puffing out his chest muscles. Jvelk barely managed to squelch a titter.

While demonstrating, she murmured, "Nothing here is cared for, including their weapons."

She poked her lower lip toward a mound of rough-hewn shafts. "Someone collected those, but never did anything with them. We will make lances for them and fix their damaged ones. They'll agree to allow us to because ours are pristine, but what we give them won't withstand the first throw. I'll show you how to make that happen. They won't find out until too late."

"Unless they use the weak lances on a hunt."

"Have you not noticed the hunters leave for days. That is how long we have to implement our plan."

"Can we?"

"I talked to Ocha while I collected grass. She will be ready before we are. I will tell her to wait for my signal." She dipped her head to a crack in the ground obscured by rocks. "Hide the good lances there, for us. We will give the others to Bruurv. If we need to delay, we'll spend our time making warm pelts."

Yu'ung shouted to Bruurv. "Bring me the hides from recent kills. Jvelk and I will make clothes. The cold is here. Your warriors will freeze before they can feed us if Jvelk and I don't make warm clothes."

As though the wind listened to her, a frigid gust blew through the camp.

"Jvelk will repair your lances after we make the pelts, so we don't starve. He will make spears that fly straight, far, and deep."

"He's a Primitive! He knows nothing of shaping weapons."

"And yet, Jvelk and I have spears while you have a pile of branches decaying on the damp soil. I argue it's you who doesn't have the skill."

"Ours work!"

"Then create your own!"

"You go too far—"

"Not far enough, I'd say." She stared brazenly into his eyes. "Before you ended Ronor's life, he taught his son many skills."

"Ronor is Chosen. We would never kill him. He was offered a place among us but preferred to abandon his son."

Bruurv unleashed a raucous laugh and strutted away.

Jvelk whispered to Yu'ung, "He lives!"

"If true, we will locate him."

Ocha may already have done so.

She said nothing about that to Jvelk as she crawled into her fresh bedding, pretending to doze while her mind churned.

Over subsequent days, small clusters of males lumbered in, bone-weary hunters, often with gashes, bite marks, or black-blue bruises that covered swaths of their chests and backs. Some carried carcasses, others stones or branches for weapons. A few met with Bruurv, hands moving erratically as they spoke. She treated the injured as she would her own, taking the opportunities to ask questions, find out where they traveled, who caused the injuries, if they saw other Uprights, all in the search of the proper cure. Few stayed in the camp long, either ordered to leave or they didn't like their Leader. That worked for Yu'ung. Overall, the total force within the camp seemed not many more than one for each finger and toe on her body.

As Yu'ung predicted, the cold air descended with a vengeance. Nights, damp gusts wrapped the fire tenders in a dense fog. Her captors whispered she could see into the future and as a result, treated her with more respect and caution than they did Jvelk. She wasn't prescient. Anyone who lived here would know, but she didn't mind using their reverence to further her strategy.

Find Ronor. Find her People.

Bruurv rubbed his arms and yelled to Yu'ung. "We freeze! Work faster! Hang more pelts on the posts."

"Then have your hunters bring more in! These are for Jvelk and me. Ours are bare. I cannot heal if I'm frozen." Every word was emphasized by a dense white cloud.

He scowled, waved a hand, and left. The fire tender—Ruarc—didn't know what to do. His gaze bounced from Yu'ung's calm face to Bruurv's fuming back.

Yu'ung helped him. "Ruarc."

That was his Tall Ones name though Yu'ung and Jvelk called him Pitted-face. The boy suffered the sore red pocks other Tall One subadults did, usually gone by adult time. This was a condition none of the People suffered so Yu'ung had no idea how to treat.

"Your fuming Leader will be fine. Ignore him. Bring the carcasses over and then give me your wrap. That hole—did someone stab you? I'll close it for you. Cold drains a man's energy and patience."

He narrowed his eyes, fingered the opening in his cloak, and hustled off to do as asked.

"Bruurv!" she called. When he ignored her, she added, "I have a new spear for you to test."

Bruurv trudged over, tried to look annoyed, but his eyes gave away his excitement. Jvelk tossed him the just completed flawless spear. Bruurv flipped it in his hands, felt the weight in the middle, tested the sharp tip, yanked on the point to be sure there was no give, then trotted to a field. The entire band joined him, eager to see if the helper slave named Jvelk could make a spear. Bruurv wasted no time throwing it at the hard trunk of a distant tree. He had a powerful arm and was skilled with the spear, better than most Tall Ones Yu'ung had seen during her scouting. It flew forward, plunged into the dense trunk, and wobbled in place. The entire band ran down the field to check the depth, that the spear was not damaged in any way. Bruurv brandished it with a flourish, the band cheered

Another clunk of plan dropped into place.

Bruurv raced back to her. "More like this!"

Yu'ung was ready for this request. "Spears or pelts? Hunt meat or prevent your warriors from freezing?"

Bruurv growled and left. That was the answer she wanted. Jvelk and Yu'ung chortled silently.

One Tall One always remained to supervise Yu'ung and Jvelk. The task was popular because Yu'ung treated the guards' injuries, scrapes, mouth problems, stomach aches, or any ailments, soothing them while reinforcing her weakness to build up their strength.

It was during one of those treatments that Ocha called. The warrior paled. Yu'ung hid her smile behind a moan.

Chapter 20

"Bruurv!" she croaked. "A Canis stalks us!"

"He's no danger to me," and brandished his new stone-tipped lance. "You kept your spear! Surely you can defend yourself, but if not, hope I'm in a good mood," and he rolled onto his side as did Ruarc-the-Pitted-face.

Yu'ung sighed, for their benefit. "It's gone. Your commanding presence must have frightened it." She spun and walked away, muttering over her shoulder, "I will forage what I need to treat your injured while it is elsewhere. I'd appreciate if you'd send someone with me, as protection."

She rambled off, moving slowly, as frantic whispers took place behind her.

"Go alone, female. As you say, the threat is no longer."

She didn't bother answering. To anyone watching, she meandered in her usual manner, but today, her aimless wandering had a specific goal. A soft woof ahead and she lazily turned slightly to her strong side, tugging a plant out here and stripping leaves there, until she made out Ocha's dark fur amidst the brush. They greeted each other quietly. Yu'ung inhaled.

"I smell Upright, Ocha. Not my tribe or Fierce's. Did you find Ronor?" A slow pant, muzzle spread in a grin, affirmed Yu'ung's guess.

She sniffed again. "And you have made friends with other Canis not from your pack."

Yu'ung needed no confirmation and it made her want to pant happily, too.

Ocha moaned and yowled softly—*It will be soon*—and slunk away, low in the grass where she couldn't be seen.

Arms laden with vegetation that would never be used, Yu'ung hid her excitement behind a mask of defeat as she re-entered camp, but motioned Jvelk to be ready.

It didn't take long. A cluster of empty-handed hunters lumbered in. Their steps dragged, shoulders drooped, a few injured by horns and claws. They muttered to Bruurv about the unusually large pack of Canis in the area. When the Leader asked, they shook their heads—*No trouble, but they watched us pass. We've never seen that before.*

The warriors crouched to eat a carcass steaming in the fire pit, bodies edgy, eyes darting along the grass and scrub surrounding the site, hiding any manner of trouble.

A shout echoed at the camp's edge.

"I come for my son!"

Jvelk jerked toward the voice. Yu'ung grabbed his arm and hissed, "It starts."

Attention on Ronor, no one noticed Yu'ung slide to the back of the clearing.

Ronor wobbled on unclad feet, supported himself on a walking stick though Yu'ung could see it once served as his weapon. He held the other arm behind his back. His body was bony, muscles stringy, but there was a harshness in his eyes Yu'ung rarely saw, so corrosive nothing short of revenge would douse it.

Bruurv advanced on the sallow-skinned skeleton that was his former partner. "You are back, and hungry."

Sharp-edged bones etched ridges on Ronor's chest, protected by nothing more than a dirty torn wrap he should have replaced long ago.

"Come. Work and we will feed you."

Bruurv thinks loud bluster makes him powerful.

His band's attention was glued to Ronor, but Yu'ung could see the worry in the tight set of their jaws, the fear that crossed Bruurv's face, his slow mind churning. Why would Ronor confront an armed group in this way?

Jvelk rose. Time to do his part. "Father! I knew you wouldn't leave me!"

Ronor wobbled as he searched out his son in the group, managed to remain upright with the stick's help.

Yu'ung chuckled to herself at his cleverness. *These brutes see a crippled old male, once one of their most respected, now too feeble and weak to live up to his vaunted reputation.*

She could see by the smooth shaft and the perfect dimensions that the lance though old was cared for. She honed in on the point.

He left it dull as a distraction. He doesn't believe his spear will be required to do what must be done.

Jvelk shook as he asked, "Father. I smell the Canis—did they follow you here? Are we at risk?"

He knew the answer, the question meant to worry his captors, and it did. As though on cue, their eyes darted through the surroundings and to a male, clutched their spears tighter.

Bruurv inhaled. Unable to come up with any reason for the Canis odor, he ignored it.

A snuffle caught Yu'ung's attention. She peeked back and many eyes blinked.

Ocha brought a pack.

Bruurv and his unkempt minions were blind to the threat, thoroughly preoccupied by the disheveled, wizened Ronor.

This is Ocha's plan.

Bruurv shuffled toward Ronor, enough of a warrior to examine the scrub behind the tattered, skeleton. Soothed by how his former partner had aged, he dismissed the threat, oblivious to Ronor's eyes, deep and dark, boring into his mind with a strength no muscles could match.

Bruurv stopped well short of the male.

He's frightened! Was Ronor once so skilled at destroying enemies that Bruurv still fears him?

"Where have you been hiding?"

A dangerous stillness enveloped Ronor. The muted response from the male who had been one of the Tall One's mightiest warrior, made it more disturbing.

"Here, to be sure my son survived, seek justice if he didn't, retribution regardless the outcome."

He brought his hidden hand to the front. It held a vine—no, a porcupine tail. A Tall One charged. Ronor swung the appendage. The quills embedded deep into the attacker's skin. Yu'ung couldn't help but wince.

That is worse than a knock on the head with a club!

The entire band was riveted by Ronor's cleverness, appalled by their bandmate's pained howls. He swung the porcupine tail at another enemy, but lost his balance. Was that planned? Bruurv slapped the makeshift weapon away with his cudgel.

The Leader yowled, as though he'd won a great victory. "When we fought together, all yearned to be you, including me. Then, you pairmated a Primitive. Now, you come to free your son armed with a porcupine tail? Is that the best you could come up with? I would do you a favor ending your pointless life, but I prefer that you suffer!"

Save the one assailant, spines embedded in his neck and face, the rest of the band advanced, their intent to deliver the punishment Ronor avoided earlier.

Ocha moaned, so softly, no one heard except Yu'ung, Jvelk, and probably Ronor. *Patience.*

Yu'ung lurched toward Ronor when the brutish warrior stabbed Jvelk's father with the dull end of his spear, but he caught her eye as he fell, held his hand up.

He has a plan.

Bruurv misjudged Ronor's gesture and yowled with laughter. "You ask us to stop?" and poked again and again. Ronor bobbed and jiggered, avoiding the massive brute as often as not, but the hits took their toll.

He's a distraction.

Bruurv chuckled and this time, slammed the shaft of his spear into Ronor's head. He drew blood, but Ronor's gaze never wavered from the huge, vicious male.

His body may be fragile, but his mind is sharper than any of his adversaries.

Through bloody lips, Ronor said, "You are too stupid to fear what is coming and too late to stop it."

Admiration flashed across the Leader's face for his former bandmate's courage when facing sure death. He disguised it with bluster. "No one will race in to save you or your whelp! We have slaughtered every rescuer you once had."

He is wrong.

"Jvelk," she mouthed as a delicious frisson of fear tingled through her. "Go to him."

Jvelk leaped forward, unleashed, slapped those who tried to block him. They laughed, unaware of the part they now played in Ocha's plot. One shoved Jvelk down, but he bounced up.

"The slave bounces!" "Do it again!" All eyes now on Jvelk.

A low bay came from the clearing's edge.

"Bruurv," Yu'ung's flat tones floated above the raucous chortles. "Ronor warned you. Now you are too late"

All stared aghast first at her and then Ocha as she padded into the clearing, head dipped, fangs glistening with saliva.

Bruurv gaped. "What is going on?"

His question was answered as the rest of the Canis stepped out of the scrub and surrounded the Tall Ones.

"It's the sound of freedom."

While the Tall Ones tried to figure out their next best step, Yu'ung flung her spear at one who taunted Jvelk. It penetrated his throat and he collapsed without a word. The others panicked, faces pale despite their sun-darkened pallor. No one went to his aid. The new lances trembled in their hands, the tips sharp, the shafts smooth and glistening with beeswax, and yet, they hesitated, pointing from Yu'ung to the dead comrade.

The spears hadn't been tested on a hunt, but her kill was convincing. If hers worked, theirs would, wouldn't they?

She bobbed her head. "This is your last chance. Choose wisely. If you assault Jvelk, Ronor, or me, the Canis will return the favor, and that, you will not withstand."

Sweat glistened on their bodies. A rancid odor of fear saturated the air. No one dared make a sound.

Except Bruurv.

He yowled. "You think to defeat us with these feral creatures? Watch this!"

He flung his lance at Ocha. Yu'ung watched the flight almost in slow motion, straight and true at Ocha's muscular furred torso. It hit with a thud, bent her pelt inward but instead of penetrating, driving into her fragile innards, the tip collapsed.

Bruurv stiffened, stunned. "This is one of the new ones!"

Jvelk laughed. "Why would we give you spears to use against us?"

Bruurv stared as understanding dawned. "We have other weapons, slave! You have accomplished nothing."

"So do we."

As the Tall Ones tugged cudgels from sacks—what they called clubs—the Canis sprang, fangs and claws tearing into exposed skin. The air around Yu'ung echoed with snarls and screams. The corroded power of the rotting Uprights cooled and died. She tossed good lances to Jvelk and Ronor and they advanced on the malevolent Leader, committed to end the evil he posed. The hate billowing from him threw her back. Before she could deliver justice for his treatment to her, Jvelk, Ronor, and others, the Canis did.

With his last breath, he hissed, "I will never forget this."

"Nor will I," but he heard nothing.

The battle ended. The oppressed won. Jvelk crawled to his father.

Yu'ung shouted, "Stop his bleeding, Jvelk," and sprinted to the milling Canis. Tails tucked, ears flat, they closed ranks around the pack. Several suffered bruises from the cudgels, some slashed by the stone points of lances.

I can treat these after Ocha. They aren't lethal.

Yu'ung penetrated the protective circle and knelt by Ocha. The Canis lay on her side, body battered. Yu'ung ran fingers through the sleek, bloodied fur, tears wetting her cheeks.

"I saw what you did, Ocha. Every threat to your pack, you placed yourself in its way." She fingered an indentation on Ocha's chest, deep enough Yu'ung's flat hand fit in it. "This one worries me."

She rubbed the raw wound with a poultice to heal the tissues beneath. By the time she rolled onto her heels, the injury was almost invisible. Ocha scrambled to her feet and steadied herself.

Yu'ung looked around for the next injured Canis, but none remained.

"Where did they go, Ocha?"

Ocha's muzzle pointed to the ripples marking the Canis travel.

"Those are good friends, Ocha. Tell them to ask any time, for anything."

Yu'ung trotted to Ronor. "I'm Yu'ung. Let me treat you."

Ronor had as many old wounds as fresh. Bruises adorned his body, his lips cracked and bloody, hair brittle, and skin scaly from bad food.

He touched Yu'ung's arm. "I am glad you helped Jvelk. You remind me of my pairmate. She and her tribe are all dead or gone, thanks to Bruurv, but they were kind."

He grasped at Yu'ung's wrap, gaze focused. He knew he was dying.

"Listen to me! My son is young, inexperienced, but loyal and skilled ... talented at making the far-throwing spear.... He can learn to track. He sees everything around...." Desperation entered Ronor's mutterings. "I wish I could be here ... as he grows into an adult." His eyes fluttered. Yu'ung feared death would take him, but he continued, halting.

"Care for him. He is worth it."

"No!" Jvelk yelled. "You promised to never again leave!"

Ronor twitched, swallowed the ache that wracked his body, and forced himself back to consciousness where his son awaited him.

Yu'ung held his hand. "Pain doesn't kill you, Ronor. Old One suffered more than any I've known and outlasted most. I'm not sure how. When he hurt, he didn't acknowledge it. Pain, he explained is a sensation the mind can shut off if you deny its presence. Focus elsewhere. It is your chance to demonstrate the strength inside your body."

He winced once more and then offered a wan smile. "It works. Your Old One is wise."

She mulched a stem, mixed in honey, and spit the concoction into her hand.

"Eat this. It will help the aches."

Jvelk tugged her arm. "Will he recover, Yu'ung?"

She scoffed. "I've seen worse. Ronor will die or live, whichever he wants. Get water, meat, and skins for compresses. While out there, confirm no Tall Ones will rise from the dead."

He raced off and Ronor smiled at her. "All right. I can see you won't allow me to leave."

Yu'ung cleaned Ronor's many and varied injuries with salves, added honey to purify punctures and sap to seal spread wounds. She was placing a slab of raw meat on one huge bruise when Jvelk thrust a thin deer skin into her hands which she tore into bandages.

"No survivors?"

He shook his head. "Not anymore. They will cause neither us nor your People more trouble."

Ronor's face clouded. He didn't argue with his son, but motioned he and Yu'ung must talk in Jvelk's absence.

Jvelk asked his father, "Why did they use the dull end of the shaft?"

"Annoying captives is a game to them. When taunting becomes boring, they flip the weapon to the point."

Yu'ung listened without hearing for a long quiet breath, then rose. "I must warn my tribe."

Ronor pushed to his hands and knees. "Your instincts are deep, Yu'ung. This battle has just begun. Many Tall Ones will be livid these deaths came at the hands of slaves."

He tried to stand, failed, and started again to bleed.

Yu'ung growled and he sighed. "Do what is necessary. I am not afraid."

She stuck the tip into the fire pit. When glowing red, she slapped it against Ronor's raw skin in each place that continued to ooze. He gasped and passed out.

Jvelk's eyes dripped. "Is he dead?"

"Unconscious. Let him be. Tomorrow, we carry him on a travois, as fast as possible. It will be difficult, but your father is tough. You should be proud of him."

Chapter 21

Yu'ung awoke before Sun. Jvelk had already bound tree limbs together and added a durable vine in front of the travois that would carry Ronor. It was in essence a lightweight land raft, similar in construction to those the People employed to cross waterways, but smaller. Ocha paced to the clearing's edge and back, over and over, hackles raised.

Yu'ung and Jvelk rolled Ronor onto the flat frame, tucked an animal skin around his frail body, and they left. Jvelk's feet worried her, but the youngster never complained or slowed. Ronor remained unconscious throughout, oblivious to the ruts and rubble. The few times he awoke, it was always with a moan so she gave him pain bark from her dwindling supply. He could point her to replacements in this strange new land when he felt better.

By often switching who dragged, they made good progress. Ronor awakened as they tucked into a cave for the night. His color had improved and he sat up without flinching. A fire crackled and Yu'ung spread food on the hot stones. They ate the fare taken from the Tall Ones and Ronor told stories to provide insight should they run into more of the enemy.

"In our past, Bruurv and I were both skilled and honored. Here, in your lands, because I pairmated a Primitive, I was underfed and overworked. They treated you well, Yu'ung, for them, because you are a healer."

He shook himself. "My pairmate had your sturdy appearance, Yu'ung, without the red hair and pale skin."

"Did you find her?'

"Her body."

Tears shone in Jvelk's eyes. Yu'ung struggled to tamp down unbidden memories of Old One, though fewer this time than others. *Life is death. Jvelk must learn grief is the cost of survival.*

Yu'ung stirred the stew, mixing in shredded meat, roots, pulses, and stalks as Ronor continued, "After the Tall Ones captured me, I wanted you to flee, Jvelk. Now, I'm glad you didn't."

Yu'ung popped an egg into her mouth, gave one each to Ronor and Jvelk, and stripped open a cat-tail stalk to reach the supple inner tissue. "How did you escape, Ronor?"

He rubbed his battered forehead. "I pretended to be weak and they ejected me."

Jvelk grinned. "You see his cleverness!"

Yu'ung offered him a gourd to share with his father. "How did you meet Ocha?"

He rested his hands on his knees. "I was starving, but wouldn't leave the area until I confirmed Jvelk was gone." The cords on his neck tightened and his face hardened. "A solution struck me. I would steal carcasses brought in by the hunters while they slumbered. If they caught me, death at their hands was no worse than starvation. To my surprise, they didn't notice, their attention fixated on a boy and a female they were following. Females are rare. I thought it must be Jvelk, teamed up with someone else, so I tracked them. I was outside when they attacked you, would have defended if necessary, but I knew they wouldn't kill you. Bruurv wanted slaves, desperately. Jvelk saved Ocha's life and Yu'ung told her to run, which she did, staggering and bleeding profusely. I didn't think she would live without help so since I knew where you both would end up, I followed her, to do what I could to help.

"At first, great sticky red drops marked her passage, and then occasional ones. They led to her den where I found her licking the lacerations. She looked at me with those unusual blue eyes, moaned, and limped away. I took that to mean she didn't want me there so I returned to your cave and spent the night eating your food and resharpening tools while devising a way to free you from a male I once knew as well as myself–except I fell asleep. When I awoke, the black Canis with blue eyes lay a hand's distance from my face. She whined and loped away with no sign of yesterday's mortal injuries. There was no doubt I was to follow. We joined up with her pack. Somehow, she let me know they planned to save you both and would appreciate my help.

"The rest you know."

When he finished, Ocha splayed herself across Ronor's legs. Within a breath, a rumbling snore trembled her lips. Jvelk refilled the gourd with the bubbling, fragrant stew and popped a sizzling piece in his mouth as Yu'ung asked, "Bruurv killed the rest of your tribe. Why let you live?"

Jvelk interrupted. "My father is known throughout his homeland. He once stopped a charging Mammoth with a spear to its eye! Another time, he impaled a deer with such force the point pierced the throat and exited the backbone."

Ronor flushed. "The one that earned me a spot on the journey to explore these lands was when I swung my club so hard it decapitated a pig."

Jvelk's grin spread from ear to ear. "Every quest welcomed Ronor the Hunter, every group more secure when protected by Ronor the Warrior."

Yu'ung grunted. "It would be a victory for Bruurv to persuade you to join him, fight for him."

Ronor splintered a hip bone and scooped marrow into his mouth. A sliver stuck between his molars and he used a thin fiber to unstick it.

"I shunned my warrior skills when I started a new life here, but thanks to Bruurv's practices, was forced to revive them, at least in part."

"Part?"

A smile flitted across his face. "In the past, I often won battles by outsmarting the enemy rather than out-brawling them." He stared into the vastness. "I forgot how good justice and retribution feel."

Yu'ung barked a laugh. "The porcupine tail was brilliant."

"An elder demonstrated this once, called it a distraction, so others could get in place. I didn't understand then why he would sacrifice himself, but now his actions make sense. I'd eagerly trade my death for Jvelk's life. You and Ocha made it unnecessary."

Yu'ung chewed bitumen and pitch, cleaning her teeth of meat and plant.

"Nap now, Ronor. Ocha will guard. Tomorrow comes early."

He required no persuasion.

Jvelk shot to his feet. "I'll check the backtrail."

"Take this." Yu'ung tossed him a pelt. "It's from the Tall Ones, but I cleaned it."

He donned the heavy wrap, large enough to reach his wrists and knees, and slipped into the dark. In his absence, she reflexively checked the tunnels for messages, found none, so snuggled next to Ocha, soon oblivious to the world.

Yu'ung rubbed her eyes. Ocha was still beside her, ears perked, muzzle forward. Her hackles were neither flat nor stiff. She whined and licked her lips.

Yu'ung scuttled to Ronor. "Wake up. It is time to go, but first, how are your wounds?" She asked while removing the pelt bandages.

"Healed," but winced as he hobbled to his feet so Yu'ung applied fresh poultices.

"If by healed, you mean no longer bleeding and no red fingers, I agree, but the lesions are raw. You'll recover by avoiding skirmishes."

He winced again, sucked in a mouthful of air to hide it, but couldn't conceal his pale face or the sweat dimpling his forehead.

"Can you walk or do you require the travois?"

His reply was to stride away while shouting over his shoulder, "I'll lead. I have explored every hill, valley, gorge, and forest while searching for Jvelk."

She didn't argue. Members always acted in the group's good.

Food and exercise will fix him.

Jvelk joined her and then Ronor. She handed both a strip of dried meat. "Eat this while we walk. We have no time for rest breaks. If you see Tall Ones, be cautious. They may be Fierce's band and my mother."

Ronor brightened. "Fierce and I will recognize each other. He will be welcome."

Yu'ung wanted to scout, but stayed with Ronor when she saw him struggle. Still, she would help only if asked.

Yu'ung said, "You came here from the shoreless sea. How near is it?"

"Not at all. We likely will meet up with Fierce or your tribe first. If we end up at your destination before reuniting with the others, it will be a problem locating them."

"Why?"

"The shoreline is huge."

"We solved that. Whoever arrives first will light a fire to announce their location."

He chuckled. "You have no concept of the sea's massive size."

"Fierce does. He spent much time exploring its shores. He knows exactly how large it is."

Ronor flushed, chastened.

Ronor and Jvelk in the lead, Yu'ung guarded the rear and sides. Her extreme sight made this task easy, but she intended to do more than lie on a high plateau. She removed her foot protection despite the cold. Her bare feet picked up the gentlest rumble and the subtle ridges of prints. If Bruurv's friends blamed them for his slaughter and sought retribution, it was up to her to stop them.

Yu'ung snuggled into the brush of the highest hill she could find and waited. She saw a dust cloud at her sight's extreme distance. It paralleled the backtrail and headed in their general direction.

A small herd or Fierce.

She debated scouting it, but was reluctant to leave a young Jvelk and weak Ronor undefended. Faced with trouble, Yu'ung doubted they could defend themselves.

Whatever it is, I must warn them.

Jvelk spoke as soon as he saw her. "Yu'ung. Ocha smells water, through those canyons. Ronor is with her."

"Something comes toward us, not quickly, but consistently. I can't yet distinguish what it is, maybe a herd heading for the waterhole you picked up. Go on our backtrail, Jvelk. Try to figure it out. I'll let Ronor know."

Trekking into the ravines felt safer than across open lands. She decided they should hydrate first, solve the dust cloud afterwards. She ran to an area marked by deep canyons and smooth, steep cliff faces. Ronor found her first.

"Ocha is ahead."

Yu'ung sniffed. "There's water in the air."

He nudged his lips down. "It's below, at the bottom of this gorge."

Yu'ung analyzed the landscape. "Can we descend?"

"Yes, but it won't be fast or easy."

Time they didn't have. Already, the hair on her neck bristled and her chest tingled.

"We're in a hurry," and explained what she saw. "Let's pass on this water. For now."

The muscles in Ronor's jaw bunched and his eyes glazed as he stared into space.

"I have another idea. Coming here, I discovered water where no one would expect it," and hobbled off, favoring his wounded side.

He limped back into sight just as Yu'ung became concerned by his absence, face flushed with excitement.

"Follow me," and he hurried along a meandering animal passage, through rugged terrain with an upheaval of hills. Short bunch grass, clumps of weeds, tussock, and scrub were the only vegetation.

How can this lead to water?

Then, a cliff appeared with a broad dark streak down its face from crest to valley.

He dropped back to her side. "The water dumps into the stream we saw earlier, at the bottom of the gorge, but there's a flat plateau partway down where it pools. That's where we'll drink so we don't have to go all the way down."

Yu'ung called Jvelk with a pre-arranged bird song and traipsed after Ronor. The path widened with the many animals descending. Ocha was already drinking when they reached the edge. They consumed as much as they could and then loaded up the hollow vines carried in the shoulder sacks to transport water. Done, they re-ascended and continued toward the shoreless sea, Jvelk patrolling and Ronor with Yu'ung.

He rubbed his neck sporadically, cleared his throat once and again, then fumbled through meaningless sounds for far too long until Yu'ung finally asked, "What concerns you?"

After a deep sigh, he said, "The same as you. There is trouble."

"I haven't forgotten the dust cloud dogging us."

"It's not a herd—"

"And maybe not trouble. We wait."

Ocha howled. Yu'ung stared at the Canis and breathed a relieved sigh. "We have shelter for the night."

Chapter 22

Yu'ung lit the fire and Jvelk collected kindling for later. After food, Yu'ung and Ocha wriggled into the thatch on the overwatch hill and lay as still as possible. When she and B'o followed herds, Yu'ung spent many fingers of time motionless. This was no different. Her breath came out in white puffs. When the cold leeched through her wraps, she loosed her abundant mane and let it tumble over her body like a fur pelt.

She muttered, "Where is Shanadar's flute? With all the prints I saw, he should be close."

Ocha didn't respond unless a snore counted.

If Shanadar lost the flute, or it broke, I'll track him down another way.

But what if her ragtag patched-together assemblage was not alone? She wouldn't lead trouble to the People.

Yu'ung prepared to give in to exhaustion when a light blinked at the summit of a nearby hill. She leaned forward and elbowed Ocha.

"It's not a herd. The dust cloud...."

Ocha's head rose briefly and then lowered. Yu'ung focused on the flicker until, lulled by Ocha's lack of interest and the peaceful night sounds, her eyes drooped. She snapped them open. The fire remained stationary as it should. She memorized the position and trundled back to the cave. Ocha remained on the high ground. Nothing would get by her.

Dry twigs crackled and popped in the hearth. Jvelk and Ronor both dozed, exhausted from injuries and endless hiking, but Yu'ung couldn't sleep. The Tall Ones' possible threat and the People's probable nearness made her edgy.

I will work.

Preparing a hide took most of a day. In this case, though, she scraped the pelt clean of gore in her time with the Tall Ones. Now, she cut it into a shirt for Ronor, a wrap for Jvelk, and laced the sides to keep the cold out. The remnants would be for bandages.

Finished, her eyes sagged, her thoughts drifted, and she passed out.

"Ronor. Go with Jvelk. I'll catch up."

With Ocha, she hurried toward the spot she'd seen the flames last night. She halted at a boulder bed.

"They hid in here. We only saw them because we were above."

She remained still, let her senses explore her surroundings. Whoever this was didn't try to hide their presence. They—and it was a group, not one—didn't expect Yu'ung and Ocha to come back to search for them.

When she was sure whoever had been here was no more, she slipped out of hiding, rolling heel to toe, and scanned for clues.

"Ocha. There's a round indent at the base of this boulder, too big for the Tall Ones' far-throwing spear."

Ocha trotted away, stopped and woofed. Yu'ung joined her.

"Prints. Let's see where they go."

She trekked through the boulder bed along a path roughly mimicking her group's route. After a short distance, she stopped, staring ahead as she tugged her lower lip.

"After spending the night here, they traced our course in daylight. Why?"

To see where we are going?

She started again. The footprints ended at a cliff.

She tipped her head up. "They climbed, probably to observe our progress from a height."

It didn't take long to identify their upward path. It was the one she would pick. She wasted no time beginning the ascent. Her toes and fingers dug into the cracks and ridges, always checking firmness before proceeding. She imitated the mountain sheep flinging themselves effortlessly from one narrow ledge to another, continuing quickly, relieved when the summit came into view. She was good at climbing, but it was taxing.

Cockiness or complacency, whatever went wrong, once started, couldn't be stopped.

The surface of the final handhold crumbled beneath her grasp. She scrambled for another and ended up hanging precariously by one hand, swinging her body to another hold, but missed and plummeted. She snatched any scrub bush or ledge available, but each time, they came loose in her grasp. Jutting edges ripped her hands, leaving a trail of her blood down the cliff face. She slammed her body into the rock wall, on purpose, hoping to somehow stick, but just bruised her ribs and thighs. A frantic yip echoed below as she thrashed, gripped another ledge only to touch scaly skin. A desperate yank away kept her far enough from the stinging tongue, but nowhere near to another handhold and she bounced off the rocks into, nothing. Air buffeted her. Images swirled through her head, of her People–B'o, Shanadar, Ese, Laak–what they would do when she never rejoined them and they didn't know why.

They will manage–

Her thoughts halted abruptly with a wrenching thud though softer than it should have been. Pain coursed through every part of her body and darkness swallowed her.

She waved a hand. "Spider. Stop bothering me!" But it didn't. *Not spider....* "Ocha?"

The Canis panted happily, drooling onto Yu'ung's cheek. She opened her eyes and squeezed them shut when ripples of pain flashed through her shoulders, back, and neck. She froze, afraid any movement would resurrect the piercing spiny throb, slowed her breathing as spasms washed through her, and then pulled back. She kept her eyes shut, sensing where her body was broken, waiting for the damage to send reports to her brain. There were bruises and cuts and scrapes, but nowhere the heavy leaden ache of a break.

A few breaths, more, and more. Everything hurt, but lying still, with shallow inhales, it seemed to diminish to a dull insidious thump.

I have to move.

She managed to sit, wiggle her arms, fingers, toes. Nothing worse than pain.

What happened? It dawned on her. "You cushioned me, Ocha."

The Canis panted again, body trembling with excitement that her pack member lived. Yu'ung carefully fingered damp sticky scrapes and cuts along her torso, ribs, and shoulders. They quivered to the touch of her fingers, or a breeze, or Ocha's hot puffs.

She forced herself to her knees. Fire bit into her neck, red and hot. She hung her head and dug into her satchel, thankfully still around her shoulder. She pawed through for bark, wincing as she awkwardly scraped the pith off and stuffed it into her mouth. The effort exhausted her and she lay back, inhaled and exhaled, once and again. The red melted away bit by burning bit. When the raw pain dulled, she managed to scrabble onto her knees, then with Ocha's help, got her feet under her.

Ocha wriggled, saying, *You're fine.*

"I didn't identify who built the fire and I'm not trying the cliff again. Let's walk along the base. If there isn't an easier route up, we wait for them to come to us."

Her woozy head made thinking a trial. Simply standing disoriented her, flooded her senses with dizziness. Ocha moaned and pranced ahead, checking often on Yu'ung. When they reached where Ronor and Jvelk had been this morning, they were gone, as they should be.

"At least someone listens when I speak! Ocha. If I collapse, find Jvelk."

Head spinning, vision blurry, they left, Ocha leading. Yu'ung shuffled because any faster exploded the simmering aches into debilitating pain. The lone good outcome of the event was that one of her many falls landed her hand on the rock Shanadar needed to stripe his face orange. He'd never met Fierce, but wanted to place the color where Fierce's was. When asked, he credited Xhosa with the placement.

Yu'ung stowed it away. "This will surprise him."

They caught up with Ronor and Jvelk that night, guided by their fire.

Ronor squinted at her scraped and tattered body. "What happened?"

She didn't mention the accident. Why would she? Talking did no good. She shrugged and asked, "What did I miss here?"

"We're fine."

He slit his eyes, noticing her wobbling walk and how often she gasped, but said only, "I am not asking how you were injured. I assume your shaky state means we must hurry?"

At her jerky nod, he said, "Tomorrow. My injuries and I are tired. Be aware, though. I will mind you as you have done me. Was it worth it? Did you find what you sought?"

"Yes." She wanted to say more, but feared throwing up if she opened her mouth too long.

After another mouthful of the pain bark and a quick check that no bones were where they shouldn't be, she changed the topic.

"The sky is clear today. Have we escaped Mountain's anger?"

She didn't hear his answer, instead toppled over.

The next day, the route flattened. Yu'ung's water was nearly gone. Jvelk's and Ronor's must also be. She hoped Ronor knew about another surprise waterhole. Ocha led them to the night's refuge. Yu'ung climbed the oversight hill, exhausted by the time she reached the crest.

I'll rest, then survey.

She found a dry spot open to the sky, and lay back, her thoughts drifting to one of her last conversations with Old One.

"Old One. What will I do when we reach the Mountain People? Ash will hide the landmarks B'o told me about."

"Watch the stars, Yu'ung. They have guided the People faithfully. Be aware their combinations alter night to night, but once you understand them, they tell everything you need to know."

Since the journey's start, the night sky showed nothing save murky smoke and clouds. She anticipated the same tonight, but was wrong.

"The stars are back!"

Shanadar must have already seen them because his last message named the star clusters to guide her.

"There's one he called out."

In spite of their injuries, her group was moving faster than the People, likely because children and elders slowed them. She surveyed the surroundings and pinpointed the twinkle.

In line with our site.

Whoever, they were too far to be a risk. Yu'ung descended the hill and curled against the cave's wall, wondering if Ese's treatments helped Shanadar.

Chapter 23

Yu'ung spent the next day hidden along the group's backtrail, watching for dust or shadows that indicated someone behind them. Often, she stopped to chew pain bark.

The group as a whole was healing. Ronor's blue-black bruises lightened to yellow-orange. Jvelk's foot sores became callouses, and her blurry vision mostly abated. The Tall Ones continued to bear down on the small group, so stoicism was required more than comfort.

Fatigue, though, had begun to worry her. It worsened with each passing day and she knew why. When herds migrated in the hot air time, the tribe replaced the salt their meat no longer provided with salt licks or specialized roots. None of those existed along this route. They passed the occasional herd, but a hunt required too much time with an enemy dogging her steps.

Finally, something only slightly less important than salt forced a decision. The air became colder with each passing day. Her wraps came from thin, lightweight warm-air fur, not only unsuited to frigid air but also ragged from the rough conditions the group faced. She stuffed her hair into her shirt for warmth, but the best Jvelk and Ronor could manage was grass, often impossible to find. By the end of most days, their lips were blue and bodies trembling. The last ember had expired in the chill dampness and striking stone against stone to create a flame tested Yu'ung's shuddering hands. She usually managed, but keeping it lit was a problem with the sparse availability of kindling. Nights became a battle to keep the fire burning enough to prevent ice from forming on their pelts as they slumbered.

Ocha nudged Yu'ung, her rat-scented breath pleasant for its heat on Yu'ung's face. She grabbed her spears and hurried along Ocha's backtrail on feet stiff from the cold, struggling to maintain her grip on the spear. The cold breeze leeched through to her skin as she pounded after the Canis, the air freezing her throat, a dense white cloud covering her face with each exhale.

She ducked under leafless branches, ice dripping off the ends. The Canis stopped, ears perked, legs spread, and melted into invisibility. Yu'ung did the same. Together, they lay on the stubble, noses forward, eyes alert. Finally, she tasted what brought them here.

Meat!

Yu'ung crawled, her pelt, despite its worn condition, shielding her skin from the grass's sharp tips. A small herd browsed ahead in their furred cold-air pelts, cautious but hungry enough to brave an open field.

Yu'ung whispered to Ocha, "Can you force them to me?"

"We will."

Yu'ung jerked around, startled at the quiet declaration behind her. "Ronor—your injuries are not healed. Go back!"

He gave her a withering grimace. "I've been worse and done better. Don't insult me. You need me, and Jvelk. Animals you miss, we won't."

She wanted to refuse, but desperation made her nod. A tremor of excitement ran through her body. There was power in being so needy you challenged the impossible.

She clenched her teeth. "Good, with one adjustment. Jvelk and Ocha funnel the herd to you and me."

Which will lessen the stress on Ronor and his injuries.

Ocha and Jvelk skirted upwind, Yu'ung and Ronor downwind. The deer's heads snapped up. Their ears tweaked and big eyes darted, but they missed the danger a few long strides away. Jvelk exploded from the undergrowth, snarling and growling as Ocha taught him, arms flailing to force the prey to go where he needed them to. It worked. The deer dashed toward Ronor, saw him and jolted a different way.

Ocha soared into the air, snarling, and forced them to Yu'ung. She flung her spear, leaning forward to add power. The chosen deer stumbled but stayed upright despite Yu'ung's lance bouncing in its shoulder. Ocha leaped and bit into the deer's bony legs with her powerful jaws. The desperate creature fell and broke its neck, dead before Yu'ung reached it.

The chase attracted Hyaena. Ocha placed her massive body between the carcass and the pack and unleashed a round of intimidating snarls. When the bravest dared move toward her, she snapped, fangs exposed, lips quivering and they slunk away but not far. Tails tucked, their gaze darted through the surroundings, trying to figure out if Ocha was with the Uprights or a larger Canis pack.

Yu'ung's heart hammered in her chest, her breath ragged gasps as she screamed her excitement, "We did it!"

A boy, an injured Tall One, a Canis, and a new adult.

They worked quickly. The blood in the air drew more scavengers, each hoping to be first. Soon, a sabre-toothed cat and a cave lion joined Hyaena. Both preferred fresh meat, but scavenged predator kills in difficult times. The carrion birds arrived, first one, then a flock, cawing threats to those below, but waiting. Jvelk and Ocha urged Yu'ung and Ronor to hurry.

They slashed the carcass into portable pieces, leaving some of the entrails for others, shouldered what they could carry, and ran. The many ravenous scavengers barely noticed the Uprights' departure or the Canis' withdrawal, engrossed as they were in who got first claim to the remaining flesh. More foragers—possibly Primitives—awaited their turn. Judging by their skeletal frames and haunted eyes, this meat promised to be the first in a while. Yu'ung left them to their business, eager for her own feast. By the time her group settled into a cave and had the hearth fire burning, daylight was gone.

Yu'ung studied Ronor's drawn face and flushed skin. He'd performed without complaint, but she could tell his enfeebled body was at its limit. As they ate, Jvelk trembled with exhaustion, but his pride at completing adult work washed through everyone. Ronor never stopped grinning, knowing he took care of his child.

"Ronor." Yu'ung couldn't hide her worry. "Your wounds are not bleeding and no worse, but now, rest. Jvelk, Ocha, and I will tend the fire."

He offered no argument. Before Jvelk restocked the kindling—an arduous and time-consuming task—Roror was snoring. Yu'ung cleaned the deer pelt, almost drooling over its thick warmth, eager to make a wrap.

"Jvelk. Check our backtrail with Ocha."

When he puffed back into the cavern later, he shook his head. "No lights."

Yu'ung eyes were heavy, but she continued. If not her, who would finish the wrap? Jvelk slept beside the fire, face relaxed. It hissed softly and a stubby log that fed it shifted with a shower of sparks. Ocha guarded the entry, at least, in position, but could she stop an invader from her back, paws dangling?

"Ocha. Are you watching for enemies or napping?"

The Canis waved a plumed tail and sent a cloud of dust into the air.

Yu'ung rubbed her eyes, listened for trouble, and drifted into darkness. For the first time in a long while, Xhosa visited her dream.

"Xhosa! Where have you been?"

"If Ocha is with you, I am. Mountain's angry smoke will soon evaporate where you are, but its damage will outlive you. Get as far as you can from here. There is much to do even after you reach your homebase."

"And the Mountain People?"

"They thrive, high in the hills where Mountain's fury can't reach them. You will never see them again. The People are your concern. They will prevail if you don't quit, Yu'ung. So don't. Much of importance occupies your future. You will pairmate, have children, and add your strength and skills to his tribe, but none of that can happen until you lead the People to their new homeland."

"Everything has changed. I have no guidelines to follow."

"Yes, Mountain's fault line fractured your life, your tribe's, but here's how to fix it...."

Yu'ung awoke to an epiphany. *I am as important to the People as they are to me.*

She lit a torch, shuffled down the tunnels, and arrived at Shanadar's marks.

Three dots....

Made by fingertips. They told her enough.

Sun bathed the land in warm rays, melted the ice frozen in shiny puddles on the ground which allowed tiny shoots of green to pop through to the surface. The group ate more of the deer to lighten the loads and departed. The Tall Ones, Mountain's explosions, Ronor's injuries, whether Fierce tricked Kriina, guiding the tribe without Old One–all seemed manageable after filling food.

Yu'ung laid the finished deer pelt over Jvelk, then crawled up the oversight hill. The strong chill breeze grew to a frigid gale, making her lips tremble. Thunder rolled somewhere far from here, announcing a storm. Judging by the dampness in the air, it came toward the travelers.

If we must be stuck, this cave is a good refuge, high enough to not flood with easy access to the waterway.

Plus, the rain would erase their prints, obscuring them from the Tall Ones on their trail.

From Fierce, too, but he goes where we go. We'll find him.

She surveyed the area, verified they were alone, and listened for Shanadar's flute. Nothing. Or its sounds were lost in thunder's swell as the storm rolled closer. She should return to the cave, had intended to until Ocha lay at her side, ears pricked.

With a jerk, awareness broke through the haze. *How did I nod off?*

Eyes slit, slight enough to prevent Moon's shine from bouncing off them, a glow lit the horizon. She pushed to her elbows. Were those trees swaying or Uprights advancing? And the noise–that was nothing out of Nature. Ocha remained at her side, muzzle forward, nose twitching.

"You smell it, too."

We haven't lost them.

Chapter 24

Yu'ung rushed to the camp. "We must go!"

Ronor scrambled to his feet, rubbing the sleep from his eyes. "Tall Ones?"

Yu'ung nodded. "Not Fierce–"

"Because he would reveal himself."

They moved quickly, avoiding known animal paths, slowing to listen before crossing waterways.

At one creek, Yu'ung grunted. "The frogs say rain is coming," but the thump of feet and a loud droning buzz soon drowned out their croaks.

"Shhh!" she hissed and motioned to an overhang in the creek's bank, stuffed with roots and abandoned bird nests, but enough space for them to squeeze in.

The steps stopped directly above them on the shoreline. If the enemy looked down, Yu'ung feared they would see a leg or arm that didn't tuck well into the tight space, but they were too busy chattering to each other and scanning the forward trail.

Ronor snarled softly, "I recognize one voice. He visited Bruurv." Yu'ung guessed Ronor had suffered at this male's hands.

She breathed out. "So they come for revenge."

Ronor leaned closer to Yu'ung. "They aren't being quiet. They want us to hear them, panic, and let our fear give us away."

Yu'ung grunted to herself. *That won't happen. How badly they underestimate us.*

One shouted, "It's done. Let's go while we have time. The fire will flush them out. What doesn't kill them, we will. None will escape!"

A chill ran down Yu'ung's spine. *Fire? They never intended to recapture us.*

Ronor murmured, "I've seen this before. Stay in front of the flames. If we try to get around them, to retreat, they will either kill or capture us."

Jvelk hissed, "Why not stay here? There's water to protect us!"

Yu'ung and Ronor responded together, "It's too shallow and narrow." "We need to get out of the fire's path."

Yu'ung twitched toward Ronor. "What happened the last time you saw this?"

"They will light the fire from a safe position. The wind is blowing our way so will race toward us. They want it to drive us out of hiding so they can pick any off that aren't burned by the conflagration. We must be smarter than that."

Yu'ung scanned quickly. "There's a copse of trees on a hillock in the distance. It should protect us."

Ronor flattened to his elbows and knees. "Keep low! Let's go."

Spears across their arms, they crawled away like oversized ground beetles, toward what they hoped would be their salvation from the flames. Damp gusts tickled Yu'ung's back. Her hands sweaty with fear, knees soon raw from rubbing against her rough wrap.

Ocha moaned and Ronor shouted, "They lit the fire!"

If only the rain would start.

The blaze spread across the field, feeding on the dry scrub. Before long, the wall of flames hid the Tall Ones from view. Without visual, they relied on the wind to spread fire over their quarry, the wretched screams of her group burning alive to their death as justice for killing those who had enslaved them. The forest was still several spear throws ahead, too far at the firestorm's speed. To the Tall Ones, the only escape from misery was death.

There's no reason not to stand. They can't see us. So she did, then raced, Ronor and Jvelk with her, but it seemed futile. The flames advanced too quickly.

Yu'ung waved her arms over her head. "Run around the fire!" An unlikely goal, but the only option.

Ocha yapped and Yu'ung signaled her on. "Go! If we are injured, come get us!"

They sprinted, propelled forward despite sore feet and weakened legs. The flames crackled and spit, close enough now the sparks threatened to singe Yu'ung's hair and skin.

"Go away!" But the fire would do what it would. Yu'ung and her group must also.

Never quit.

Without warning, the heat, the noise, and the blistering gale behind them evaporated. Now, the wind blew in her face. Surprise nearly stopped her, but instead, she ran harder for the salvation ahead, ever closer. Finally, the ground's elevation rose, the surface now mushy and soft, and Yu'ung scrambled up to the crest. Once in the relative safety of the copse, she pivoted to see if the Tall Ones or the inferno was the greater enemy.

Neither.

"Ronor! Jvelk! The fire veered!"

It now raced back in the direction it came, even faster than at first. The conflagration recrossed the charred field, breached the initial point where the Tall Ones started the blaze, and chased the enemy. They were now the ones in a flight for their life, the goal, the river. Yu'ung didn't think they would make it. The flames now flanked the Tall One warriors, licked the flying feet of those in the rear. Screeches echoed and then glowing pyres announced the carnage. Those in front never looked back, didn't need to. The rancid smell of burning flesh told them everything. They ran harder, ignoring the devastation as the flames picked off the next row of warriors and the next, one after another, until those who hadn't succumbed finally dove into the waterway, some ablaze.

Ronor stood beside Yu'ung, watching. "Better to have burned," and pointed to the huge scaley lizards that slid across the river, their destination the desperate males. Wide jaws, a frenzied screech, and they rolled below the surface where both disappeared. There were more Gators than males. The Tall One's' only hope was to reach the opposite side while the Gators fed on their band mates. One after another, shrieking Tall Ones were dragged under.

Finally, the fire burned itself out and the crimson water cleared except for more sated Gators than Yu'ung had ever seen in one place.

Charred bodies littered the blackened land. It seemed all life touched by the inferno had been extinguished.

Yu'ung slipped down the hill to another woods, this one on the opposite side of the rise. There, she hid in case somehow, an enemy lived. Ocha greeted her. Ronor was steps behind, but Jvelk remained crouched above on a roomy, sturdy branch in the canopy.

He called to Yu'ung, "I see no life. The Gators ate those who escaped to the water, but a few might have made it across."

There was no compassion in his appraisal. Why would there be?

Ronor steadied himself against a tree. "Others will come after us, outraged so many of their band died."

Yu'ung swallowed. "Why chase mere slaves? We are soon, if not already, beyond their territory."

He shivered. "They are my kind, but nothing about them is me. I've seen their type in my former homeland. It is why I left and warned Jvelk about Tall Ones."

"How many are there like them, unlike you and Fierce?"

"Too many, and quite a few here."

Yu'ung patted her array of weapons. "We will be wary. Jvelk," she called up the hill. "You watch first."

He climbed higher into the canopy where the view was less obstructed.

Yu'ung tipped her head up. "Wake me when you're tired," and lay by Ocha.

Jvelk woke her by tumbling through the branches and landing in a heap at her side.

He scrambled up, rubbing his arm. "I passed out."

"And fell." She craned her neck, squinting to see where he started. "Are you all right?"

"I was climbing down and stopped to rest. That's the last I remember." He yawned. "It's your watch."

Yu'ung rubbed her eyes and said, "I'll skip the tree," and headed up the hill.

The rain had come and gone. When the Sun peaked over the horizon, it revealed the extent of the fire's damage. Even with her extreme sight, she saw nothing more than swaths of blackened land as far as the horizon, but something didn't sound right. A piercing silence, then faint hums far in the background. She couldn't pin down what it was, but it sent an edgy shiver through her body.

She hurried down the incline. "Skip the watch. We must go. Now. Fast."

No one questioned her. Ronor injured his leg running from the firestorm, but Yu'ung said nothing. If he required help, he'd ask.

"Stay on the edges."

Yu'ung motioned everyone to the shadows on the field's border as Ocha dashed off.

When Jvelk and Ronor asked what was going on, she snarled, "You are loud." Ronor choked out a few garbled mutterings before clamping his lips shut.

Yu'ung murmured, "Don't you hear it—the soft rattle of pebbles dislodged by something brushing too hard against a rock face, the crunch and rattle of gravel underfoot. Someone is here, but I don't think they know we are."

Sun was high by the time Ocha reappeared. The somewhat stiff hackles told Yu'ung she found danger, but not close, or not serious. Yu'ung climbed another hill, this one with a view in the opposite direction. When she saw no worrisome signs, she sighed, relieved.

"Whoever it was left."

Ocha headed in the general direction of the shoreless sea and the rest of the group followed. By the downside of the day, a wave of cold air rolled over them with a vengeance. Yu'ung wrapped her shirt tight. Ronor and Jvelk did the same. Occasionally, she spoke as a bird. Tall Ones, if any were around, would think it a native, but Yu'ung's tribe would recognize the difference and know it was her.

Nothing.

Ocha woofed and pawed through a layer of branches.

"What do you have, Ocha?"

Hope bloomed that it could be the People and then wilted. Tears pricked Yu'ung's eyes and her head pulsed.

Will this ever be over?

Jvelk rushed to her. "More Tall Ones. How is it possible?"

Yu'ung cringed. *They must know where we are headed so no matter how we divert, they find us.*

But she said none of that, instead smiled at the subadult who depended upon his adults for safety and security.

That mollified him and he resumed scouting.

For the remainder of the day, they moved carefully, hiding in the grass or within the forest's trunks. Yu'ung came to an overhang, small enough body heat made a fire unnecessary. Ocha dropped a rat amidst the group. This with cold stems from Yu'ung's travel food would be the day's meal. Afterward, Ocha and Yu'ung lay prone by the entry, hidden in shadows, to observe and listen. At first, normal nighttime sounds soothed her, and then, the abnormal told her trouble stalked them. Lights flickered in the distance and Ocha raced off. Before long, a Canis howled, then another and another.

Jvelk slunk to her side. "What's happening?"

Whoever is out there is too big for one Canis so Ocha found help.

But she didn't tell him that. It wasn't the People. Her kind wouldn't light a fire in the open with enemies around. Besides, it came from behind, not in front.

She said neutrally, "Ocha gathered a pack to investigate."

Jvelk clutched his spear, ready to throw. "These could be the prints Ocha found, more Tall Ones coming after us."

Yu'ung rubbed her eyes, bleary from focusing. "It will end soon. We will unite with the rest of my tribe, or Fierce's band, and they will not risk attacking such a large group."

She hoped Jvelk believed her words because she didn't. When her father, Dhar, led the People, he often sent small clusters to scout. If they didn't return, he sent large groups to take care of the problem.

Howls filled the night complemented by snarls, yowls, and screams.

Jvelk tensed. "Is Ocha in trouble?"

Yu'ung narrowed her eyes. "Someone is." When silence again reigned, she muttered, "Rest until daylight arrives, Jvelk. We will move fast tomorrow."

Jvelk slipped inside and Ronor came to relieve Yu'ung.

He asked, "What should I know?"

"The fires vanished."

She tried to sound confident, but her voice pinched with worry.

She dozed, lulled by the scuffling and slithering of night creatures, woke when Ocha pressed her body against Yu'ung's. She opened her eyes to see Ocha wag.

Yu'ung gasped. "Do you know one of your ear tips is missing and there's a raw, ragged puncture in your flank?"

Yu'ung wasted no time treating both. Ocha stretched, shook herself when Yu'ung finished, circled several times before dropping, flipping over, and snoring. She didn't move even when Yu'ung lumbered to the front to join Jvelk and Ronor. No one said a word as she searched for the enemy who injured Ocha.

"Ocha should rest today."

Ronor grabbed his lance. "Jvelk and I will scout."

They didn't reappear until Sun was high overhead, Ronor with the carcass of a small Boar around his neck and Jvelk with a hare. Ocha still slept. Yu'ung started a fire, confident its light would blend into the day. The aroma of sizzling, dripping fat woke Ocha and they shared the feast. Yu'ung checked the Canis. Both the puncture and the torn ear were almost healed as wounds did on Ocha. Yu'ung surveyed the dark. No flames flickered.

Several days later, as they rested from a long march, Ocha scratched her back on the prickly dead grass, whimpering with joy. Then without warning, she scrambled to her paws and took off. When Yu'ung caught up, the Canis was trailing a solitary Mammoth calf. The People didn't hunt calves or cubs unless abandoned by the adults. Those would die anyway.

Ronor stamped one foot then the other. "The calf might lead us to the herd."

A Mammoth herd meant not only plenty of meat, but thick pelts for clothes and fat for the cold.

Yu'ung agreed. "It's worth the delay."

Ocha snarled and the calf bellowed for its mother. No response comforted it or warned predators to keep their distance. The youngster tried again with the same result. Jvelk scrambled up a hill and then came back.

"It is alone."

It trundled onward on squatty legs, its trumpeting call more desperate with each step.

The baby will die without adults. We do it a favor.

As she pondered how to proceed, it stumbled into a stream, sucked water into its trunk, and sprayed the cool liquid over its head and back.

Ocha's hackles stiffened and Yu'ung backed into a copse of trees edging the water. Ronor did the same, tapping his nose.

"Jvelk! Find who else is chasing the calf. If our kind, we will split the flesh with them."

He hurried off, but not for long. "Tall Ones and they head here." He scratched. "I think they're after the calf, not us."

Yu'ung eyed the youngster as it stepped out of the water, weary and frightened, and promised, "You will die painlessly, little one, and we will wear your pelt with pride at your memory."

She stepped to the copse's edge, arm raised to fling her spear, but too late. Other lances found it first. The calf screamed and collapsed, dead before hitting the ground.

Will we never get away from these Tall Ones?

She withdrew into the shadows, forced to watch as the Tall Ones took the food meant to fuel Yu'ung's tribe. After they left with all they could carry, Yu'ung and the rest retrieved the substantial leftovers. They sliced with speed and efficiency, determined to be gone by the time the Tall Ones came for another load.

Dismemberment completed, portions shouldered, they hurried along the shore, the water high enough to obscure their tracks. When it became too shallow, they switched to the rutted shoals that edged the coastline. This circuitous route was longer but safer and they stumbled into their camp as Sun dropped out of sight. The firepit sparked to life. Slabs of mammoth overflowed the stones and fleshy shreds were tossed into a stew with stalks and roots Jvelk had found. It was the best in days. Yu'ung planned to repair a tear in her wrap, but passed out before that happened.

They left early the next day, in silence, soon lost in the endless unvarying trunks and shadowy recesses of a vast forest. At length, Yu'ung followed badger tracks out. By the time they freed themselves of the forest's gloom, daylight had run its course. They found a refuge littered with detritus from other tribes. They ate, then rested while Yu'ung lit a firestick and strode into the tunnels.

Shanadar's etchings were damp with fresh colors, cautioning of Tall Ones everywhere. The freshness of Shanadar's message meant he was near. Surely, they would soon reunite. That was the best protection against the Upright enemy.

The message looked incomplete, as though Shanadar wrote more on a different wall, but something inside Yu'ung told her to return to the cavern.

If everything is fine, I will return, find the rest, and hurried back to the front.

Ronor and Jvelk stood shoulder to shoulder, backs to her, faced off against weapon-wielding warriors.

The Tall Ones.

When she appeared, one yelled, "Seize her! She killed Bruurv!"

Chapter 25

Fierce, the Tall Ones, and Aynoh

The sparkles Aynoh saw disappeared without revealing their source. Fierce guessed it was from water on their forward trail. He had been warned to fill up before beginning the ascent up the mountain, that little to none was available afterwards so they did, drinking at every waterhole they found before heading deeper into the new land. As though proving the point, with each stride, the air became drier.

Aynoh had been scanning the surroundings, as she did migrating, when she jerked at an unexpected movement far ahead on the forward path. She squinted and then shouted.

"Deer! There–headed toward the foothills!"

They needed this. There'd been no meat since the last Moon.

Fierce's head snapped and Grub bellowed with joy.

Fierce had been teaching her to use the far-throwing and bowed spears. She learned quickly and was excited to test the new skills. The deer led them on a torrid chase across the flatlands, up the slopes, and then down a narrow ledge with more curves than should be allowed. One side of the ridge plunged into a canyon, the other abutted a rough wall that ascended to a summit far above.

Each of the band hurtled fearlessly along the shelf, single-file, but always the sure-footed animal disappeared around a curve before they could take a shot. Running full speed in an effort to catch up despite the personal risk, Fierce cocked his spear to throw when a mud-caked, scrawny figure emerged from the cliff-side scrub and flung a snake at Deer. The panicked creature leaped off the trail and tumbled over the cliff. The serpent slithered after it, but stopped at a ridge an arm's length down. The hunter, a female of the People's kind, blocked the passage, one arm clutched against her torso, and stared without fear at the Tall Ones.

They skidded to a stop, unsure how to respond to one whose weapon was a snake. Fierce lifted his spear to his waist, level with the ground, hoping it communicated power without threat. The female–no older than a subadult–sneered.

"Go!" She shouted, glaring, sweat drenching her hair. "I and my tribe will allow you to live, but do not presume to share our meat!"

Did she have a bad experience with Fierce's kind?

The youngster's eyes slit in distrust when Grub shuffled toward her, though she didn't back up. Aynoh stepped toward Grub to motion him away. His innate grumpiness would certainly worsen the stranger's already brittle temper, but Fierce stopped her.

"Let him go. He has another side you've never seen."

To Aynoh's surprise, the blocky, rugged, muscle-strapped male who smiled less than a rock, exuded good humor as he studied the stranger with obvious approval.

"You're right. We contributed nothing. Your trick with the snake–I never saw that before."

Grub stuffed his bowed spear into his shoulder sack, a simple action that relaxed her more than any of Aynoh's planned words would have. Though the young female still glared, her anger lessened, replaced with curiosity about the huge male with the radiant smile.

Aynoh played along. "Her courage is impressive, to stand boldly against a threatening foe the likes of you, her only weapon a serpent."

Grub beamed, missed Aynoh's sarcasm, and Aynoh asked Fierce, "Is this how he acts around females not me?"

Fierce muttered, "Once before."

Grub called out, "I'll process the carcass. Slay the snake if you can–"

"No!" from the stranger. "It isn't poisonous. I hunt with it often, and Deer–I can manage it myself!"

Even Fierce grinned. "I think … Grub … prefers you not die in a one-armed cliff descent."

He motioned Eknilk, Crevkukk, and Braanroorv to retrieve the body. Aynoh shuffled sideways, noted the female's backtrail, listened for sounds beyond the band behind her, the strangers' shallow breaths, the rattle of rocks dropping down the cliff as the males descended.

"Fierce," she murmured, face neutral, attention never leaving the stranger. "There are no tracks behind her. She may be from a tribe, but today, she is alone. And hungry."

The youngster glared, unintimidated. "Yes, I hunt by myself today, but it was I who brought death to Deer, and if you steal it, when I tell my tribe, they will stop you before you leave this mountain."

Grub beamed. "How do you salvage the carcass with a broken arm?"

She stomped a foot, but her eyes shone wet.

Aynoh responded for her. "By taking her time of course."

The stranger reluctantly made a wise decision. "My tribe is small. We won't need all of this. Take your fair part for helping."

Aynoh cocked her head. "What do I call you?"

"Wik."

"I am Aynoh. This is Grub. That's Fierce, the Leader of this band."

Aynoh waited for Wik to explain more, but she said nothing, unmoving, gaze frozen on Aynoh as though she wanted to talk but didn't know how to start.

There isn't a tribe.

Aynoh stepped closer, hands out, palms up at her sides. "I don't blame you for claiming a tribe, Wik. A female by herself must be careful."

A tear dripped down Wik's cheek. "You, One-called-Aynoh, are my kind. Why help these savages?"

Her statement was fearless, eyes alive with intelligence.

"They have become my friends."

Aynoh started to explain when Crevkukk, Eknilk, and Bhidid scampered up the cliff like mountain goats, deer parts bouncing off their chests. Wisely, they'd left the entrails, head, and hooves for scavengers. As Bhidid passed Grub, he snatched a chunk of the carcass and tossed it to Wik. She snagged the slippery flesh reflexively with her good arm. Her face softened in thanks and lips quivered with the ravenous hunger that etched her bones.

Grub ripped a wedge from the deer haunch and nodded to Wik as he chewed. She nibbled, eyes fixed on him, unblinking.

He swallowed and asked, "Snake was a brilliant strategy. How did you come up with it?"

"How else would you stop prey who runs faster than you?"

"With my spear."

"Before you could, Deer would escape around a bend. You don't hunt often in mountains, do you?"

Grub blinked. "I don't. You could teach me."

Turning to go, she peaked at him from the narrow corner of her eye.

She wants him to stop her!

Aynoh did it for him. "We are here for salt. Others we ran into suggested we contact a local guide. Is that you?"

Wik's steps faltered. "Possibly, if worth my time. I'm busy."

Fierce chewed as Aynoh asked Wik, "How did you break your arm?"

"A Tall One—his kind—massacred my tribe and left me for dead. Then, he stole the food, water, and furs we set aside for the cold. I trailed him, intending to steal them back, but never had the opportunity. Since then, I prefer being by myself."

Her balled fists and dark eyes screamed the lie.

Fierce clenched and unclenched his teeth. "They may be our kind, but they are nothing like us. Be assured of that, Wik."

Aynoh asked, "Where did he go?"

She shrugged. "Vanished into the mountains."

Fierce whispered to Aynoh, "I explained earlier, my band came to explore, but others came to conquer. Most, we never saw again, assumed were dead. Many were as Wik describes. They take a life for no reason except they want to."

Aynoh squeezed the subadult's wounded arm, testing. Wik winced and tightened her lips.

"Wik. If I don't treat your arm, you could suffer the rest of your life."

Wik grunted. "Tribe members with this injury hurt daily as you say."

"Did you have a healer, before.... ?"

"He died."

Aynoh inclined her head. *She is a subadult who acts like an adult.*

Wik said, "If you fix me, I will help you."

Aynoh switched to her healer tone. "I need—"

Something thudded at her side. "These," and Grub stepped back, but not far.

My healing treatments and a stick to support her arm. Grub paid attention.

"Where can I get clay? And large leaves?"

Wik jutted her lips down the passage. "The water hole where Deer planned to drink."

"I'll get it," from Crevkukk, eager to be noticed by this young female.

Grub rumbled, "You have work to do, with the carcass."

Crevkukk stuttered *Yes-but* as Grub beamed at Wik and left.

By the time he reappeared, hands overflowing, Aynoh had coated Wik's arm with a poultice.

"Grub. Pat clay on this."

When he ran out, he raced off for another armload. Aynoh layered on leaves and more of the sticky sludge.

"Let it dry. By the time it crumbles away, the arm will be usable."

Wik stared into Aynoh's eyes. "It already hurts less. I will guide you and the murderous enemies you call friends." She twitched toward Grub. "Though, this one is different. I never saw a Tall One help before."

He said, "Grub. My name is Grub."

Wik studied him with her level eyes. "You told me."

Another Tall One shouldered past Grub. "And I'm Bhidid."

Aynoh huffed. "I will check your arm, so it heals properly as we travel—"

Grub interjected, "Tell me if you need more of whatever." His face reddened, but other than that, he didn't notice how odd he sounded.

Wik's face flushed and their eyes met. "I'd appreciate the support."

Fierce rolled his eyes and clumped off to find kindling for the fire.

Aynoh smiled at Wik. "He isn't angry. He is distracted by Leader requirements," and added, "He's my pairmate."

Wik gasped.

Chapter 26

Fierce dropped twigs into the fire and turned back to Wik. "We have exhausted our supply of salt, but are told you have some here."

No one understood Wik's mutterings so Aynoh prodded. "Can you take us to it?"

Wik answered gruffly, "It is beyond these peaks. You're fortunate to have found me. Only one path winds through the hills. If you miss it, you end up at the mountain's crest where you'll freeze."

Grub sniffed and drooled. "First, food."

Eknilk placed deer chunks on flat stones in the fire. When the stone heated, the meat sizzled and fat bubbled, drawing everyone to the pit. Much to Aynoh's amusement and Bhidid and Crevkukk's frustration, Grub crouched near Wik. He offered her bites from his serving, frowning in confusion when she refused. There were few opportunities to mate. Wik would be the first since Aynoh arrived. Bhidid might think he and Grub could share Wik, but Aynoh doubted that would work, not after watching Grub. Besides, Wik wasn't an adult. How did they not notice that?

Fierce asked, "Why does it matter?"

"Among my kind, females don't mate until bleeding starts."

Wik wiped her fingers on her shirt and strode forward. Aynoh joined her while the rest took their usual positions in the column. Aynoh talked of being a healer, her daughter Yu'ung now the People's

Alpha, pairmating with a Tall One, her long ago life with the Primitives, her goals to reach the shoreless sea and a new homebase, and that Fierce's band was here to explore not conquer.

Finished, she asked, "Can you tell me about this region?"

"It will crush you if you aren't careful."

Aynoh swallowed her disbelief, asking simply, "How?"

"You have never felt such brutal cold. It oozes through any opening in our wraps. Mine the salt and depart. Don't waste time. Don't stay longer than necessary or you will be trapped."

"If that is true, why are you here?"

"This is my home."

Aynoh let the silence hang, memories swirling through her mind of a homeland she'd never again see.

Before beginning the steep part of the mountain, they stopped at a small lake.

Wik said, "Drink as much as you can. There is no more water after this."

"You live on the opposite side. Where do you get it?"

"Here. There is one source where we live, but each time we collect water there, someone dies."

"Why?"

"It's in an ice cave. Chipping pieces to melt often collapses the roof. Doing nothing more than breathing causes hunks to dislodge."

"How long does passage to your salt take?"

"Too long for today."

Wik led, Grub with her, Bhidid and Crevkukk behind, the rest in between single file. At an intersection of trails, one tilted down, the other to a lofty bluff. The choice seemed obvious. Without discussion, Fierce started, but Wik stopped him.

"That ascends—"

"It *descends*."

"Briefly."

"Your alternative runs into a cliff."

Wik stomped away and vanished behind a section of the rock wall covered in drooping vines. Grub tore after her and he too disappeared. When Aynoh reached the spot, Wik poked through the vines and revealed an invisible tunnel, taller than any of the People and by all appearances, not wide enough for Grub's broad shoulders.

"It is a shortcut." With a backward glare, she snapped, "The last person must obscure the opening."

Grub bumped Fierce. "She's a smart one."

Wik studied Grub. "Can you shrink yourself?"

"Of course!"

But Aynoh squinted at him. How would he become smaller? Slide sideways? Raise his arms? She shrugged.

He'll figure something out.

Debris and dead insects layered the ground, the rocky sides heated by the Sun's rays. Wik's murky shape lumbered ahead, brushing away Spider's webs.

Few travel through this. And then, *Grub did somehow shrink.*

Leaves rustled and the sweet aroma of flowers soon permeated the air, as did the distinctive odor of fresh dung. She tightened her grip on the shaft and wondered if Wik was leading them into a trap. She sped up, face flushed, eyes darting over the enclosed tunnel. She careened around a corner and popped into a verdant pasture hemmed by bluffs, warmed by a gentle breeze. The meadow was huge, its edge farther away than a spear throw.

"The Equiis live here, but are no danger to those I call friends," Wik explained. "The branches are filled with birds. At times, the singing deafens me."

Wik brushed her hand over the forehead of a magnificent black mare. Her coat glowed with health, hindquarters dappled with Sun colors. The beautiful Equiis dipped her head, flipped her elegant mane, and drew a circle with her nose. Neighs rewarded Wik's giggles and a great stallion galloped toward her. He skidded to a stop only when almost on top of her. Aynoh felt the spray of sweat from his sleek pelt. Legs spread, ears back, his proud head shook as steam blew in a cloud from his nostrils.

Wik said to Aynoh, "These Equiis guard ingress and egress to the field. They recognize my scent and tread. Not yours, though. I reassured the leader you are not a foe. If you came without me, he and his herd would trample you before you entered the field."

Bhidid strode into the clearing, the last Tall One out of the tunnel.

His face beamed as he gripped his spear. "Look what we have. We will eat forever now!"

Wik screamed at Bhidid, her fury joined by an enraged bugle.
The Stallion.

Wik slapped Bhidid's arm away. "No!" brandishing her broken limb. "Do not hurt them. They are friends!"

Grub muttered under his breath, "Of course she befriended Equiis."

Hand raised above his head, Fierce shouted, "I apologize, Wik. Tell the Equiis we are strangers unaccustomed to your habits."

The stallion tossed his head and galloped with the mare across the pasture, tails in the wind, and plunged into a shadowy corridor on the opposite side. Wik hurried after the graceful creatures, Grub caught up to her, their arms touching, and whispered too quietly for Aynoh to hear, then they both took off. Aynoh and the rest of the band kept her pace, often ducking under low branches. The broad field behind them, they now traveled single file, the same as they entered. The ground was looser here.

When it leveled, the Equiis nickered farewell.
They wanted us gone. I don't blame them.

As they thundered back to the meadow, they toppled Bhidid, who was frantic to avoid the lethal hooves.
I guess he deserved that.

Outside of the tunnel, the cold was absolute. Scree covered the flanks with scarce vegetation to break the blustery gusts. The frigid chill penetrated the seams in Aynoh's wrap and cape.

Fierce inhaled then licked the air. "Salt! And a lot of it!" His words a breathy explosion, but Aynoh wasn't excited. She was worried.

The overpowering scent blocked all other indicators that would usually describe the surroundings. Her stomach tightened and she wanted to run away, not satisfied the Tall One who killed Wik's tribe wouldn't show up. She wound around boulders, avoided crevices, and slid on her butt, grabbing branches for balance when that was her only choice. Wik paused on a plateau with an expansive view below—a greenish-blue lake, shore sparkling with white crystals, surrounded by stately summits shoulder to shoulder with no exit save the passage through which they entered.

Fierce murmured, "This reminds me of shoreless sea but smaller and more salt," his tone awed.

Wik muttered absently, "I have seen nothing similar anywhere. Father said water must seep in from beneath. He tried many times to tap into the source, but never managed to track it."

"Do you catch the fish—"

"No fish. No plant life, not in the lake or along the shores. Just salt. Endless salt."

"Wik. I see birds...."

Wik rubbed the side of her head. "The last few. They depart when the cold arrives. What they feed on is a mystery. The sole sound then is the gusts howling over the lake's surface, like an injured animal. Without scrub to anchor the land, the dust beats against your skin. Do you see the tiny white ice floes? The cold causes them. When it's hot, they are mosquito swarms."

She strode sure-footed despite the loose gravel. As they approached, the lake switched colors, from blue at times to green, or practically black. The nearer the shoreline, the more stagnant and heavy the air, and dry. Aynoh's mouth felt like the inside of a cat-tail.

Beyond the foothills, the land was cracked and dead, absent of the usual droning insects or bird song. The sky held not a single cloud, but a faint mist covered the lake, from where, Aynoh couldn't imagine.

Fierce headed for the first salt patch he could see. "The sooner we complete our harvest, the faster we move on."

The silence was eerie, as though life itself had been erased. Wik's endurance spoke to her strength. By the time daylight waned, Fierce declared they had enough salt to get them to the shoreless sea.

He heaved a tired sigh. "Let's rest—"

"No." From Wik. "Look."

White clouds gathered at the crest of the mountains. Aynoh tasted a dampness in the air absent before.

"Didn't you say it never rained?"

"Not here, on the opposite side. We get the dust, often too thick to breathe. We must get inside now or we will be in trouble."

In the short time she took to explain the dilemma, standing proved difficult without bracing themselves with their digging sticks.

Wik shouted, "This came on suddenly. My refuge is too far. The sole shelter we can reach is the ice cave."

Aynoh stiffened. "The perilous one, where someone always dies?"

Wik grunted. Fierce grumbled, "Will we?"

Wik paled. "Many have."

"And here?"

"No one can survive this. The salt crystals will cut you to pieces."

He cast a skeptical eye on Wik, but answered, "Lead," with a sweep of his arm.

Chapter 27

Wik sprinted toward a dark smudge on the cliffs. Grub kept up while hauling more salt than anyone else. They stopped at the opening to what must be the ice cave. Wik obstructed entry, waiting for everyone to gather.

Grub yelled, "Leave the salt outside. Be quiet inside. Wik says loud sounds crack the ice and send chunks crashing down. Anyone hit by those will not survive."

One by one, they entered, sidling through the icy piles. The hollowness of the interior soon made the tempest no more than a memory. They huddled together, awed by the dazzling white on the walls, ice piled high on the floor. Huge stalagmites rose above their heads. Stalactites dripped from the ceiling, many almost blocking passage. Aynoh touched one shining surface. It felt smooth and slippery, not damp as she expected.

Crevkukk asked, "Can we build a fire? It's freezing."

Grub hissed, "Of course not! You'll bring the whole mountain down on us!"

Wik glowered. "We are not here permanently. As soon as the storm ends, we leave."

Grub licked at the mist from a glittering stream trickling down the wall. "Can we drink that?"

Wik bobbed her head as though happy to say yes. "It will be the most sumptuous you ever tasted, but don't chop or chip."

They trudged to the crystalline liquid, wary of the blocky boulders strewn about. Aynoh drank slowly, the liquid freezing her throat, but the purity gave it a flavor like nothing she'd ever tasted. The shivering group tipped their vines beneath the flow, one at a time, then huddled together to share body heat.

The outside finally quiet, Crevkukk hissed, "The storm is over. Let's get out."

He strode forward, jumped over a shiny lump, but in so doing, slipped on the slick floor. With a yelp, he flailed his arms to prevent tumbling into a crevasse. His hand smacked a stalactite and the stocky spike cracked loose with a noisy clatter. Worry flooded Wik's face as Grub roughly yanked his hapless bandmate to his feet.

Oblivious to the jeopardy he placed the entire assemblage in, Crevkukk called, "Sorry! Everyone be careful!"

Grub slapped a hand over Crevkukk's mouth to silence him, but too late. Aynoh's warning to be quiet died in her throat, drowned by an ominous rumble.

Wik yelled, "Run!" Terror drenched her scream.

As though on cue, the ground quaked, followed by a crack and the thunder of ice cascading. A block bounced off Crevkukk's head. He squealed, but remained upright. Wik lost her balance, tumbled to her knees, and Grub hefted her atop his wide shoulder.

"I have you, Wik."

Crevkukk faltered, woozy, but managed to stumble forward. His leg bled profusely, but Aynoh's bigger concern was the gash on his head and slack face and glazed eyes.

Aynoh shouted, "Crevkukk! Do you need help!"

He shook his head, too slowly, like a Bear shakes. "Go, Aynoh … I'm right … behind you.…"

Aynoh's People said what they meant, so she believed Crevkukk and pounded toward the entrance. An ice ball plummeted to the floor. She dodged it, but it sent Crevkukk sprawling.

She tried to help him, but slid on the icy floor so settled for shouting, "Get up, Crevkukk! Keep running!"

He responded with, "Ummm," shook his head, and tottered to his feet.

Bhidid also dropped. When he couldn't push to his feet, Grub snatched him up to the shoulder without Wik.

"I needed that, to balance the weight!"

As he raced onward, he shoved Eknilk out of the way as an icy missile shot by. Then Grub soared past Fierce, dragging Braanroorv up from a fall, shouting at his band to *hurry, hurry, hurry.*

Fierce yelled for Aynoh and she answered, "I'm behind Grub, but Crevkukk isn't!"

Another booming roar. When she darted through the disintegrating cavern, she couldn't see Crevkukk.

He must be out.

She fell forward on her hands. Grub started to come back for her, but she waved him on and crawled the last short distance. He escaped, gently lowered Wik and Bhidid to the ground, and then vomited. His face was pale and blood poured from the top of his head.

"Grub!" Aynoh pawed blindly to locate her sack as she crept to her band mate.

Wik stopped her. "Tell me what to do."

"Push against the gash. Don't let up. I'll come back as soon as I can!"

Grub didn't worry her as much as some of the others. Head wounds were notorious bleeders.

Wik leaned over the giant as Aynoh scrambled to Bhidid. He hadn't moved from the disheveled heap Grub had dropped him in, but shallow breathing indicated life. She ran her hands along his limbs—nothing broken, but one laceration pumped crimson blood. She pushed hard with her hand.

Fierce yelled Aynoh's name.

"I'm with Bhidid!"

The male's eyes fluttered. He covered his gash with a paw the size of one of Shanadar's Canis and motioned to Aynoh. "Go. Help someone in need...."

She lurched through the destruction, bouncing off the occasional boulder-sized ice lump, until she reached Eknilk and Braanroorv. They managed by now to wobble to their knees.

They weren't bleeding so she asked, "Does anything hurt?"

Before either could answer, Wik yelled, "Aynoh!" A desperate plea. "It still bleeds and his eyes are white."

Eknilk waved her off. "Nothing hurts," he said with a flinch. "We are catching our breath. Help Grub." So Aynoh scrambled back to the male who had saved so many of his bandmates.

"Grub! Talk to me!" She must hear him speak.

He garbled something about Wik and the cave-in, mostly slur but enough to show he was aware, and then, with shocking clarity, he said, "Crevkukk. Where is he?"

Crevkukk!

"Wik–keep Grub talking," and she jolted to her feet.

A quick scan turned up no Crevkukk, which left one place to look. Ice blocked the entrance so she dug, fingers quickly numbed, hands torn by the ice's sharp edges.

She yelled, "Crevkukk is still inside!"

Another cave collapse….

Fierce pulled her away. "Stop, Aynoh. He lives a warrior's death, one that would make him proud. Others need you more."

Aynoh listened for Crevkukk, but heard only an eerie creaking. Anyone not out would never escape. Grub howled, his voice cracked, the sound raw and hollow. She felt his anguish for one who could never be replaced, how she would feel without Yu'ung, or Fierce.

She stiffened her back. "Everyone is surprisingly well, with the exception of Grub."

"Losing Crevkukk will hurt worse than a lump of ice. Crevkukk filled the spot Qad never could, and Grub was Crevkukk's mentor. His father called him lazy. He almost believed him. When both parents perished in a stampede, no one cared about the boy. Grub took pity on him, maybe because he saw much of Qad's misfit nature in him, and adopted him as a warrior trainee. His one requirement was that Crevkukk do as Grub told him. I didn't believe it would work until the day Crevkukk proved us wrong.

"Grub dispatched him to collect limbs for arrows and he didn't return. When Sun neared the horizon, Grub and I went after him, finally saw him far down a field, surrounded by another band of our kind. Even if we tried, we couldn't reach him in time. As we tried to figure out how to help, Crevkukk brandished his spear and shouted Fierce's name–though he couldn't possibly see us–and faked communicating with a non-existent Group. He pretended so well the brutes left, frightened. Bullies never like fair odds. Such an audacious move in the face of disaster made Grub realize the boy's value."

Aynoh didn't respond, distracted by the courage required to stand firm against impossible odds.

Fierce continued, "That changed Crevkukk. He adopted a never-quit attitude that made him a favorite among the warriors. He tagged along when Grub hunted, explored, scouted, or even scavenged. No one was surprised when he joined Grub on this expedition."

Wik tugged Grub into her lap and folded herself on top. He didn't stir.

Aynoh wobbled over and checked his head. "Grub. Are you nauseous?"

When he mumbled, she grasped his muscular shoulders and shook, gently. "Look at my eyes."

He tried to focus, but his eyes spun in his skull. "My head hurts.... "

Aynoh turned to Wik. "Can we go to your refuge? Get Grub out of the storm?"

"It isn't far."

Arm around Grub, she struggled under his bulky frame, but managed. "We must hurry. Another storm is almost upon us."

Not long afterwards, they tumbled into Wik's haven where she started a fire and heated the deer remnants along with grubs and grass stalks that Aynoh guessed had been her planned meal. Aynoh tended wounds. Most were scrapes and abrasions, a few deeper lacerations. Fierce refused her salves and pain treatments because he wanted to remain alert. She didn't fight him, expecting his injuries to be better by daylight.

When they awoke, the gales had blown themselves out. A supple mist clung to the ground. Without discussion, the entire band trudged to the ice cave and hollowed a passage to the interior. They uncovered Crevkukk's foot, frozen solid. Shouting, no matter how loud or long, didn't budge it. They dug until Sun sank below the horizon and then clattered back to Wik's homebase, exhausted, no one bothering to do anything except sleep.

They left early the next day, weighted down with salt, water, and grief, the group smaller with the loss of Crevkukk, larger with the new female. Grub, no surprise to Aynoh, acted normal other than occasionally pressing his palm against his temple or squinting. At some point as everyone slept, Wik striped her face with his colors. Now, she walked straighter, head higher, her damaged arm forgotten.

The return trip was faster. While resting at the waterhole, Grub and Fierce slayed a Boar. All ate it almost as duty and then continued. Mountains gave way to endless flat scrubland stretching from the craggy hills behind them to whatever would take them to the original path. No rain fell since their passage out so the backtrail was obvious. Grub scouted and Wik addressed every question Aynoh asked regarding the former healer's treatments.

"I have another, Wik. You hid from us when we first arrived and then revealed your presence. Why?"

"If you were sent by the Tall One I escaped, I wanted you to think no one lived here any longer. Once you were closer, I saw you were female of my kind and wasn't worried, though traveling with Tall Ones confused me. I decided to intercept the deer where you would see me and find out."

Wik stopped suddenly, focused on the distance.

"What do you see, Wik?"

"We're bypassing a shortcut that would save us time. Should I tell Fierce?

Wik's cutoff was faster and easier than the original route and the cave they stayed in for the night held a message from Yu'ung.

Old One is gone. I have a new member.

Aynoh mouthed to herself, "We too lost one and gained one."

Wik was eager to meet Grub's Chosen, but worried about being rejected.

Grub guffawed. "Aynoh is not my kind, but is my band." He curled around Wik's smaller body. "Besides, anyone who rejects you, I will–" At Wik's glower, he grinned and finished with, "Change their minds."

The day ended in a recently-used refuge. Fierce and Aynoh gathered tinder for the night. They were almost back to the cave when Fierce hissed, "Aynoh! There are Upright tracks."

As though on cue, a scream and a growl split the air.

Chapter 28

Yu'ung

The Tall One snarled at her, eyes burning with hate, intent on revenge against Yu'ung for the deaths of so many of his kind.

"You killed Bruurv, but we both know that was luck! Never could you beat his spear work if he was prepared."

"I was a prisoner—"

He chortled loudly. "My warriors are killing Ronor right now. The Canis who saved you last time are gone!"

"Yet you start by yelling at me? You go first. Attack now that we are both prepared."

He charged. Instead of running as he expected, she stepped into him, lance forward, and he speared himself on her shaft. With a gasp, his hands flew to his stomach to staunch the blood. She yanked her point free and raced away, no interest in his health or death, her attention on the battle outside.

Tall Ones were strewn across the clearing, most dead, a few crawling away leaving crimson trails in the dirt. Jvelk strutted up to her, his youthful body coated in a red mist interspersed with smeared bloody streaks. His hand clenched a spear not his own.

He won the battle.

Surrounded by bodies, pride swelled within Yu'ung. Jvelk did an adult's work defending his tribe.

"Jvelk. You and Ronor excelled."

"Without Ocha's pack, we'd have been overrun."

"What happened?"

"The Tall Ones struck while Ocha was hunting, but she returned with reinforcements. Ronor and I had left our weapons in the cave." He huffed. "Lesson learned."

Yu'ung scowled. "Never be unarmed."

"They mostly asked about you. We pretended ignorance, but I'm a poor liar. The Leader ordered me slain so Father would talk–"

Jvelk twisted around. "Where's my father–"

A strangled cry erupted as Jvelk morphed from a mighty combatant staving off the enemy to a desperate boy racing to a slumped figure. Ronor's eyelids fluttered and closed. One hand rested on a shaft embedded in his abdomen, the other, a lance that penetrated the body of a Tall One.

"Can you save him, Yu'ung?"

A voice at the clearing's edge replied, "He died a warrior, young one. We will bury him as one."

Yu'ung stiffened. "Fierce!"

"And me."

"Kriina!"

"I am now Aynoh, of my pairmate's band."

Aynoh. I must remember.

Behind Kriina–Aynoh!–strode Bhidid, Grub, Eknilk, Braanroorv.

Fierce was explaining, "I permanently stopped a few … enemies … before they could go for help."

Yu'ung peered beyond the new arrivals into the scrub. "Some are missing?"

"Crevkukk left us a hero, Qad ... for ... other reasons."

Aynoh will explain those cryptic comments later.

Yu'ung sniffed injury blood and unfamiliar female bleeding. "Someone is hurt and you have a new female."

"Bhidid will recover. The new adult Wik joined us."

"These are the Canis Ocha and subadult-now-fighter, Jvelk. Ronor." She indicated the body beside her. "Jvelk's father, was valued."

Fierce examined the older Tall One with interest. "I knew him. He was always an explorer first, a warrior if necessary."

Yu'ung stared into space, eyes tinged with fatigue. "Tall Ones chase us," hastening to add, "They are enemies, not friends."

Fierce grunted. "We will take care of them."

Ocha padded up to Aynoh, tail sweeping the air, panting, ears tucked.

Aynoh stooped. "I greet you."

Yu'ung rubbed an open hand down Ocha's supple fur, the muscular shape ready for anything.

"Ocha belongs to Shanadar's tribe and now mine." At Aynoh's confusion, Yu'ung explained, "When I went to accept Fierce's offer to join your migration, you were gone. Shanadar was there ... for ... complicated reasons I can explain later. He offered to guide us. His tribe is Canis, including Ocha, but he is our kind. The others in Ocha's pack went with the People, but she joined me to deliver Old One to the Mountain People."

Aynoh shook her head, puzzled. "Old One lives?"

Yu'ung's throat tightened. She didn't want to explain this, not now. "I tried to get him to the Mountain People, but he didn't make it."

Images flashed through her mind—Old One's struggles, dragging the travois, the Elder by the stream, the friendship with Grg's Primitives....

Did the tracks Dag located lead to a herd? Is Ak doing well as healer? Has Zug's rash improved? Have they found a new homebase to live out Mountain's anger?

She forced those thoughts aside—stories for later—and said simply, "I honored where he wished to end his life."

Aynoh scrutinized Yu'ung. "You have changed, daughter."

Yu'ung straightened herself, knowing she was no longer the child of a vaunted healer. She was Alpha, the leader of an important tribe.

"You have, too, Aynoh. I look forward to sharing our stories."

Then, Yu'ung and Fierce said in unison, "But later. Daylight is dying."

Fierce's brow puckered and then smoothed as he evaluated what had just happened. Her relationship with Fierce, too, had changed. Where she recently deferred to the muscular, assured Tall One Leader, now, after what she lived through, she considered them equals.

Jvelk scuffed his feet, gaze bouncing between Yu'ung and Fierce. "We have mammoth cooking on a fire."

Fierce blinked, his gaze taking in the youngster-now-adult's pain, his mixed heritage, and made a decision.

"First, Jvelk and I have a job." He slung Ronor's body around his shoulders. "He was a warrior. We bury him with respect."

Yu'ung joined them. "There's a spot."

She lit a torch and entered the dank passage behind the cavern. After a short distance, they stopped on the lip of a dark crevasse. Fierce tossed what was no longer Ronor and his spear over the edge. They thumped against the distant floor.

Jvelk asked, "Why waste a good weapon?"

"Tall Ones—the Chosen—like your father are unsure if those who depart life require food or fortification where they go. I include a tool so Ronor can feed himself if necessary."

Without additional ceremony, they gathered around the hearth. After the meal, Yu'ung pawed through her sack for glue to repair the broken tip of her lance. She found the leaf that should hold the hard slab, but it was empty.

Old One taught me how to wrap the point onto the shaft. I've never tried it, but I watched him once.

She was concentrating on her thoughts and missed the quiet footsteps.

"I can help with that."

Yu'ung jerked upright. "Fierce."

He pulled a shiny black substance, like a frozen puddle, from his shoulder sack. "It's from bark I haven't seen here, but we use in my homeland."

"How does it work?"

He placed a small piece on a hot surface in the flames. When flexible, he peeled the material off and wrapped it around the point.

"By tomorrow, the seal will be so hard, the tip will never break off."

"We use a similar glue, but I can't always find it."

As he hafted stone tip to shaft, she flashed to Ronor's caution that many Tall Ones hated the People, the exception being Fierce. Yu'ung promised Ronor she would warn Aynoh that though Fierce may be trustworthy, other Tall Ones weren't.

What if Fierce changed since Ronor knew him? She glanced at Ocha, sleeping, lips trembling, eyes mere slits. *She trusts him, but his kind is recently our enemy. Jvelk and I must be cautious.*

Yu'ung squinted into the night, blinded by the fire, waiting for her night sight to return.

Aynoh noticed her quiet. "Are you worried about Fierce or his band?"

"Not them. His kind. It is they who captured Jvelk, Ronor, and me. We escaped. Since then, many have tried to stop us. Fierce seems a friend, but will he side with us when our enemies–his kind–strike? Because they will. *That* is what worries me."

Wik stretched a hand forward, palm down, fingers spread. "I had a similar worry because one of them slayed my entire tribe. Now, I call Grub pairmate."

Aynoh pulled her voluptuous hair behind her shoulders. "Fierce will tell you his kind are as likely to kill Uprights as we are not to. You must decide for yourself, Yu'ung, how much you wish to worry about that, as Wik and I have."

Yu'ung wanted to believe, but an Alpha must be right, not guided by emotion. She drew a finger over the bright stripes on Aynoh's face.

"Describe again why you wear these colors."

Wik answered for both of them. "They show we are unavailable for mating. I prefer this system to ours."

Yu'ung cocked her head, remembering pairmated females taken for mating because the lusty male didn't ask. Visual identification was a good idea.

Aynoh added, "Plus, they are obvious from afar, and announce to other Tall Ones who we are."

Old One warned her to be resilient. Was this what he meant?

Fierce stirred a finger through his stew and said, "Why not ask me those questions that bother you, Yu'ung? I will answer anything and what I say may surprise you," his tone a balance of patience and tamped-down irritation.

Of course he's irritated! We talk about him as though he isn't here!

Ocha woke up at his voice. She remained by the fire, but her blue eyes stared at him as though waiting to hear what he said.

Why not ask? I will know if he says other than the truth, as will Ocha.

"Fierce. Why are you—and Ronor—unlike other Chosen?"

He swallowed a mouthful of stew. "Your appearance and strength intimidated those who came before my group. They determined it better to battle first, ask later. I'm not like that. I observed many of your tribes and realized you never used your physicality for dominance, only survival."

He thinned his lips, but Yu'ung could tell he had more to say so she remained quiet.

Finally, he added, "It's not true with mine."

She heard his words, but they didn't make sense with what she'd seen. "Why abduct my mother, the People's healer, if you are peaceful?"

Aynoh snarled, "Have you forgotten I came voluntarily, as Fierce's guide?"

She told me that, but neither B'o nor I believed her. Old One did. I should have given it more credence.

"Why did you?"

"Why wouldn't I? When your Alpha duties end, you will join a pairmate's tribe. Without you and Old One, I have no one. Yota had Old One. He had you and me. When I become an Elder, too infirm to complete my duties, no one will remain in the tribe to care for me."

"That will never be the case with me, or my band." From Fierce. "We consider Aynoh a spirit. Her Tall One name means that. Our healer, Seer, saw in a vision how she heals illnesses no one else can in ways no one considered. Age has nothing to do with that. Seer's many wrinkles record his experience as they will for Aynoh. She will be valued, pass her skills on to others in the band, be honored in death when that day arrives."

Yu'ung tilted toward Aynoh. *What is he talking about? Our healing skills are not uncommon.*

Aynoh as usual, saw her thoughts and grinned. "I explained to Fierce my treatments are based on intuition–instinct–but he doesn't believe me."

Aynoh leaned into Fierce, but kept her gaze on Yu'ung. "I am interested to meet this Seer, talk with him about healing. Fierce promised if living in his homeland doesn't work for me, he will return me to the People."

He faced her, head lopsided, "Or stay with you in your new homebase if you choose not to go to mine."

Aynoh pulled her head back and opened her eyes, wide, catching his, then nodded.

She didn't expect that. Nor did I.

Jvelk wriggled toward Fierce. "My father, Ronor, mentioned spirits. I'm unfamiliar with them."

"They are beings my kind relies on to do the impossible. Seer talks to them. Since he saw Aynoh from afar, he assumed she did also."

Was Aynoh a spirit? Were Xhosa and Ocha?

Yu'ung hadn't discussed Xhosa-who-might-be-a-spirit with Aynoh, but surely the blue-eyed Canis stood out.

More stories for later.

Jvelk fixed his damp eyes on Aynoh and spit out what Yu'ung wanted to know. "Are you?"

Fierce wrapped his hand around Aynoh's arm, gentle and firm, affection never displayed by the People. For a breath, Yu'ung felt envy, or yearning, and rejected both.

Aynoh brushed it aside. "If I am, no one told me."

Yu'ung's eyes flattened. "Why does Fierce require a guide to return to a spot he already knows? Why not follow his backtrail?"

Fierce answered, "You know this answer, but I'll explain anyway. We, like you, rely heavily on the Moon, Sun, and stars to guide our travels. Mountain's anger obscured them as well as many other signs we might have turned to for direction. Though we now see the night sky, the landmarks have changed from when we arrived, covered in ash or gone. Plus, because of our side trip, we approach what would be our backtrail from a different direction. Everything is new. Aynoh might not recognize a specific hill or gully, but she can place it in context with the landscape she does know and in so doing, direct us where we must go."

Aynoh smiled. "I have tricks, like using ash as I would snow."

"Our homeland has no snow."

"I discern the direction the wind blows, how it matches what I'm accustomed to."

Bhidid crouched by the fire. "We wouldn't be able to reach shoreless sea without Aynoh."

Yu'ung's face burned. It was clear her mother was valued by these strangers in a way none of the People ever did. She wanted to change the subject. Fierce did it for her.

"Jvelk. Why did the glue you used on the spears you made for Bruurv fail?"

Yu'ung and Jvelk both howled, talking over each other as they explained their devious plot to weaken the captors' lances and work with the Canis to rescue the captives."

Fierce chortled while Grub examined the substandard tip. "It looks normal."

Yu'ung fidgeted, excited to teach their trick. "We didn't mix in the ingredient that stiffens the glue—"

Jvelk interrupted, "I did for the first one I gave Bruurv. He declared it better than any crafted by his warriors."

Fierce chuckled despite himself. "I never considered the benefits of weak glue," and glanced at Yu'ung with new respect. "The glue to affix points to shafts and caulk a boat uses a special sap. We don't know where to find it but it seems you do as well as Aynoh."

Yu'ung's body tingled. "Why waterproof a craft? Logs float."

"Not always. One log, the right kind of tree, but many attached together can be problematic."

Her head spun. Another topic she didn't understand.

Fierce said, "If you'd like, you can help caulk them when the time comes."

Grub trudged inside to join the group around the lively blaze and Eknilk left, to replace him on guard duty. Grub rubbed his chapped red hands together and Wik offered him stew. He blew on it. When cool, he snatched out chunks of meat and vegetables with his fingers and gulped the liquid.

"Whoever made this—I've never tasted anything better," and scooped another portion into his gourd.

Yu'ung wiped her palms on her wrap and rose. "I'll assist Eknilk. Jvelk will swap with me after he sleeps."

Fierce waved her away. "No need. We have a schedule. Better you and I plan tomorrow's departure."

Yu'ung pattered in a small circle and then squatted again by the fire. "The People are close. We saw their prints and Ocha picked up her pack's scent. It was fresh, a few days old. Shanadar scratched messages into the walls of several caves with instructions to the shoreless sea."

"He goes the same place we do. What did he tell you?"

"Keep Sun's nest to our dominant side. Head toward the river."

"Which river?"

"The one before shoreless sea."

Wik giggled. Fierce huffed. The knots inside Yu'ung loosened.

"We're to look for two free-standing trees on our dominant side where they aren't part of a woods or forest. Align each with the other, stop when they are one."

"What?" Everyone was confused.

Yu'ung spun Fierce until he stood an arm's length from Grub both in front of the same wall.

"You are trees on my dominant side. If I proceed as though to walk between, both of you continue to show, but if I walk alongside, keeping you on my dominant side, the farther I go, the more you seem to approach each other until at a certain point, I see one tree, not both—"

"We—the trees—are lined up. One conceals the other."

"Shanadar says at that point, put the one tree to our back and walk away. That route leads to the shoreless sea. He will be along that corridor between here and there."

"If he isn't?"

"He will be. B'o is with him. And the rest of Ocha's pack."

Fierce clenched his fists, eyes dark. "How does Shanadar know? Did he visit the shoreless sea?"

Yu'ung shook her head.

"Then how?"

Any explanation begot more queries so she settled on, "Ask your Seer to explain."

Aynoh recognized Yu'ung's discomfort and asked, "When did the People start their migration?"

A tingle ran through Yu'ung and she bit at her lip. "At the same time Old One and I left to meet up with the Mountain People, after you and the Tall Ones headed out. You should have run into B'o, Shanadar, and the People."

"We would have except we took a side trip to get salt."

Yu'ung straightened. "You have salt?"

Fierce tossed a bag to her. She dipped a finger in, sucked the grains, and passed the bag around.

After everyone was satisfied, Fierce asked, "Have you checked here for a message?"

She leaped to her feet. "I did find a message, but I was interrupted."

Torch in hand, she and Aynoh hurried into the tunnels. Her mother glowed with energy in a way Yu'ung had never seen before.

"He is good for you, Aynoh."

"I hope for such a pairmate in your future, too."

"I have no time to pairmate," not with the weight of leadership. "Besides, I've never experienced what you describe, never deemed it possible."

How could it happen?

They swept the light along the walls, past the first message Yu'ung had found, and as expected there was one more, on a wall farther down around a curve. This one had an interlocked square and triangle scratched into the face.

Aynoh said, "He wants us to hurry."

She started away, but Yu'ung stopped her. "You left this in the Tall One cave."

In her hand was the necklace Fierce gave Aynoh and she dropped in the tunnels for Yu'ung to find.

Aynoh's eyes glistened. "It felt good knowing you held what I once wore, Yu'ung."

Yu'ung removed another from her shoulder sack, similar to Aynoh's.

"I made this for myself to tell others you and I are together."

They both slipped the strings around their necks and shuffled back to the spacious entry. Bear's claws clickety-clacked against Eagle's talons telling all that each protected the other.

Chapter 29

The united group left before Sun awoke, Fierce and his band toward the shoreless sea while Yu'ung, Jvelk, and Ocha tracked the enemy back to see where they came from, if they were alone or part of a larger group. The trail led to a river. Muddy steps exited, a wide swath of many heavy warriors, the round impressions from spears mirroring their prints.

Yu'ung murmured to herself, "About as many as we killed."

The river was wide and fast moving, but not as deep as a male was tall. They'd tied a vine to a tree on each side of the river, gripped it to keep from being washed downstream, a common way to cross if you didn't have a raft.

Yu'ung sliced it.

"Jvelk. If there are more warriors, they should soon come looking to see what happened. I'll wait here. Tell Fierce what we found."

"But you'll be alone."

"Restringing the vine will take a while. I'll leave when they start, if they do. If I get into trouble, Ocha will come for you."

Jvelk did as told and Yu'ung climbed an overwatch hill, hid behind a thick hedge, and waited, stayed longer, and then more. When Sun was less than both hands above the horizon with no activity, she left, comfortable the Tall Ones decided further pursuit was not worth additional deaths. She sprinted, slowed to a run to catch her breath, and caught up to the assemblage as they crawled into the night's refuge. Jvelk was with Grub on overwatch.

Fierce touched Yu'ung's necklace. "This is similar to Aynoh's."

"Hers inspired it. Is that a problem since I am not your tribe?"

"You are Aynoh's which makes you mine, Yu'ung."

Yu'ung fidgeted, her eyes darting through the spacious cavern.

"Several of my males would pairmate you."

"That is not my destiny."

She bit her lip, wanted to ask if he and Aynoh had spoken more about her future with the Tall Ones, but was not ready for an answer she wouldn't like.

Fierce asked. "What makes you chew your lip?"

Yu'ung scowled, annoyed he'd seen her discomfort, and had no intention of telling him the truth.

"These do," indicating the bowed spear and tiny arrows he carried over his back.

"The bowed spear? Have you seen it in action?"

His eyes sparkled as they always did discussing weapons, warrior skills, and hunting.

"No. Aynoh likes them. Will you teach me before you depart?"

"Of course. I won't abandon you, Yu'ung."

Grub and Jvelk trudged into the cavern. Thick white clouds cloaked their faces with every exhale. Their hair and wraps glistened with ice. Bhidid and Eknilk left to replace them as guards.

Grub warmed his hands. "We are being observed. Jvelk, Braanroorv, and I tracked the prints, but not far. Jvelk said it's not the same direction he went earlier today, toward the waterway. We feared a trap so we came back. Braanroorv remained where we saw … it."

Jvelk added, "Only one set of tracks."

Wik handed Grub stew. He tipped his head to swallow the contents, his body alive with energy, hands tapping the container, but eyes distant. Ocha's lips twitched, hackles slightly stiff, and her tongue swept her muzzle for remnants of her last meal. Grub refilled his gourd and slurped until he again emptied the bowl.

He wiped his mouth with his hand and studied Ocha. "You and the Canis work as though partners. How, Yu'ung?"

Yu'ung pondered this. How did they? The Canis were smarter than many Uprights–People or Tall Ones–but explaining Ocha required a discussion of Xhosa and an explanation for the blue eyes.

She shrugged, "We just do."

Grub chewed the succulent meat, staring out while licking the flavorful juice from his fingers.

"We have Canis in our native land. Why don't we hunt with them?"

Yu'ung swallowed. "Ocha, Ragged Ear, White Streak, Ump— Shanadar says they joined him by choice. Have you ever asked yours?"

Curiosity flashed across Grub's face.

"Is she listening now?"

"Yes."

Ocha's muzzle dropped between her paws and her tail swept side to side. As always, her body exuded an air of suppressed energy she gave voice to now with a low elongated yowl.

"Ocha reminds me it was she and her pack who found Shanadar, not the other way around."

Grub stared at Ocha, eyes soft, flickering. "How do I get found by a Canis?"

Yu'ung slid her eyes away. "Ask Shanadar when you meet. Be prepared for the unusual."

When Grub continued gazing quietly at Ocha, Fierce said, "Our healer, Seer, is unusual. He relates to few yet predicts events with frightening accuracy. Does this also describe Shanadar?"

Yu'ung thought about that. He arrived just in time to rescue her, easily persuaded B'o to co-lead the People, and knew where they must go. Did that mean he could predict the future?

When she didn't reply, Fierce asked as though her response was unnecessary, "And why—despite you just met him—entrust him with your tribe while you took Old One to the Mountain People?"

Yu'ung ate the beans Wik soaked most of the day, and stuttered, "B'o is with him. I trust him more than anyone I know."

She could see in Fierce's face he wanted more. He waited, chewing, eyes on her.

It's time to tell him about Xhosa, but memories flashed through her mind, of dreams that seemed real, of watching tribes in caves when she couldn't possibly have been there, of helpers promised by Xhosa who came true. *Who would believe that other than Shanadar?* But Fierce, because he knew Seer, might listen to stories of how quickly Ocha healed, her ability to go days and nights with little sleep and less food.

She glanced at Ocha, hoping for some sign, got none, and decided to delay revealing these secrets.

Fierce sensed her struggle, her mind closing down, and heaved a sigh, as though seeing her decision.

"I understand. With my kind, distrust often precedes trust. Whatever instinct inspired you to trust Shanadar, I will wait to experience that, but tell me this. Has Shanadar always been unusual?"

"He fell on his head as a child which was when he developed the ability to communicate with any life he comes into contact with."

Fierce picked up a dark shiny stone and a cutting tool like those Yu'ung used. With practiced strokes, he struck the tip, over and over until sharp enough to cut through hide.

As he worked, he asked, "Does that explain where he got the odd name 'Shanadar'? It is unlike others among your kind."

"Others?"

"In your new homeland, I spent time with a tribe of your kind. They had names like Mook … Druyl … Turk … Liis.…"

Yu'ung pondered those. They sounded familiar, but how was that possible?

"Shanadar said his came in a vision."

Fierce flinched. "A vision.… That's where Seer learned his name."

"It also led him to the flute."

"A flute?" From Wik.

"A hollowed-out cave bear femur on which he plays beautiful songs that start in his head."

"How does someone play music heard nowhere but inside them?"

"I'm not clear. All I know is the vision directed him to guide my tribe and the flute is part of that."

Ocha jerked upright, growled once, and slipped into the night. Fierce crept into the shadows at the cave's mouth. Yu'ung did the same, on the opposite side.

Her next question was unnecessary, but she couldn't stop herself. "Bhidid and Eknilk. They are good scouts?"

As soon as she spoke, she flushed, but Fierce figured out her real concern. "You mean to teach Jvelk. Yes, or I wouldn't entrust the child of an honored warrior to their care."

"He's my responsibility. He already wields the far-throwing lance skillfully. Ronor taught him."

"Then he will help train. Can Shanadar also?"

Yu'ung shrugged. "He did save my life."
They both grunted. *We are more alike than I imagined.*

The repetitive drone of night insects lulled Yu'ung to sleep, not a deep invigorating slumber, this a doze, under the edge of awareness but short of full consciousness. Her hand rested on her spear, thoughts on the Tall Ones, convinced a problem she couldn't see was almost upon them.

Chapter 30

Yu'ung woke before the rest. She mumbled to Fierce about checking the prints Jvelk and Grub found last night and trudged away, slowly, as Sun sent its light over the landscape. The spot was obvious and she fingered the prints.

One individual. My kind. The impressions are deep so he stood here a long time.

She returned to the cavern and sent Jvelk to track him—or her.

He was back soon. "Whoever left the prints goes toward the herd Grub and I discovered earlier."

Yu'ung snapped her head to Jvelk. "A herd! Where?"

Jvelk squinted. "Not close. Not far."

Fierce yelled, "Grub just told me. Let's go!" and took off at a sprint.

Grub led, with Eknilk, Bhidid, and Fierce. Braanroorv stayed behind in case the enemies showed up. Yu'ung and Jvelk kept pace, but after a few hands of travel at Grub's fast speed, she struggled. Her tribe typically stayed within a day's range of their homebase. If the hunt took them farther, they established processing sites to prepare the carcasses, toss parts they wouldn't use, and portage what remained the next day. Fierce's band didn't mind going longer distances, even in the dark.

Ocha panted at Yu'ung's side, excited to be back to hunting.

Yu'ung giggled to herself. *Hunting with Ocha will be unusual, but there's no sense warning him.*

As they approached the meandering herd, Ocha's fur stiffened down her spine and she took off.

Yu'ung trotted up to Fierce. "I'll go with Ocha."

He looked like he wanted to ask why, but settled on a grunt. "We'll stay with the herd."

Ocha howled, somewhere beyond a rise. *Is she in trouble?* Yu'ung was about to call when the Canis fell silent and simultaneously, a Giant Pig bawled from beyond a thick hedge of scrub.

Ocha handled her problem, so Yu'ung took off after Pig, found it frozen in place, stiff-legged, gaze locked onto something Yu'ung couldn't see. She didn't care about the reason. Motionless prey were easy kills. She flung her spear, determined to claim Pig before a mystery hunter could. Losing Mammoth to Tall Ones remained a distressing memory. As the lance neared Pig, a brindle-colored blur leaped out of the grass and grabbed the shaft mid-flight. Yu'ung howled in frustration and then chortled as an agile, athletic Canis bigger than Ocha sprinted away, Yu'ung's spear in its mouth, toward where Fierce stalked the herd. Pig fled squealing the opposite direction, not so traumatized it must realize the Canis had saved its life.

That's Ragged Ear!

Yu'ung met Ocha's packmate only once, but how many blue-eyed Canis had a torn ear? She took off after Canis-who-must-be-Ragged-Ear, in case he decided to drop her weapon before destroying it.

Why did he take it? Does he want me to follow?

A chorus of Canis caterwauls merged with One-who-must-be-Ragged-Ear, joined by birdsong.

Shanadar.

She skidded around a corner and stopped at the sight of Fierce and his band, spears up but uncocked. The why became obvious as soon as she glanced over the field. Dead carcasses littered the ground, throats torn out.

The Canis did this.

Ocha gamboled in front of Canis-who-must-be-Ragged-Ear while Fierce jogged to Yu'ung. Anger mixed equally with confusion on the Tall One's face.

"Did Ocha's friends just steal our food?"

"No. They slayed it for their pack."

His jaw fell open. "What?"

"You asked about hunting with Canis? This is how."

He stomped in place, staring at the backend of the escaping Pig. "No sense going after Pig. We have more than we can carry with what the Canis killed."

Yu'ung corrected, "Technically, they hunt for Shanadar, the People, and Ocha. You played no part in the kills so you must request a portion. Tell everyone that, and to consider the Canis friends."

A vertical wrinkle formed between his eyebrows and he punched his chin toward the opposite side of the field.

"If that's Shanadar across the field, then you're right. He is unusual, maybe a match to Seer."

Yu'ung's entire body tingled with relief at the curly red hair, knotted in a twine behind his neck, face striped in fresh colors as though knowing today, he would reunite with Yu'ung. Ocha and Ragged Ear flanked him, Ocha bobbing, Ragged Ear preening, a proud Alpha.

Shanadar rested the flute in his lap, fingers still moving over the small holes.

As Yu'ung approached him with long strides, he shouted, "Laak and Ese took the rest of the People to your space."

Yu'ung sucked in a breath. "Laak?" *Assigned adult duties?*

Shanadar slapped the bone flute against his thigh and then stuffed it into his satchel so he could rub both Ocha and Ragged Ear. "He is no longer a reckless boy. Fierce was right."

Fierce jogged up to Yu'ung's side. "Was it Laak last night?"

Shanadar smiled thoughtfully. "His discretion skills are weak. I'm sure you can teach him. B'o and I have been … busy." He paused to study Fierce. "We've met through Laak. He often talks about you. Your time together was significant to him."

Fierce cocked his head. "As was your brief but weighty time with Yu'ung. You remind me much of my healer, Seer."

"Seer … a familiar name."

Ocha pranced around Shanadar, tongue hanging.

Shanadar roughed up the fur on his back and shoulders. "I missed you, too."

Ragged Ear wound through Shanadar's legs to lick Ocha's face. If Canis smiled, Ocha did.

"Ragged Ear brought your spear...." He jerked his head, confused. "At least, I thought he did."

The stick was gone.

Fierce nudged his chin at the other Canis burying Ocha in greetings. "These also are Ocha's pack?"

"Ump and White Streak. They will share the meat if you ask."

Fierce harrumphed. "We earn what we eat." He waved an arm to his scattered band. "Let's get to work on these carcasses!"

The Tall Ones disarticulated the legs and ribs with gusto, ignoring the Canis who ate as they pleased while lazily surveying the industry surrounding them.

Preparations completed, Shanadar beckoned. "Daylight is practically gone. Let's take the shortcut."

What shortcut?

Without waiting for approval, he left at a fast trot. Everyone slung what they could manage over their shoulders and necks. Any leftovers were loaded onto the Canis. Yu'ung caught up to Shanadar, hoping to talk, but Ocha monopolized him. At the cave, Ese and Aynoh with Laak and Wik organized the cooking. The youngest among the People, Ruk, toddled through the space, doing chores for the adults.

The Tall Ones and the People's females were eager to meet. The People rarely welcomed outsiders, the exceptions being Fierce's band and Wik, both thanks to Aynoh. Everyone asked Wik about the stripes on her cheeks, her insights on Tall Ones, what habits differed from the People, and–the most popular topic–how she convinced Grub to pairmate.

Some eyed Jvelk, grown from the subadult skulking around a mating ritual to a capable adult. No one asked where his tribe was, but they would over future days. Laak befriended Jvelk, addressing his endless questions regarding the People, what it meant to be Lead Warrior, and if Jvelk could be one also.

Yu'ung asked Shanadar about the unfamiliar youngster crouched along the crowded cavern wall. Shanadar beckoned him over.

"Xad trailed us a long distance. Any would consider him our scout, which was his intention. But if they paid close attention, they realized no one talked to him and he ate our throw-away food."

Shanadar nudged him. "Tell your story, Xad. Yu'ung is your Alpha. Fierce and his band are friends. These are now your tribe. Let them meet you."

Xad leaned against Shanadar, legs shaking, one arm hugging his chest, one hand pressed to his jaw.

"Shanadar left fr-esh f-flesh for me one night."

As Xad stumbled through his explanation, White Streak plopped onto his feet, making it impossible for the youngster to move without bumping her. Oddly, Xad calmed.

"I devoured it. When I raised my head, I saw Shanadar. He asked what happened to my tribe so I explained no tribe would take in a lone boy even though I promised to work hard and cause no trouble. No one had food to spare.

Yu'ung scratched her cheek. "It is a difficult decision, who to feed with insufficient resources."

The boy's eyes dampened. "Not for Shanadar."

Shanadar placed a hand on the boy. "You were willing to work. We needed males with that skill."

Xad relaxed, and in doing so, winced. Yu'ung knew why.

She flattened her hands to her thighs and squared her body to Xad. "You say you will work, yet tonight, you slouched against the wall, watched others prepare the meal rather than assist."

Ese slipped up to Xad, her shoulder touching his. "I think so many new Uprights frightened him."

Yu'ung brushed a hand to the side. "Jvelk! Show Xad how to decide which jobs best suit him."

As they walked away, Jvelk was explaining, "It's not difficult. Notice what needs doing. Do it."

Yu'ung went outside. When she crested the overwatch hill, Laak and Ragged Ear were already prone. Both stared at her as she pawed through her sack.

"Here is the orange color you asked for," and handed Laak the rock she found.

Laak's eyes glistened. "Will Fierce mind?"

"Ask him. Tell him B'o says you have been an adult since my departure. When we settle in our new homebase, he offered to help you learn what you need to become a Lead Warrior."

She rose, fatigue filling her voice. "We'll talk later," and left him to his thoughts, the crunch and rattle of gravel marking her passage.

One task more before I relax.

Xad squatted by White Streak, scraping pelts and preparing travel food, sporadically rubbing the back of his cheek. At Yu'ung's steps, he snapped his hand away and pasted a smile on his face.

"Jvelk explained I do what needs doing. He will answer any questions I have."

"But?"

"No but. It is good." His response was too quick, hand again on his jaw.

"Always tell the truth, Xad. I can't make decisions based on lies. Open your mouth."

She was too tired to be patient. When he refused, she leaned in and sniffed.

"It is rotting."

"I live with it. Please, don't expel me. I can do any work. This injury will not slow me!"

"Being sick and in pain will. Let me see what you're hiding."

It turned out to be an abscess. If untreated, it could ruin the tooth and then the entire jaw.

While digging through her healing supplies, she asked, "How long have your gums hurt?"

"They just started," he said, unaware of his contradiction. Yu'ung wasn't and it gave her more respect for the youngster. Not giving in to the chronic ache told her a lot about who he was. Xad added, face contorted, "Please don't send me away."

"You need treating, not ejecting. Chew this. Don't swallow," and handed him mold. "Save this for later." She gave him another leafful of something that stunk like spoiled vegetation.

Xad scrunched his nose and stuffed it away.

Yu'ung grunted. "It's noxious, but works. Tomorrow's tomorrow, come to me so I can confirm it is healing."

The rich aroma floating from the cooking slabs called her. She took a birch bark tray from the pile, to be repurposed as kindling after the meal. Eating over, those not guarding gathered around the hearth, Tall Ones with the People. Hides were scraped by holding them in their teeth and dragging a wide bone over the surface. Clothes didn't last in the People's rigorous lives. Making new wraps took time. Elders proudly displayed the stripes on their incisors, the result of this work. Some tribes applauded those with the most prominent ridges. Anyone not cleaning and scraping preserved the meat, the smaller pieces tossed into an organ bag for later.

As all became acquainted and re-acquainted, Yu'ung beckoned Fierce, B'o, Shanadar, and Ump to join her on the plateau above the cliff. Shanadar didn't, choosing instead to play his flute. Evening shadows transformed from blue to purple and then gray as daylight waned. Being together again with her People, especially B'o and his sage wisdom, filled Yu'ung with gratitude.

Fierce started, "Let's catch up—"

Yu'ung interrupted, as though they planned it. "Then figure a solution to the problems—"

"Issues," he corrected.

Yu'ung chuckled. "*Issues* we face."

Fierce described the salt the Tall Ones mined, how he cherished Aynoh, the agony he faced when Grub's sibling turned on her, the pain of losing Crevkukk, and Wik's invaluable service traipsing through unknown terrain. Yu'ung shared how she and Old One spent time with Grg's kith, how Old One chose where to die rather than continue a climb that might kill both of them.

B'o explained how Shanadar guided the tribe through areas familiar to them and then those no one had ever visited, how Laak accepted adult duties without argument, how the Canis always brought birds, rabbits, or ground squirrels despite the smoky air, barked and snarled at creatures invisible to the People.

"The Canis saved our lives often."

He stopped, dipped his head, and picked at his shirt.

Fierce and Yu'ung said together, "But...."

"Shanadar is ... unsettling. He is confident in his ability to get us to the shoreless sea, but performs ... oddly ... most days." B'o huffed, shoulders drooping. "I'm glad you're back."

"Explain." Fierce and Yu'ung said in unison.

"Evenings, he vanishes into the tunnels or onto a high plateau and does ... I don't know. No one is allowed to go with him. In the morning, he insists all keep his pace. If not for Ump and White Streak, we would struggle."

Fierce asked, "Has he ever mentioned Seer?"

Worry lines framed B'o's mouth and tugged at his eyes. "Yes, and someone named Xhosa. No one understands those names."

Fierce rested his elbows on his knees. "Seer in my homeland also sees what no one else can. The guidance he gave before we departed called Shanadar one we should listen to."

Yu'ung asked, "Does he bother anyone?"

B'o shrugged. "No, in fact, his confidence puts most at ease. They recognize we are where we are—on a good course to a new homebase—because of him. Whatever his plan, which he can't seem to articulate, they accept it works."

Fierce's eyes lit. "Your Shanadar and my Seer are as different as they are the same."

B'o's neck muscles relaxed. "I'm relieved you consider him normal, but why does he allege our new homebase smells of death?"

Fierce brushed his concern aside. "All life does. Do you think the end of your time will be something else?"

"If he means that, why not say it?"

"Seer claims we are unable to handle his visions. Maybe Shanadar does, too."

Ump opened his eyes and stared at Fierce.

The Tall One Leader murmured, "Why do the Canis have blue eyes?"

Yu'ung knew, but it would be better if Shanadar replied.

The group parted, filled with well-being. Yu'ung never expected easy. Living meant facing problems. She lay down, Ocha at her side, the People's scent soothing. Soon, she slumbered. Somewhere during the night, Ocha's odor receded.

She went to be with her Canis kind and then Yu'ung sank into a dark dreamlessness.

Chapter 31

An owl startled Yu'ung awake, and then Shanadar's beautiful flute, replicating the sound. Ocha trotted over, a dead eagle in her jaws. Ragged Ear was beside her, his muzzle, too, exploding with feathers and wings, though smaller than Eagle. Ocha slapped her feet on the ground. Within a breath, Shanadar exited the cavern, dust from the tunnels covering his body. He gutted the elegant broad-winged bird and stuffed the carcass into his satchel, sticking one dark feather in his hair.

Eyes glued to the distant horizon, he said, "We have little time."

Behind him, came scuffling and muttering as walking clusters formed. Aynoh and Wik joined Ese. Fierce directed his band to scouting positions. Xad slipped in with Laak and the subadults.

I'll check his jaw later.

"Jvelk!" Fierce shouted, deer meat in his hand. "Go with Grub. He will describe what it means to be a warrior."

Fear tightened Xad's neck. "I'll go, too," and raced after them.

As Fierce and Yu'ung proceeded, B'o asked, "Why does Shanadar say time is limited?"

"He seems to think I know, which I don't."

B'o walked with her as they often did when talking through problems. Yu'ung's step bounced, so happy was she to again rely on her level-headed partner.

"I've missed your leadership, Yu'ung."

"And I your counsel. Fierce and I must gather wood to replace my far-throwing spear."

"Stones if you find them. We are low."

Accompanied by Eknilk and Bhidid, Yu'ung and Fierce went toward a forest she'd seen and hoped it had the right trees.

"Yu'ung!" Wik shouted. "Grub wants the special sap, and beeswax."

Fierce waved. "I know."

As they harvested the wood and supplies, Yu'ung whispered to Fierce, "We are not alone."

"Tall Ones. I see them."

Yu'ung and Fierce finished their harvesting, careful to keep their weapons available, the strangers' positions always in mind. They didn't appear threatening, more like another band trying to find their way out of Mountain's danger.

When they rejoined the group, the Tall Ones slowed to the group's pace. They didn't threaten, and maintained a decent separation. Yu'ung looked around for Shanadar. Maybe he'd seen this band before, but no one had seen him all day. He didn't reappear until the group had settled into a cave for the night and then with Xad and Ump. His body was damp with sweat, face flushed from running, and hair matted with grime. He squatted between Yu'ung and Fierce and dipped a gourd into the stew.

"Tall Ones are close."

"We know."

"They need help."

Fierce squinted. "I'm not convinced. Many of my kind are devious—"

"These are in need. We observed them," he said, waving a circle over Xad, Ump, and himself.

He peered up at the waning daylight, and then at Yu'ung, his question clear.

She shrugged. "We'll check tomorrow."

Shanadar rose. "It will be too late," and pointed up to the gathering carrion birds. "Something is wrong right now."

He trotted into the dark, accompanied by Ump.

Fierce huffed, exasperated. "The Tall Ones we saw didn't bother us because we are their kind. Shanadar is not. Seer will want me to keep him safe."

He stuffed meat in his mouth and raced after Shanadar, Yu'ung behind. If Shanadar's trail vanished in the diminishing light, the squawking circling vultures would show their location. The Tall Ones came into view, pelts tattered, frames too skinny to subsist.

Yu'ung and Fierce stopped to study them. "These are the ones who trailed us while we harvested supplies."

They were scavenging a ragged carcass, one eye on the work, the other on the hungry Hyaena pack, either oblivious to the presence of Yu'ung and Fierce or uncaring as they slashed wildly with dull tools and waning strength to disjoint the limbs. Hyaenas' fangs dripped saliva as they shuffled closer to this unexpected prey.

Yu'ung and Fierce, joined by the rest of the Chosen, crept up to Shanadar and Ump. They had a good position, screened from prey and predator by a hedge of thick grass.

Fierce touched Shanadar. "Let them work. They will get meat."

Shanadar grunted. Since he made no move to interfere, Yu'ung took that as agreement.

The strangers, increasingly anxious, stripped the shreds of old meat from the carcass, trying to finish before the other scavengers attacked. Heads bobbing between watching the circling carrion birds and the approaching Hyaena, the sense of desperation increased as though this pathetic remnant was worth dying for.

Maybe it is. Maybe they haven't eaten in a long time.

Hyaena padded nearer and the vultures circled lower, the Tall Ones ever more frenzied.

Yu'ung started to ask Fierce if there was any reason to help this band when a rumble rolled across the landscape, then the ground shook and fractured. The Tall Ones snatched what bones their weak arms could carry and fled. One moment, smooth ground, the next, a honeycomb of deep gouges. They were forced to leap across wide gaps and around too many cracks. One female darted back, to save a subadult swallowed by a rift, only to be yanked away just in time. Her savior yapped something Yu'ung couldn't hear, probably, "Run or die, too!"

A loud crash echoed through the clearing and a crevasse snapped shut, crushing whoever lay inside. The Tall Ones raced off. Yu'ung and the Chosen remained in relative safety until the earth-shaking ended and then they scurried back to camp. The devastation had been local, only where the Tall Ones scavenged. The People said they felt mild trembling, but nothing serious enough to even knock them off their feet. Shanadar didn't return all evening. That didn't bother the Canis or they were used to it. As soon as they ate whatever they'd caught for their meal, they curled into a heap and slept.

Fierce led when Shanadar didn't re-appear the next day.
Is he helping the Tall One survivors?
She slipped to Fierce's side, but he dropped his hand below his waist, level with the ground.

"The Tall One strangers are here. Shanadar gave them food. Now, we'll never get rid of them." Lines formed between his eyes and mouth. "They should offer help, not skulk on our backtrail begging."

Yu'ung wasted no sympathy on Tall Ones, not after what they did to her, Ronor, and Wik. This group seemed inept at best, ignorant at worst.

She asked, "Will they be trouble?"
"No. I will not let them."

Available shelters had diminished the nearer they got to the shoreless sea. Thankfully, the air warmed and they comfortably tucked under an overhang. Shared body heat was sufficient especially with the Canis furred bodies tight against the furless ones. Yu'ung fell asleep, oblivious to the grunts and groans of mating. She awoke briefly when Shanadar showed up, but not long enough to ask about his night.

The sound of vomiting, running, and Grub's muted pleas woke Yu'ung with a start. She scrambled to her feet to hear Aynoh hissing, "Wik is fine, Grub," as she offered the young female leaves to settle her stomach.

Everyone chattered except Grub and Wik who just looked confused. By the time the day's march commenced, Wik strode, head up, proudly ignoring the discomfort. She attached herself to Aynoh. As a new adult, her questions were endless.

Jvelk scouted with Bhidid and Braanroorv. Xad stayed with Shanadar after Yu'ung declared his tooth healed while Laak joined

Grub, Fierce, and Yu'ung. Laak modeled Grub, convinced it would make him the warrior he intended to be.

Eyes darting through the landscape, nose twitching, he asked, "What am I supposed to find, Grub?"

The Chosen warrior took a deep breath and spoke with a calm albeit forced smile, "Be Lead Warrior all day every day, Laak. Locate danger before it finds you. Become feared because you miss nothing, know everything. Be menacing when poked, lethal when attacked. Demonstrate what happens when power meets weakness. Always listen when called for."

Laak rolled his shoulders and raised his head exposing his neck. "What is the lesson today?" he asked, his face open.

"Replicate what you hear, but with a slight imperfection to identify it as you."

"Like Shanadar's flute."

"If you have one, use it. Otherwise, train your voice." He mimicked several birds, Hyaena's huff, and Canis' moan. "Now go. Show me where you are with your voice."

Yu'ung watched Laak. He looked back once, tripped over his feet and fell, regained his balance, and disappeared from sight. But not from sound. His thudding steps crunched through the dry grass, at one point, sending a flock of ground birds into the sky. She looked at Grub out of the corner of her eye. Mouth set, feet spread, she cocked her head.

Grub grumbled, "I better go with him," and took off.

Yu'ung and Fierce established a fast pace, eager to end this journey, but also to lose the Tall Ones who shadowed them. They seemed to have decided living off Shanadar's kindness was a good survival strategy. Even if they tried to obscure themselves—which they didn't—the stink spewing from their rotting wraps gave them away. Not only did the People not wonder where they were, neither did anyone else.

How have they survived? More likely, most didn't.

Chapter 32

Inevitably, the strangers one night built their camp within view of the People. Yu'ung studied them, her new far-throwing spear in hand. Fierce stood with her, stripes bold on his face, eyes glued to the uninvited outsiders.

Shanadar passed them, hands overflowing with stems, roots, bark, worms, and scraps of flesh. White Streak and Ump joined Shanadar, fangs exposed, tails low.

Yu'ung called to Shanadar, "White Streak and Ump don't like or trust these Tall Ones!"

He pivoted, walking backwards now toward the strangers. "The purpose is not what it seems."

Yu'ung and Fierce looked at each other, confused, as Shanadar twisted and made his way across the clearing, into the Tall Ones rough camp. The female took the foodstuff while he spoke to the males. Yu'ung couldn't hear them, but no one looked friendly. The more time Shanadar spent with the males, the more the Canis rumbled. The one who must be Leader—whom Shanadar called Kruutud—threw a rock at Ump which he easily dodged though not without a yowl of warning. Shanadar placed himself between Kruutud and Ump. Kruutud showed no respect, nothing but disdain for the Canis, which might be why Ocha padded up to her Alpha, head dipped, a rumble vibrating in her chest.

"Time to join my packmate."

Yu'ung followed, close enough to listen and make sure Kruutud and the other burly male saw her far-throwing spear, smelled her power.

Kruutud twitched a trembling finger toward Ocha. "Is that one going to be a problem, too?" dismissing the threat posed by Yu'ung. He tried bravery, but a wet throaty snarl from Ocha backed up by Ump made his lip quiver.

Yu'ung answered for Shanadar, "Not if you aren't."

When Ocha's rumble became a growl, Shanadar took her advice and left.

Yu'ung lifted her lance to her shoulder, to remind Kruutud she was armed with more than the Canis, and returned to her group.

"Did you learn anything, Shanadar?"

"Enough. They want to know about us and tell nothing of themselves. Kruutud and Vobar are Tall Ones and Asvulk our kind. That is why they call their tribe the One."

"Why are they here?"

"I asked, but—"

Fierce interjected, "They must leave. Their stink—scavengers will track them here, to us."

Shanadar smiled. Strands of dirty hair escaped the tie behind his neck. Eagle's feather peeked over his ear. Females offered to groom him and mate which he always refused. The only companion he tolerated was Xad.

"I will tell them next time." He walked away, shirt frayed, thin hide shiny where the fur wore off.

Ese stomped up to the group and wrinkled her nose. "We smell them inside the cave!"

"Shanadar promised to talk to them."

"He can't talk firm." She patted the fire starter and the pelt scraper in her shoulder sack. "I'll do it."

Yu'ung said, "Shanadar is giving them food."

Ese groaned and marched over to the Ones' camp. Unintimidated by the males' glares, she dropped the fire starting tools at what they were calling a hearth. Asvulk shuffled over to take them, head down but with surreptitious peeks at Ese. Vobar snatched the kit, but Ese grabbed it back. Yu'ung watched Ese explain its purpose, noted

Kruutud's dismissal of her, adding a glare at Yu'ung, then marched away. Ese said something to Asvulk and left.

Yu'ung pounded the end of her lance into the ground. "They weren't receptive."

"Asvulk was, but the males–they dislike you."

"Why?"

"Your youth, female-ness, and Alpha status."

"That's all?" She giggled.

Ese scoffed. "They're the ones starving, not us. That should tell them everything they need to know, but their minds are shut."

Kruutud and Vobar trotted up to Yu'ung and Fierce, interrupting their preparations for another day of travel. The whiff of rot enveloped them, but not as bad as the prior day.

Yu'ung scrounged through her shoulder satchel and tossed an organ sack to Kruutud, assuming him the Leader. He looked inside.

"What are these?"

Yu'ung tilted her head. *How does he not know?* "Leaves, to neutralize the stench of your poorly prepared wraps. Either rub them on the hides or leave our area. You have become a danger to our group. You attract predators with your rotting carrion stink."

He yelled behind himself, "Asvulk!"

She hurried up, peeked in the bag, and brightened. "I ran out of these, Alpha Yu'ung." That earned a scowl from Kruutud. "I am unable to locate the right tree."

"I have enough to share, for now. Shanadar thinks I will find more on the trail to the shoreless sea."

Kruutud dismissed Asvulk–Yu'ung, too–and directed his conversation at Fierce. Asvulk hurried back to the hearth and began to clean her wraps. Yu'ung remained exactly where she'd been, gritting her teeth and feeling the skin on the back of her neck prickle.

He is trouble.

Kruutud spoke to Fierce, staring brazenly into his eyes. "We know this area well, Leader Fierce. We can help you find your way."

Fierce scratched his side and then nudged his chin to B'o who had joined him. "Tell B'o."

"He is a Primitive!"

Fierce squared off to Kruutud, his eyes dark flat pools. "And you are starving Tall Ones begging for help. What is your point?"

Kruutud gaped, and then with Vobar lumbered over to the gathered group of Tall Ones.

Fierce mumbled to B'o, "Don't let them out of your sight."

"I don't trust them, either," he said and joined Eknilk and Braanroorv to scout.

When Kruutud and Vobar stood in place, confused, he waved. "What are you doing? There is no time to waste! Follow me," and he took off at a fast trot.

Kruutud yelled after B'o which didn't even earn a twitch. Then, spit flying from his lips, he yelled that B'o was going too fast. B'o snapped at him to keep up.

Grub chuckled and called to Fierce, "Bhidid, Laak, and I will find meat," and left.

Yu'ung and Fierce matched Shanadar's fast pace in the direction of the shoreless sea. Asvulk now alone, Ese and Aynoh beckoned her to join them.

At daylight's end, the hunters trundled in with a young Okapi carcass which they added to the day's largess. Behind came the scouts.

Yu'ung gestured to Grub and B'o, "Any problems?"

Grub shook his head and B'o tugged his lower lip. "They were too busy watching the landscape to talk to us. I said if they knew this area as they claimed, they must know the location of waterholes. That made them sprint ahead, out of earshot. They muttered together then dropped back to my position, saying tomorrow we would come to a ravine with a river at the bottom. They would show us the way."

Yu'ung asked, "But?"

He tugged his lip again. "I feel a trap."

"The ravine?"

"Probably not. They must know we would descend in groups, some remaining behind to control the high ground. Telling us about the river was to garner trust. They need something from us. I asked Vobar his plan. He claims it is the same as ours, to reach the shoreless sea, but he lied. Ese says Asvulk is a captive or pairmated against her will. Who would do that?"

Fierce huffed. "We'll guard the overwatch tonight, see if the Ones try to contact others."

Instead of preparing food, Kruutud and Vobar sharpened spears and tools. Asvulk spread empty hands to her pairmate, brow furrowed. He bellowed at her and she shuffled away.

They have nothing to eat.

To reinforce her conclusion, Asvulk brought tinder to Ese, face flushed. She refused to make eye contact.

Did Ese invite her to join us?

As Yu'ung approached, Asvulk was saying, "Our children ... before ... played a game yours might enjoy."

Aynoh smiled. "Let's ask them."

When the youngest gathered, Asvulk explained, "This we call predators and prey. I look away while you conceal yourselves—"

One bounced excitedly. "Where we see you and you can't see us—"

Another interrupted. "Cover yourself with leaves and slit your eyes!"

Asvulk grinned. "So you know this game?"

Some shook their heads, some nodded. One responded, "Not since leaving our homebase."

Asvulk opened her mouth in mock surprise. "Then we must play. If I see you, I point to you and you stand. The last one is the next predator."

At first, the children forgot the ruses of the past. Asvulk always explained what gave the one she found away—light bounced off eyes, colors mismatched in the background—and suggested methods of hiding better. By the time food was ready, Asvulk could find no one.

Aynoh motioned a spot next to her. "Join us, Asvulk. Your help with the children is welcome."

Between mouthfuls, the youngsters chattered, sharing trickery for subsequent games.

B'o leaned into Fierce, not worried if his conversation was overheard by Asvulk, "Kruutud and Vobar care only about themselves, but something makes them edgy."

"What makes you think that?"

"For example, they say the One has no Leader, but no decision comes without Kruutud's nod. Why hide the Leader from us?"

Before Yu'ung could ask more, Vobar and Kruutud lumbered up to Asvulk, ignoring her, and proceeded to eat the People's food with gusto. They skipped the customary request to partake of a stranger's hearth and brought nothing to share.

Fierce asked while he chewed, "You take our sustenance yet gathered none of it."

Vobar bobbed his head, chewing with more relish than the food warranted, then nodded toward Asvulk. "She did."

"Yes, and not you."

Vobar glanced at Kruutud out of the corner of his eye, stuffing another tuber into his mouth, and answered despite chomping harder, "The water–"

"We have not yet found that."

Kruutud popped a slug into his mouth, spit it out, and barked, "You will. That is our contribution," his response tinged with irritation.

He reached for a slab of meat which Fierce grabbed first. "You won't be staying. That's our ... contribution ... to your future."

Vobar eyed the food, but didn't take more. *I guess he got the message.*

Finally, Kruutud sighed. "You don't trust us. It is not our fault incidents out of our control separated our group."

"What are those?"

Vobar spread his hands. "The usual, events we can rectify with your help."

Yu'ung thinned her lips and Ocha's hackles rose. "Where are they, Kruutud?"

"They?"

"The rest of your ... tribe?" From Fierce. "The ones you say became 'separated'?"

Kruutud paled, his jaw twitching. "At shoreless sea."

Sweat broke out on Vobar's forehead, and he refused to meet Fierce's eye.

Fierce remained calm. "The same place we go," he said, his voice hardening. "Which you already know."

Kruutud leaned in. "You're Tall Ones. You must want to shed these Pr— Uprights."

Yu'ung interrupted, no longer hiding her antagonism, "Asvulk is my kind, as is Fierce's pairmate."

Kruutud kept his attention on Fierce. "We must reach an island offshore. Shanadar promised to guide us. Surely, he told you."

Ump flattened his ears and Fierce bristled. "Shanadar is not the Leader."

"Or Alpha," Yu'ung added.

Kruutud sneered at Fierce. "What is an Alpha?"

Asvulk sat straighter. Her eyes glowed with new respect as she answered, "My kind calls the tribe's leader Alpha. I've explained that, Kruutud. It's temporary, for emergencies like Mountain's explosion. Rarely is that position held by a female. Yu'ung must be extraordinary."

Kruutud reached for another block of meat, but Fierce slapped his hand away. "What did Shanadar say?" His eyes blazing.

Kruutud crabwalked backwards. "Ask him! He will tell you!" But Shanadar was nowhere.

And then he appeared. "I did say we would help the One reach the shoreless sea and provide what assistance we could to reunite them with their tribe on one of the shoreless sea islands. The reasons why that is a smart decision will be obvious later."

Yu'ung pondered Shanadar's comment. *He knows something we don't.*

Fierce's cold gaze told her he agreed.

She straightened her shoulders and settled her spear in her lap, in both the One's sight. "I agree, Shanadar, though Fierce's and my motives may differ."

He looked at her with a smile. "Or not."

That brought the meal to an end without explanation from Fierce or argument from Kruutud. The One left, Asvulk with food Aynoh stuffed surreptitiously into her shoulder sack. Yu'ung's assemblage bent to the work of repairing tools, sewing holes in hides, and talking about the nearness of their new homebase. Yu'ung joined Ese, Grub, and Wik drying meat.

"Ese. You spent the day with Asvulk. Do you have an opinion?"

"She fears them, but won't say much more."

"B'o said they don't talk openly and when they do, they lie."

Yu'ung rose. "Grub. Let's you and I find out what it is they keep to themselves. I may change my mind about allowing them to travel with us, despite Shanadar's support."

Ocha scrambled to her paws, head cocked, and strode with Yu'ung toward the One.

Chapter 33

Yu'ung crouched by Asvulk who scooted over to give her more room. Ocha squeezed in beside them. Grub wedged between Kruutud and Vobar, beaming across the fire at the female One. Asvulk gulped and Kruutud glared. Grub enjoyed discomfiting others, claimed their reaction was useful for uncovering the truth. Yu'ung choked back a laugh.

Kruutud snapped, "Your Leader told us to leave. Why are you here?"

"Lucky for you, he and I co-lead." Yu'ung snatched the One's weapons and tossed them to Ocha. "She will guard your spears while you convince me working together is beneficial."

Kruutud's eye when he caught Yu'ung's was toxic. Before becoming the People's Alpha, before she fought and beat Upright enemies, fear would have frozen her in place if a male looked at her that way. Now, she forced herself to not stab him with his own spear.

"I am the People's Alpha, as Asvulk explained, on par with a Tall One Leader. Fierce and I share the same authority. If we are to reach an agreement to travel with you, I must speak to one with similar authority. Who would that be?"

Kruutud and Vobar communicated something between them that caused Asvulk to squirm and Ocha to snarl. The males wriggled farther from the Canis.

Kruutud said, "Either of us will do," his manner disinterested, dismissive.

"Good." Yu'ung twisted to face the now-terrified Asvulk. Ocha moaned with pleasure.

"Asvulk. Are you a slave?"

Asvulk's mouth fell open and her face paled. "No! Of course not! I mean—"

Kruutud interrupted, "She is not a Prim—your kind. Her mother was," and muttered to himself, "Nor is she our peer."

Asvulk didn't react, as though accustomed to such comments, but Yu'ung saw a glint in her eye, a flash of fury that said there was more to this female than Kruutud expected.

Yu'ung covered her real thoughts with a veneer of calm. "They treat you subservient."

Asvulk straightened her back, knees touching. "Kruutud is Leader and my pairmate. We are equal." With a peek at him, asked, "Aren't we?"

Her *equal* pairmate slapped her viciously.

Tears sprang to her eyes, but to Yu'ung's surprise, her back stiffened and another flush of fury raged over her face, this one, barely controlled.

After a ragged breath, she murmured, "Not *equal*. How could I say that?"

There was sarcasm in her voice which Kruutud didn't like. He raised his fist and Grub seized it, crushed it in his brawny grasp.

"Don't."

Kruutud stopped, rigid with fury, but unable to do anything.

Yu'ung slouched to catch Asvulk's eye. "I know what equal is. My mother, Aynoh, my kind, pairmated Fierce. She is never hit or muzzled."

Kruutud and Vobar glowered at Yu'ung. Vobar recovered first. "Fierce pairmated Aynoh? Not mated?"

"I struggle to be worthy of her."

When did Fierce get here?

And he brought B'o, Shanadar, and the Canis.

He expects trouble.

Kruutud breathed out, a slow measured exhale. "We would like to make an arrangement with you."

"Then answer our questions."

Kruutud slumped. "Anything." He waited, hands on his knees. The brittleness in that one word gave away his fear.

Fierce and Yu'ung took turns. Kruutud and Vobar's responses never matched their bodies. The more they talked, the brighter Yu'ung's internal warnings flared. She felt trust from Fierce, in Shanadar. This wasn't it.

She caught Fierce's eye and spoke to him silently. Fierce studied Kruutud as Yu'ung would prey in the field.

Finally, he said, "We don't believe you. Go away. You are not welcome with us."

Kruutud scrambled to his feet, hand outstretched. "Hear me, Leader Fierce. Our stories are not so different. We too lived along shoreless sea our entire lives. Like you, Seer sent us to locate a homebase outside the grasp of Mountain's anger. We became stranded, hoped to cross the shoreless sea by hopping from one island to another or, worst case, live on one until rescue arrived. We built a raft."

"What happened to your original craft?"

"It crashed. We are not experienced sailors like you. After that, as I was about to say, we built a raft because that's all we knew and sent a small crew to search for a habitable island. They returned telling of birds flying from over the horizon. We provisioned a new raft and sent it out."

Yu'ung said, "Let me guess. You never saw it again."

Kruutud didn't disagree and Fierce ended the story for him. "If your sailors missed the island, they may have ended up in your homeland or along a shore you haven't yet searched."

"Or dead," Grub added neutrally.

Fierce overpowered Kruutud's angry response. "Most likely. The shoreline along the shoreless sea is rough, dangerous for inexperienced sailors. You know that. Still, you sent them."

Kruutud sputtered, ignoring Fierce's inference. "We believe they are stranded. We need to rescue them—."

"No. You can't use our boat, but we will help you construct a sturdier raft."

A glint sparked in Kruutud's eye. "We appreciate your offer but," he tried to get Shanadar's attention, but he was talking to the Canis. "Shanadar indicates your destination has changed since you arrived, that the vessel you stowed is unnecessary."

Fierce glared at Shanadar. "No one uses our craft except us."

"They could be starving!" He paced a tight circle until his breathing slowed. "We will prove our value and loyalty. We start with guard duties."

He left, body stiff, Vobar and Asvulk with him.

Yu'ung watched them leave. "Ocha and I will take overwatch."

Shanadar said, "That is unnecessary. The shoreless sea is huge. You are safe until they identify where along the endless coast you stowed your craft."

Aynoh said, "I treated a gouge in Vobar's arm, before he realized I spoke Tall One. It is as you suspect. They intend to behave until they find Fierce's craft. Then, they will steal it."

Yu'ung giggled. "They underestimate Fierce and me."

Fierce guffawed. "It was challenging to shroud such a large craft. Its true protection is that few can sail it."

B'o asked Fierce, "Why didn't he take you up on building one with them?"

"All Chosen recognize ours is exceptional. It took long to construct and sails farther than any water craft. He doesn't want a boat. He wants ours."

"Why did you need such a creation?"

"Our homeland has many expansive lakes."

Yu'ung caught Aynoh's eye. "Not as big as the one near Aynoh when she dwelt with the Primitives."

Fierce huffed. "To circle some of our lakes takes a full Moon. We can sail so far out that land vanishes leaving nothing but water on all sides. Aynoh's couldn't be as large."

Aynoh stared into the distance. "And yet it is."

When Fierce had nothing to add, Yu'ung asked. "You don't need your boat to get us to our new home?"

He faced her. "No. That is on this side of the shoreless sea, but the coast juts and bends. The land route is much slower than water. Once we deliver you, we need the vessel to reach our homeland."

Grub grunted. "For those going."

Fierce dropped his head. "For those going."

Daylight came and went, again and again, until Yu'ung heard a sound she couldn't place.

She asked Fierce, "What is that?"

He chortled, unable to contain his enthusiasm. "Waves crashing along the sea. They explode onto the shore, pull back, and repeat. Some are above my head. Their power covers the sea in white foam.

"We are almost there."

Yu'ung narrowed her eyes, but before she could disagree, Shanadar raced up. "A storm comes."

The group raced to the top of a ridge with a long view of the shoreless sea. Fierce studied the horizon, the dark billowing clouds, fire splitting the sky, endless gray foam separating the shore from sea. White tips danced on the undulating surface and manic waves crashed along the beach. Yu'ung stared at the frothy water, and sucked in the scents of damp plants, wet feathers, dung, and a tang absent from the homeland lakes.

Fierce cupped a hand around her ear and shouted, "Do you taste the salt?"

Shirt billowing in the wind, hair whipped in the storm, he grinned and motioned to Grub, "Tell everyone to join us. We will try to make ourselves easily seen. Then, when all are gathered, we will shelter onboard the craft. Yu'ung, see if you can find the One or their band. We need to know how much trouble they will be!"

Rain had started, the drops quickly becoming sheets denser than a waterfall as Grub headed toward the main group while Yu'ung searched the landscape. Other than gusts slashing the vegetation into shreds, tearing it out by its roots, all she saw was the rabid treacherous storm stretching out to the horizon and drenched groups racing toward Fierce's position, but none of the strangers.

Shanadar struggled up to Yu'ung, Aynoh in tow. Arms and feet bare, he should be cold. Grub yelled from a distance, Wik and others around him, but no one understood what he meant so he waved them to him.

Fierce shouted, "That's a higher hill. Maybe he sees the boat from there!"

He wiped water from his eyes and with Aynoh, ran along the crest, keeping themselves as visible to others as possible. Yu'ung hung onto whatever she could find to keep the gale from blowing her away. Insects swirled, flying into her nose and eyes. Birds screeched in a frantic search for shelter.

B'o and Ese slogged up beside her, panting, just as the tempest flung her to the ground. She crawled until she could regain her footing, and then chased after them to the top of Grub's rise. Fierce was already there. Everyone gathered in a circle, heads dipped together as elephants did in storms.

Grub shouted, "The boat should be ahead, but I can't see anything through this storm!" His voice barely louder than the roar around them.

He started to say more when Laak, Eknilk, and Bhidid stumbled up the back flank, away from the shoreless sea and partially protected from the storm. A gash on Bhidid's head bled and Eknilk's jaw clenched.

They were alone. They should have been with Kruutud and Vobar.

Chapter 34

"Eknilk. Where are the One?"

The gusting wind roared in Yu'ung's ears, whipping her wrap tight against her body, her long red hair tangled around her face.

Eknilk's arms hugged his body as he leaned into the group. "The storm worried Kruutud. He was to meet his group here, along the shoreless sea, but they weren't anywhere. Laak and I agreed to look for them one direction, Bhidid and the One the opposite. If Kruutud's band members ran into trouble, we'd help if possible, but the storm was much worse. It seemed likely they sheltered somewhere until the storm abated which was what we should do. After not finding them, we returned to the meeting place and found Bhidid in an unconscious heap and the Ones gone. When he came to, he said Kruutud knocked him out."

Yu'ung scanned the surroundings, but could see nothing through the sleet.

Grub shook water off his body. "Whatever their plot, it is happening now."

Fierce turned to Yu'ung. She knew what he would ask before he spoke a word. *I can't put the People's lives at risk over a fight among Tall Ones.*

She bellowed to Fierce, "What does the One stealing your boat have to do with the People?"

She looked at Aynoh, busy treating Bhidid, and Ocha, hoping for support but got a curious glance instead.

It's my fault. I considered Fierce and his Tall Ones the helpers Xhosa promised, like Shanadar and the Canis. Maybe they aren't.

When no one came to her defense, she shouted, "I didn't know you helping us would endanger my People, Fierce. I can't do that!"

Surely he understands!

Fierce leaned into Yu'ung. "I have used others for my goals in the past. I am not that individual anymore. I promised to stay until you were safe. I will, no matter what that takes."

Aynoh whispered, "Even if that's forever?"

"Yes." He scratched his head. "How can I be clearer?"

The wind howled. A tree crashed to the ground and exploded. Gusts thrashed, flinging dirt and gravel into the air. The rain blew sideways, attacking Yu'ung's exposed skin as cinders do bursting from a hearth fire. Her breath steamed a diaphanous cloud with each exhale. She rubbed her arms, but it did nothing to keep the frigid gale from seeping between the stitches of her wrap.

She didn't notice after what Aynoh asked next.

"Fierce. When you go home, do I go with you?"

His wide-eyed gaze darted to Grub. Yu'ung might call it frightened, but she'd never seen Fierce afraid of anything.

"That is more complicated than you think."

Wrong answer, Fierce.

Suddenly, the storm didn't exist.

"It's a simple yes or no." Aynoh's voice was soft but Fierce and Yu'ung heard her clearly.

And as important to me as any words you've ever said. How he answered was key to what Yu'ung would do next.

Grub shrugged. "Wik insisted I reply also."

Fierce roared, "Yes! Yes! Yes! I want you with me, in my homeland or yours, until my end!" He howled, louder than the storm.

Grub grinned. "That's what I said, too."

"But this storm is worse than any I've ever seen. It will break the boat's moorings and drag it out to sea. We will have few options if I can't secure it!"

Well done, Fierce.

Movement drew Yu'ung's attention down the shore. "Fierce! There they are—the Tall Ones."

He jerked where her lips pointed. "Where?"

Yu'ung spun him around. "Heading toward that bouncing blob on the edge of the shoreless sea."

"That's my boat! They're trying to launch it, but don't know how!" He took off with Grub and Eknilk.

"Stop!" Fierce bellowed. They heard him, looked his way, and ran faster.

By the time Fierce got within spear range, they'd cut the vines fastening the craft to the shore and shoved it seaward despite the tree-high waves. Those who could, leaped onto the deck.

"Sailing in this storm is suicide!" Bhidid shouted as he took off, Yu'ung and Aynoh with him.

A wall of water plowed into the bow and swept the raiders overboard. Mouths opened in screams, but no one tried to help. Instead, more boarded and tried panicky maneuvers to force the vessel out to sea past the tumultuous waves.

How stupid they are.

Fierce shrieked, "Let me keep it afloat!"

The One and their thieves ignored him and soon, the carcasses of all those who couldn't hang on littered the sea's turbulent surface. Some pled for help, cries falling on deaf ears. Others were flung against the boat's sides, their flaccid forms sucked to the seafloor where they drowned. The bow smashed someone's head, the boiling water soon red with his blood. A few tried to swim away, but it was obvious most didn't possess the skill.

Behind, further along the shore, Yu'ung heard faint yelling. She jerked around, ready to defend, but it was the People, jumping, pointing to a massive swell that roared toward the shore. She snatched Aynoh's hand and flew from the impending tsunami of water, digging her toes into the sand and shale.

"Fierce!" she yelled, but he saw it, too and abandoned efforts to save his craft, focusing instead on his band. The thieves either missed or discounted what would end their lives, intent on the absurd task of sailing the broken wreck into the storm.

The wall of water slammed into the shore and thrust the heavy vessel high into the air. Bodies dangled from the flanks as the monstrous waves catapulted the hulk forward and dropped it almost on top of Yu'ung. The smooth decks splintered and the tightly-hewn sides collapsed. What Fierce called a mast snapped off as easily as a bird wing from an overcooked carcass. The supports for balance shattered. A final rotation and the ruined colossus landed atop rocks, mounds of scree, and in some cases, Tall Ones. Fierce fell to his knees.

The storm blew itself out leaving the survivors to slog up the beach, accompanied by growls, frantic gestures, and brandished spears, a clear message to those who spoiled their passage home: *You are the enemy.*

Yu'ung shouted, "B'o! Take Laak, Jvelk, Jhat and get those who can walk out of the water and up the shore. Aynoh, Ese, and I will help the wounded."

Kruutud had scrapes and lacerations, but nothing serious. Not so with Vobar. Aynoh knelt by Asvulk to comfort her, but Kruutud forced her away, his eyes shooting fire. Yu'ung and Aynoh left after telling Asvulk to let them know if she needed anything. They rejoined Fierce as an unfamiliar One strode toward them, arms swinging, lance gripped. He ignored that Fierce, Aynoh, and Yu'ung were deep in discussion. At his approach, they fell silent. Yu'ung no longer trusted these One, but stayed, for Fierce. The rage burning in her throat couldn't compare to the fury on his face.

The burly unknown One stared down his nose at Yu'ung and then faced Fierce. "I am Gevol. Vobar is dead. I am now Lead Warrior. You deal with me."

The power of Fierce's wrath was almost physical, like a whirlpool pulling Yu'ung under, his fury for the One choking whatever he wanted to say. She stepped forward to give him time to shake off the emotion of all they cost him.

"You are not welcome here. Stay away from the Chosen and the People."

Fierce stepped up to Yu'ung's side, a dangerous scent spilling from his body. With his diminishing reserves of control, he murmured, "You joined Kruutud to assault us. You destroyed our way home. Go or we kill you and whoever remains of the One."

Braanroorv joined him, every bit of his muscle-bound body ready and eager to take on this enemy.

Gevol's mouth dropped open.

He doesn't know.

She took advantage of his confusion to slap the lance from his hand. Ocha snarled, plopping atop the shaft. Her saliva splashed on his shirt and fear washed his body.

Yu'ung touched Ocha. "She dislikes you. That is not good for your lifespan."

Without warning, Ocha snapped the spear into pieces with her powerful jaws, blue eyes never leaving the pack's enemy. He coughed, visibly trembling.

Tone now conciliatory, he said, "We are not the ones who assaulted you. They are dead. Kruutud says you agreed to let us use your boat."

Fierce's shoulders hardened. "Our screams didn't reveal the lie in his words?"

"We thought you warned us to beware of the storm." He tried a smile. It failed.

"That's the story you expect me to believe?"

Grub and Ragged Ear trotted up. Gevol cringed, probably not at the sight of Grub though he stood a full head taller and at least a hand wider at the shoulders with muscles that rippled where Gevol's were best described as firm flab. No, doubtless, it was the massive feral-eyed Canis next to Grub, gliding with purposeful steps toward Gevol. The Tall One backed away and fell over Ocha lying behind him, hackles raised, fangs exposed.

Eknilk yelled, "You need help with this scum? I'd love to do that," and strode toward Fierce, knocking Gevol down as he tried to rise.

Gevol managed to push to his feet with the help of his cudgel. Ragged Ear took that as a threat and leapt. Fierce snatched the Canis by the scruff of his neck, stopped him from doing what couldn't be undone, but let him rip a piece of Gevol's already frayed shirt from his trembling body. Gevol stepped on Ocha, still stretched out, and she tore a swath out of his leg, almost as an afterthought.

Yu'ung made no move to help.

Both Ocha and Ragged Ear spit the shreds aside as though they tasted rotten and howled.

"Fear empowers Canis."

Gevol swallowed a scream, but couldn't hide the wobble in his steps as he scurried away.

Eknilk spoke through clenched teeth, "He refused to help his injured. Who does that?"

Yu'ung brushed hair from her face. "Have you seen Shanadar?"

Grub skimmed the crowd. "I see Xad, but that's all."

Yu'ung wrapped a hide strip around her hair to keep it behind her back. "Find Ump and White Streak. He'll be with them. Let's gather all of our weapons."

Fierce glared after Gevol, watched him arrive at the One group. They closed around him and Kruutud in a lose circle, faces confused. Gevol spread his hands, hissing frantic words Yu'ung couldn't make out. Kruutud responded with angry orders, finger poking, leaning into first Gevol and then the others, casting sidelong glances at Fierce and his group, making no effort to hide his revulsion of the male he'd been sent to rescue.

Fierce turned his back on these enemy, speaking in low tones to his assemblage. "The Ones will use this chaos to strike. Grub. Determine how many remain to carry out this threat."

Grub hurried off, saying, "I'll tell the rest."

"While Grub does that, I'll emasculate the head."

Fierce and Ragged Ear strode up to Kruutud, glad all One eyes were on him, and knocked their Leader down. Ragged Ear snapped his jaws around the terrified male's wrist to hold him in place. Yu'ung followed with B'o and Ocha.

"You lied to Gevol."

Kruutud flailed his free arm. "I was confused."

Yu'ung spit on him and Fierce hissed, "Tell me what's going on or Ragged Ear bites harder."

"When you didn't come back to the homeland, we came to rescue you. That's why we are warriors, not explorers. We thought you were in trouble. We did our part. Now help *us* save *our* stranded members."

Fierce's eyes slit. "You came here for us?"

Kruutud searched for how to convince Fierce while telling only the absolute minimum of truth. At least, that's what Yu'ung thought. She waited, wondering how deep Ragged Ear's teeth had penetrated, enjoying Kruutud's discomfort, remembering wise words someone told her.

Kruutud was whining now. "You are the band's apex predator. Seer was sure you lived."

The hair on Yu'ung's neck tingled. Ocha growled and dipped her head.

Fierce's eyes narrowed, watching Kruutud, but something the male said made sense, at least to Fierce.

He motioned for Ragged Ear to return to his side and asked, "Why not say something when we first rescued you?"

"We feared Yu'ung coopted you," his voice unsteady, a stream of blood dripping from his wrist.

Fierce shoved him away. "Go! We will tell you our decision tomorrow."

Kruutud sighed, hands spread. "We will re-earn your faith and build a new boat with you under your command. We are too few to cause problems. Recognize this! Honestly, you are no longer important to our goals. It's those stranded, waiting for help for too long that concern us."

Fierce ignored Kruutud's pleas and the One Leader shuffled away, toward Asvulk and the others who survived the storm.

In the morning, after discussions with his band and Yu'ung, Fierce told Kruutud the good news.

The conclusion to the *Savage Land trilogy*

Balance of Nature

A tribe haunted by the past. Lies that threaten a new beginning. A reason to find the truth.

Here's a preview:

Chapter 1

75,000 years ago
What we now call Gibraltar

Shouts woke Kazeb and Turk before Sun's arrival, screeching about a long boat headed to the Clan's shores. The brothers had waited long for this news, Kazeb with excitement, Turk with dread. They flew across the grassland, leaping over crevices in the dark, their width and size familiar to the males, and scrambled up Big Rock's towering cliffs, over jutting ledges, grabbing the tiniest of finger- and toeholds with speed mountain goats would envy. Its height dwarfed every other in the area, overshadowed only by the distant mountain range that separated the Clan from neighboring tribes. From an occluded position off the lip, they waited for the vague elongated shadow floating on the inky black surface to reveal its intentions. Kazeb gritted his teeth so tightly, he thought he'd break a tooth.

Is it them? After all this time?

He clenched his sturdy hirsute fists and glanced at Turk's square face. Fury stole whatever words his brother wished to say. As Sun's arrival erased the darkness, the sea below shimmered in shades of blue. Waves crashed against the coastline, gravelly scree in places, sand in others. The incoming craft must pick the right mooring spot or risk disaster.

If it is them, they will.

The brisk and cold breeze atop the promontory whipped Kazeb's dark red hair across his face, but he scarcely noticed, thoughts fixed below.

Turk whispered, "It must be them, Liis. They're headed for the cave."

Kazeb's Clan name was Liis, but he preferred "Kazeb," the title awarded him by Fierce for agreeing to guide the Tall One group across the sprawling landmass to Sun's waking place.

"They are too far to tell," but if this were Uprights without knowledge of this cove, they would head to the plains, not the cliffs.

Kazeb scanned a full circle, from the flat grassland bordering one flank of the massive outcrop to the sea surrounding all other sides. The morning sun colored the sky in pinks and blues. Birds plummeted into the crystalline blue water and the fish with no desire to be food dove deeper. Far down the clearing, Pig rooted through the grass for a meal and a herd feasted on fresh grass, protected from most predators by the mountain range that blocked access to this spit.

When we're done here, Turk and I will hunt.

Visible on the clearest days, a faint brown outline shadowed the horizon. Fierce called it home, where his Tall Ones started their journey of exploration.

Kazeb turned back. The vessel remained beyond the white peaks that marked the beach. The Clan's scouts said they had watched it much of the night. It floated far out there, made no move to approach.

Those aboard awaited Sun's light to guide it in safely.

Only Uprights here before would be cognizant of the underwater shoals.

It veered for the cove, jogging around a darker patch of water, to a spot where one like it beached long ago. Kazeb gripped his spear tighter. He waited many Moons for this moment, afraid it would never arrive, but Fierce had promised and Kazeb trusted the Tall One. Fierce earned that confidence in his brief time with Kazeb's People by sharing valuable hunting knowledge and treatments for illnesses.

Kazeb watched the prow plow through the water. Shivers ran down his body.

It's not the same craft, but who else would come from that direction?

Soon, a line of Uprights materialized out of the dim light, working paddles, the interior space just wide enough for them to stand abreast. In front, the stripes and confident stance of a slender male made Kazeb stiffen.

The other males could be Fierce's band except one, a female of Kazeb's kind.

Did he find another guide?

Her legs spread for balance, shining flame-colored hair flying in the wind, as she scanned the Big Rock.

Her gaze stopped on Kazeb, as though she spotted him.

But that is impossible.

He'd muddied his skin to match the brush behind which he hid and squinted his eyes.

She shouted to One-who-might-be-Fierce. He turned and she pointed.

At Kazeb.

Turk muttered, oblivious to the drama, "It can't be them. Why return to where they caused so much trouble?"

"We don't know they caused it—"

"Who else?" Turk's voice harsh.

Kazeb fell silent.

As the vessel approached, he admired its sleek profile, its quick movement, so different than the flatter, smaller ones the Clan built. It beached at the base of the cliff where the brother's hid and Turk let out a strangled yelp.

"These *are* those who killed our tribe, Liis," his voice fiery but quiet. "This is our chance, why we survived instead of dying with the rest."

2 *years ago*

Liis and his brother Turk though new adults represented the core of their small Clan. Besides broad muscular shoulders, brawny limbs, and thick chests, their quick minds connected events in ways others in the Clan didn't. When unrelenting cold pushed the tribe from their ancestral homes, despite their youth, the Clan appointed the brothers co-Alphas to find the Clan's new homebase. Alphas temporarily led during emergencies, empowered to make decisions all members must abide by.

Liis and Turk, with the entire Clan, followed the indigenous herds along a corridor edged on one side by rugged peaks and deep valleys, the other by never-ending water. When the herds finally stopped on a field of lush grass as far as Liis could see, the Clan did too.

If this promising area was indeed a new homebase, the emergency could be declared ended and life revert to a leaderless community where each member did what he or she determined necessary for the group's welfare. But this area was nothing like those familiar in the past, not even to the Elders. Despite the plethora of living creatures, despite the surprisingly comfortable temperatures, they must overcome the absence of drinkable water, shortage of caves, and a confusing array of strange food. The Clan decided Liis and Turk with their penchant for bringing calm to chaos should remain Alphas until potable water sources were identified, reliable food sources located, and a living habitat selected.

The brothers solved the first problem by following the animals who instinctively knew where to find ponds not tainted by the salt from the surrounding seas. The second—food—would require more than the small herd now grazing a spear throw away. Despite relentless exploration, few other herds inhabited what appeared to be these lush grasslands. After considerable experimentation, the brothers discovered that despite being undrinkable, the water offered an endless supply of fish similar to those eaten in their previous homeland. With the limited herd meat, the limitless fish in the water, tidepools, and crawling on the beaches, the bounteous supplies of small birds, tortoises, squirrels, pigs, and other sea-based creatures, no one went hungry.

The last problem was to find a homebase.

In the past, the Clan moved when they exhausted the area's food supplies, but with the abundance of food in this environ, that proved unnecessary. The question became should they live in caves as in the past or open air sites like those used on hunting trips?

Liis and Turk argued about this.

Liis: "The protection from enemies and predators of rock walls would be nice...."

Turk: "But we have seen no foes and few even of our kind since arriving."

Liis: "The hearth fire warms an enclosure better."

Turk: "Hardly necessary as the days and nights are comfortable."

Liis: "When daylight darkens, the light of fires allows us to continue our work."

Turk: "Fire pits vent better in open air."

Liis: "We don't have materials for the enclosure."

Usually, they pounded tree trunks into the ground and then strung hides between them to block out the cold air and prevent entrance of unwanted predators, but that required the huge skins of mammoth and bison. They didn't live here.

Turk: "The only caves are in Big Rock, at the tip far from fields, plants, pigs, ground birds, and most sources of food other than fish. I think we both agree living there is not the best decision."

Liis tipped his head up, focusing on the summit of Big Rock. "Clan members on the crest would be concealed yet have full view of all land and water routes, ready to alert us to a menace before it threatens. We would have plenty of time to prepare a defense or find refuge."

After many discussions, each arguing different opinions, they decided on the grassland, with the Big Rock as overwatch.

Over time, the danger they worried about never arrived. The brothers thought about visiting the brown mirage on the horizon, but the channel between the landmasses churned with rough water and deadly waves. The Clan's log rafts crossed similar distances but not in storms. Well, they might make the crossing, but it was just as likely they wouldn't. With no critical reason to test it, they didn't.

The scouts, in their explorations, focused primarily on the land route that led to the former homeland. Why wouldn't other tribes follow the same passage here? The Clan must be prepared.

Moon came and went over and over without the arrival of other Uprights. The tribe settled into a predictable, safe lifestyle. Liis and Turk called the group together with the intention of announcing they would step down as Alphas.

That's when a subadult male raced into the camp with the news of an approaching boat.

The brothers scrambled up the craggy sides of the Big Rock. The treacherous path tested their skills, but as usual, they traversed it quickly. When they reached the peak, they dropped immediately, concealing themselves in the brush.

"Turk! They are mooring!"

The scouts who had originally noticed the vessel stole through the prickly dry stubble until they were directly behind Liis and Turk.

They gulped, in unison murmured, "It was only just in sight when we first observed it. How could it move so swiftly?"

The form resembled a hollowed out tree trunk rather than the tied-together logs that comprised the Clan's rafts. The sides were higher, Liis thought to keep the rough sea's water out. Something stuck out, for what reason wasn't obvious. Many paddles pushed the craft through the water, driving its pointed nose directly for Big Rock.

We cannot aim for a specific place. We end up where the surf take us.

This close, the Uprights were clearly visible. They stretched tall in the boat's interior. Their heads were larger than any among Liis' kind, foreheads higher, and faces flatter, without the brow ridges that kept rain and sun out of Liis' eyes. Bright colors striped their dark skin like the bands on Badger's face or a young Boar. One male stood spread-legged in the front, unbothered by the rocking deck, hands on his hips, eyes fixed on the cliffs that edge Big Rock.

Liis whispered to his brother, "Let's gather our males, our weapons, meet the strangers when they disembark, tell them they are not welcome! Let them think we are many to their few, that they can't defeat us."

Turk huffed and started down the rock face.

Liis stiffened. "Turk! Where are you going? Only mountain goats use this passage!"

When fishing, they approached this cove not by crossing over the crest of Big Rock but traveling along the shore. He expected Turk would retreat down Big Rock's shallower slope, loop around and come up behind the vessel.

Turk hissed, "Then call on your inner goat!" but added with a chuckle, "There's a shortcut not far ahead. The intruders will wonder how we appeared out of nowhere."

Without another word, he hurried forward, leaving the rest scrambling to catch up.

They descended slowly and deliberately, each step a cautious probe of the loose debris, some crumbling into gravel under their feet, others skittering away. One slid, arms flailing for grip, and regained it quickly. By the time they reached the bottom, Liis' calves burned, his knees pulsed, and his back ached from keeping his balance, but the group managed to slip down the rubble-strewn rock face without being seen. Turk motioned the Clan to hide, including Liis and Turk, with the exception of a small contingent who would stand in the open, spears down.

He whispered, "Don't look frightened or intimidating. Interested is good."

Liis began to understand Turk's plan. *Confuse the strangers, find out their intent, before we reveal ourselves.*

The Uprights disembarked, noted the visible Clan males without interest, as though aware they represented no more than a ruse, and scanned the beach.

As they did, Liis studied them. *Taller and slimmer than they appeared from above.*

They moved awkwardly as though more comfortable running than fighting.

Maybe they've been on the sea so long, they forgot how to walk!

This close, he could tell the stripes on their faces and necks were not the natural ones of Badger but like those the Clan left on cave walls, to tell others of the area threats and food sources.

What is their purpose when drawn on a body?

The newcomers carried stone-tipped shafts, but unlike the Clan's, slender rather than robust.

A mosquito whined by Liis' ear, but he remained motionless. There were more Uprights than Liis had guessed from the top of Big Rock. He ticked them off on one hand and ran out of fingers, but not more than both hands. It didn't worry Liis. Clan males' physical strength and powerful spear skills meant they easily penetrated the tough coats of prey. These Uprights would be easy to defeat, if necessary.

The male who must be Alpha ferreted out Liis' hiding position and strode toward him, shaft gripped but level with the ground. Liis and Turk stood which didn't surprise the Alpha even a little. Liis gesticulated to the rest of the clan's hunters to remain obscured. They may need this subterfuge.

Not expecting argument, Liis said to Turk, "I will talk to One-who-must-be-Alpha," and stepped toward the tall, rangy stranger, replicating his hold on the Clan's heftier lance, intuiting it as a power play. The stranger gargled sounds Liis didn't understand, but hand movements and a pleasant smile made it clear he meant no harm.

Liis motioned toward the craft. "What is that? And where do you come from," waving down the length of the sea to where Sun awakes.

Between his words and hand motions, probably mostly the movements, the male seemed to understand. He placed his weapon on the ground and pointed to the brown bump revealed above the skyline on clear days. Liis did his best to hide his surprise, but the look on the Upright's face said he failed.

We considered the land in that direction too far away and the water too rough for any to attack!

Tall-One-who-must-be-Alpha smiled again at Liis, jabbered something which made his group drop their spears though their eyes maintained the gaze of predators hunting.

Liis beckoned Turk. "Whatever their reason for being here, it isn't to fight."

"How do you know?"

"Because they disarmed."

With that, Liis stowed his lance in his shoulder sack and placed a hand on his chest. "I am Liis. This is Turk," he explained with hand and body movements. "We are Alphas of our Clan," though he didn't think that message got through. He was about to try again when Tall-One-who-must-be-Alpha placed a hand on his chest.

"Fierce. Leader for my band," then pointed at Liis. "You are Leader—Alpha—for your band--Clan."

Liis bobbed his head. "Yes!" Then signaled to his brother, "With Turk. We are both Alphas."

Turk grunted, turned abruptly and headed up the trail that ascended Big Rock. Liis' gaze darted from his brother to the Upright Alpha and shrugged.

"Come," with a hand flourish and a grin. "Turk invites you to our camp."

Fierce craned his neck upward. The precipitous drop of the rugged cliff made ascent appear impossible.

Fierce motioned, "We go to the crest?" The implication that there was no path.

Liis grinned again. "How do you think we got down here?" and followed Turk.

He didn't have to check to see if the strangers followed. He heard their noisy steps, rearranging the scree and crunching the debris. Luckily, this was not a test of the intruders' silence, rather their strength and abilities, traits Liis needed clarified before engaging in a relationship. If they survived this climb, Liis would ask many questions around the hearth fire starting with why this beach, not one of the others.

The strangers carried spoiled meat that no surprise attracted the attention of a bevy of rats.

He spoke over his shoulder without slowing, "You brought meat, One-called-Fierce."

Fierce looked confused at first and then figured out the question. "We came from far away and didn't know if meat animals lived here." He waved a hand between his sailors and Liis' group, bringing up the rear of the assemblage. "We would like to share it with you."

"Your rats can have what remains. Bringing it would make ours angry. There is no shortage of food here."

Fierce laughed after processing Liis' meaning, then jabbered something that persuaded his band to abandon the fetid meat.

"We didn't mean to bring the rats. They follow us onto the boat every time we stop for water or plants."

To Liis' surprise, the Tall One's words began to make sense.

He turned to caution Fierce of the soft ground ahead, that he should be careful, when without warning, the hillside beneath the newcomer gave way. Fierce shouted in surprise as he slid down the hill. Liis grabbed for his hand, missed it, and careened after him. He yelled at Fierce to grab something—anything—to stop his fall when a root caught the Tall One's foot, slowing him. One of the other Tall Ones—was his name Grub?—grabbed for him, missed, and then he too fell, sliding headfirst downward. Liis flung himself after the males, oblivious to the danger to himself, intent on catching these scrawny males before they killed themselves.

Questions You Ask

Were Neanderthal lives boring?

Well, they did spend a preponderance of time searching for food, concocting meals, knapping tools, sewing clothes, and migrating (activities deemed 'boring' by some), but using fire (for warmth, protection, and seeing in the dark) and inventing cooked glue and stitched clothes saved Neanderthals time. This they used to ask why events happened and draw conclusions based on reflective deliberation as well as instinct. Artifacts support the idea Neanderthals discovered art and music and may have credited something greater than themselves for life events. Such cerebral advances made everyday existence anything but boring.

Describe Neanderthal appearance

Based on skeletal remains, Neanderthals stood about five-five on average with robust bones, a spread rib cage, a sloped forehead, an expansive nose, a brain size moderately larger than ours housed in a skull smaller in front than back. Their hair was probably straightish and dark with a percentage of redheads.

No surprise skin color doesn't preserve so scientists disagree whether Neanderthals were white, brown, or black. Their homelands were Eurasia with its less direct sun. That supports the presumption they were light-skinned.

A note: cellular mtDNA provides species data over 100,000 years which provides much information about our Neanderthal ancestors.

Neanderthals aren't dumb cave dwellers.

The time-tested Neanderthal image of mentally challenged hominids who carried clubs over stooped shoulders has long been debunked by evidence. Neanderthals cooked glue, made fire, sewed clothes, talked, played music on various 'instruments', created art, and possessed other skills shared by modern man, but applied them in ways suited to a rigorous physical life lived in a world with a high value on physical strength.

A study in <u>PLOS ONE</u> explains the complex cognitive control necessary to knap the Neanderthal hand axe:

"For the first time, we've showed a relationship between the degree of prefrontal brain activity, the ability to make technological judgments, and success in actually making stone tools," says Stout. "The findings are relevant to ongoing debates regarding the origins of modern human cognition, and the role of technological and social complexity in brain evolution across species." Most hand axes produced by the modern hands and minds of the study subjects "… weren't up to the high standards of 500,000 years ago," Stout says.

Could Neanderthals talk?

Most evidence indicates yes: 1) They had a hyoid (a prerequisite to speech), positioned above ours which fueled speculation among scientists that it pitched their voices higher than modern man. 2) Ears had evolved to listen for voices. 3) Tasks often require collaboration, difficult without the ability to speak to a group. In Savage Land, *I've given Neanderthals voices enhanced with body language.*

An addendum: Thirty-two geometric signs have been found in caves throughout Europe for over a hundred thousand years. Research hints Neanderthals (like the story's People) communicated via common-to-them geometric signs, more Chinese or Japanese symbols than Roman or Cyrillic letters. The translation is lost in time, but not to them.

You say they squat rather than sit?

Nominal physical evidence includes tell-tale divots in the Neanderthal femur, tibia, and ankle bone likely from squatting a lot. This shouldn't surprise us. At least a fourth of modern man habitually crouches in a deep squat both at rest and work. Squatting is far more natural for the body. It doesn't require anything extra to make it happen—like a chair or bench. We simply stop walking, bend knees and rest. It is also much quicker to get out of should danger strike and a fast departure be required. Chairs arrived less than 6,000 years ago. They probably were for royalty and rulers, something the wealthy could afford and commoners couldn't.

How did Neanderthals tell time?

Like today's primitive communities, Neanderthals possessed no concept of hours or minutes. His metric was how much daylight remained. Characters indicate time in two ways: 1) future time by indicating a place in the sky where the sun would be, the inference, "Return when Sun reaches here in the sky." 2) present time by placing fingers next to the sun. A finger represents around fifteen minutes, the time the sun takes to cross the sky a finger's distance. A hand is four fingers or an hour. Test it yourself. Place a finger alongside the sun. The sun takes approximately fifteen minutes to cross to your finger's far side.

How did Neanderthals navigate without a map, GPS, or compass?

They used a process called Natural Navigation. This describes the ability to maneuver through geographic terrain without technical tools, using instead a pensive brain and a problem-solver's attitude. Both rely on the eleven million data bits received every second by our senses to assess, extrapolate, and guide. They are commonly ignored today, though popular among hunter-gatherers, survivalists, and nature lovers.

If you're interested in the topic, search "natural navigation" in your browser.

Can Neanderthals run down prey?

Yes! Scientists call the ability to run endless distances the "Endurance Running Hypothesis." Our ancestors ran slower than herds but harder—all day or longer. The Homo genus (which includes Neanderthals) evolved a stable head, loose hips, shock-absorbent joints, and springy feet. These made them—and us—well-suited to continuous running. Further alterations meant humans neither tired nor overheated as fast as most mammals. Most animals sprint short expanses before forced to catch their breath and cool their bodies. Evolution corrected that flaw in man.

Did Neanderthals count?

The short answer is: He didn't, at least, not the way we do. Modern primitive tribes— as recently as the early 1900's—had little need for exact counts. "One," "two", "some" or "many" sufficiently described a herd, fruit trees, or distance. They recognized when a tribe member was absent by noticing the smaller size of the group and/or by a missing scent, relying on an exceptional memory, comparing current impressions with the image stored in memory to tell whether a single object is missing in a group. This is comparable to listening to a piece of music and noticing when the musician leaves out a measure. You can't say how many measures are in the piece, but you know one was omitted.

60,000 years ago, in western France, a Neanderthal cut nine notches into a hyaena femur, scientists speculate to count regardless most evidence indicates Neanderthals were anumeric. Numbers were unimportant in pre-agriculture societies.

Did Neanderthals store water in ostrich egg shells as the story indicates?

A human can stand on an ostrich's eggshell without breaking it. As long ago as 105,000 years, early man collected rainwater in these shells. Today's Kalahari San use them as a canteen. They puncture a small hole in the end, clean the inside, fill the shell with water, and reseal the gap with beeswax or reeds.

Did Neanderthals play music?

Shanadar's flute is modeled on the 60,000-year-old Divje Babe bone flute produced from a hollowed-out cave bear thigh bone, among the oldest musical instruments. It has three holes on the top and one on the underside, with both ends open. In an expert's hands, this ancient musical instrument plays pretty much any song our sophisticated modern ones can. If interested, click for a video (not available in print books). Be prepared to be amazed.

Besides this amazing flute, earliest man—including Neanderthals—had the brain power to turn natural elements around them into music, such as rocks, hollow trunks, and stalagmites/stalactites. Here's a video (not available in print books) where you can listen to organ-like music from stalactites in caves Neanderthals considered home.

Did Neanderthals use fire?

Fire played a key role in our genus' evolution. It provided heat and protection, cooked raw food, made glue, and availed us of activities in what otherwise is darkness. The question becomes whether Neanderthals made fire or captured it. No one disputes whether Neanderthals were clever enough to create fire—using rocks most likely—but that doesn't preserve so scientists are reluctant to draw that conclusion. Still, here are clues that did preserve:

- *Stone circles deep in Bruniquel Cave (in France) show fire used to light the dark.*
- *Neanderthals cooked food, boiled stews and bones in water.*
- *Neanderthals cooked pitch (does not appear naturally in nature) and bark to create a glue to attach stone tips to wood shafts for spears.*
- *Neanderthals hardened the ends of lances and digging sticks with fire, still used by primitive tribes today.*

Did Neanderthals care for their sick?

The injuries suffered by Book 1 and 2's character, Old One, are modeled on a Siberian Neanderthal named Shanidar. Skeletal evidence indicates he suffered a serious blow to his left eye socket which might have blinded him or resulted in brain damage. His right humerus broke and healed in two places. He lost his right forearm. His right foot revealed fractures. Osteoarthritis in his leg joints made moving painful. Despite these infirmities, he survived until older than fifty. University of York researcher, Penny Spikins, says: "… he was looked after for about 10 to 15 years."

Another example: A Neanderthal with a bent spine, a long-broken clavicle, a healed broken femur, osteoarthritis, and lung disease survived for fifty-plus years. He too must have been cared for. A final famous example is the Old Man of La Chapelle-aux-Saints, missing many teeth and suffering severe periodontal disease in addition to joint degeneration in his hips. These injuries entailed daily care from others.

Additionally, food remnants indicate Neanderthals self-medicated with chamomile—an anti-inflammatory—and yarrow—a natural astringent.

Did Neanderthal genetics affect who we are?

Modern humans are 2-4% Neanderthal. Roughly 30% of the Neanderthal genome is preserved in ours, albeit spread throughout our population. As a result, many Neanderthal traits persevere today. Most among us today—everyone?—descend from humans alive 50,000-80,000 years ago. Why might it be all? We possess two kinds of DNA, one derived from both parents called simply 'DNA', and another from only the mother called 'mtDNA'. mtDNA tracks our genetic heritage back 100,000 years for those able to read it.

Are story elements drawn from prehistory?

Yes. First: The Neanderthal's Book 1 Asian home—before they are driven away by Nature—was in what we now call the Iranian-Russian Altai Mountains, what paleo-archeologists know as Denisova Cave. This is a long-researched site most famous for evidence indicating Neanderthals and Denisovans co-existed.

Second: this story's fictional Old One's closest Elder friend, Yota, is drawn from a historic discovery by the University of Cambridge. They retrieved sufficient skeletal remnants to reconstruct a 75,000-year-old Neanderthal who inhabited Iraqi Kurdistan, close to where this story's characters lived before migrating to the Mediterranean and Gibraltar. She might have belonged to the Neanderthal tribe in this book called the People. Her death according to the archaeologists in situ was due to a cave-in, maybe the same one that killed Yota. Here's the event's story and the Netflix docudrama (links not available in print books) trailer detailing how scientists reconstructed her skeletal head.

Is Shanadar's cave on Gibraltar authentic?

While Gibraltar is home to one of Europe's—or the world's—extensive cave systems, the tunnels to Shanadar's Gibraltar caves (in Book 3) are based on two subterranean habitats occupied not by Neanderthals but other prehistoric species that co-existed during the timeframe of the Neanderthals. The first is the Rising Star system in South Africa, occupied by Homo naledi *(not Neanderthals) circa 300,000 years ago. The second is Bruniquel Cave in France, built by Neanderthals circa 175,000 years ago. There is evidence the interior was illuminated by fire (no surprise—it was far from natural light), and Neanderthals transported two tons of stalagmites three hundred meters, broke them into four hundred similarly sized pieces, and arranged them in a circle—for no obvious reason. A prominent theory is spiritual/religious. Whatever the purpose, it demonstrates Neanderthals mastered the dark as well as symbolic thought.*

Did a natural disaster destroy Neanderthals?

Toba erupted around 75,000 years ago in Indonesia, ranked by many scientists as the worst natural disaster experienced by our genus. Some contend this volcanic eruption ushered in what is called a "volcanic winter", defined by World Atlas as—

"a dramatic drop in temperatures experienced globally, in the aftermath of a massive volcanic eruption... As a result, typical winter conditions are amplified while the winter season becomes longer."

It spanned six-ten years (or shorter, or longer, depending upon who you talk to). The eruption's plume exploded twenty-five miles upward, depositing a six-inch ash layer as remotely as India. Climate models suggest the planet cooled 3.5–9 °C with a 25% reduction in precipitation. Most volcanologists deem Mt. Toba the most destructive eruption ever in man's existence.

This story fictionalizes this historic Mt. Toba eruption, how it devastated Savage Land's *Neanderthal People and inspired migration to Gibraltar.*

Did man's population decline around the time of *Savage Land*?

Around the Toba Eruption—featured in Savage Land—*a genetic bottleneck almost triggered man's extinction. At first, scientists blamed Mt. Toba's eruption. Today, many dispute the causal effect, instead blaming conditions no one agrees on.*

Explain the face stone Shanadar carries.

Shanadar's Wise Stone is modeled on the 250,000-year-old Berekhat Ram, a palm-sized volcanic scoria colored by charcoal. Grooves around the neck are caused by both natural elements and deliberate modifications. The indentations accentuate the female shape. The artifact's age suggests it was created by Homo erectus *(Xhosa's species, predecessors to Neanderthals).*

Were Neanderthals religious?

Proof is marginal either way. Shamanism existed, rooted 100,000 years ago, before Neanderthals time in Savage Land. *Because they created the circular man-made structure in Bruniquel Cave, we speculate it represented their curiosity about the hereafter, spiritual beings who control the natural events around them, and make miracles possible. There is evidence they buried the dead, maybe with flowers.*

In this trilogy, I explore religion's roots without drawing conclusions.

Are the Canis (proto-wolves) spirits?

I leave the decision regarding spirits unclear. Throughout time, spirits have been nebulous creatures, Gods or gods.

Is prehistoric fiction boring?

If you enjoy adventure, death-defying odds, and humans who routinely do the impossible, the answer must be "Not even a little." We first categorized the Man vs. Nature trilogies as "prehistoric thrillers" because the characters and plots share both historical fiction and thriller traits. The individuals you meet in Savage Land consistently outsmart bigger and stronger enemies.

I'm reading the books out of order. Will the story make sense?

Each book in the trilogy includes details on prior events. As such, they can be consumed in any order you choose. You may enhance the experience by reading the three trilogy books consecutively. Here's a quick accounting of the three books:

Endangered Species *(Book 1)—how the worst volcanic eruption man ever lived through forced the People to abandon their homes.*

Badland *(Book 2)—the People and the Chosen leave the Altai Mountains to migrate beyond what we call the Mediterranean Sea.*

Balance of Nature *(Book 3)— A tribe haunted by the past. Lies that threaten the future. A reason to find the truth*

Bibliography

Allen, E.A., The Prehistoric World: or, Vanished Races Central Publishing House, 1885.

Berger, Lee and Hawks, John, Almost Human: The Astonishing Story of Homo naledi and the Discovery That Changed Our Human Story National Geographic 2017

Boismier, William, et al (editors) Neanderthals Among Mammoths: Excavations at Lynford Quarry, Norfolk English Heritage 2012

Allen, E.A., The Prehistoric World: or, Vanished Races Central Publishing House 1885

Brown Jr., Tom, Tom Brown's Field Guide: Wilderness Survival Berkley Books 1983

Caird, Rod Apeman: The Story of Human Evolution MacMillan 1994

Carss, Bob The SAS Guide to Tracking Lyons Press Guilford Conn. 2000

Cavalli-Sforza, Luigi Luca and Cavalli-Sforza, Francesco The Great Human Diasporas: The History of Diversity and Evolution Perseus Press 1995 Conant,

Charles River Editors The Pleistocene Era: The History of the Ice Age and the Dawn of Modern Charles River Editors 2020

Humans Dr. Levi Leonard The Number Concept: Its Origin and Development Macmillan and Co. Toronto 1931

Diamond, Jared The Third Chimpanzee Harper Perennial 1992

Everett, Dr. Daniel Don't Sleep There are Snakes Pantheon Books 2008

Gooley, Tristan The Lost Art of Reading Nature's Signs The Experiment 2015

Gooley, Tristan How to Read a Tree The Experiment 2023

Mather, Tamsin Adventures in Volcanoland: What Volcanoes Tell Us About the World and Ourselves Hanover Square Press 2024

Mead, Margaret Letters from the Field 1925-1975 Perennial 1977

Mithen, Steven The Singling Neanderthals: The Origins of Music, Language, Mind, and Body Harvard University Press 2006

Morris, Desmond Naked Ape Dell Publishing 1999

Morris, Desmond The Human Zoo Kodansha International 1969

Paabo, Svante Neanderthal Man: In Search of Lost Genomes Basic Books 2014

Pattison, Kermit Fossil Men William Morrow 2009

Rezendes, Paul <u>Tracking and the Art of Seeing: How to Read Animal Tracks and Sign</u> Quill: A Harper Resource Book 1999

Saenger, H. G. *Neanderthals: Unraveling the Secrets of our Ancient Relatives* 2023

Slimak, Ludovic *The Naked Neanderthal* Pegasus Books 2024

Stringer, Chris, and McSahn, Robin <u>African Exodus: The Origins of Modern Humanity</u> Henry Holt and Co. NY 1996

Tattersall, Ian <u>Becoming Human: Evolution and Human Uniqueness</u> Harvest Books 1999

Thomas, Elizabeth Marshall, <u>The Old Way: A Story of the First People</u> Sarah Crichton Books 2008

Tudge Colin <u>Time Before History</u> Touchstone Books 1996

U.S. Army Survival Handbook

Vogel, Shawna <u>Naked Earth: The New Geophysics</u> Dutton 1995

Vygotsky, Lev <u>The Connection Between Thought and the Development of Language in Primitive Society</u> 1930

Walker, Alan and Shipman, Pat <u>Wisdom of the Bones: In Search of Human Origins</u> Vintage Books 1996

Wills, Christopher <u>Runaway Brain: The Evolution of Human Uniqueness</u> Basic Books 1993

Wragg Sykes, Rebecca <u>Kindred: Neanderthal Life, Love, Death and Art</u> Bloomsbury Sigma 2020

About the Author

You can reach Jacqui Murray on her **blog**:
https://worddreams.wordpress.com

X:
https://twitter.com/WordDreams

LinkedIn:
https://www.linkedin.com/in/jacquimurray

Instagram
https://www.instagram.com/jacquimurraywriter/

Newsletter
https://jacqui-murray.aweb.page/p/46e8c9bf-eaed-4252-8aad-3688e233a4cc

Reader's Workshop Questions

Setting

- Why did Neanderthals occupy such a wide swath of geography—from Europe to Asia?
- Did Neanderthals have a preference for climate type—cold (like Siberia) or warm (like Gibraltar)?

Themes

- Discuss how Neanderthals respect animals. Why? Was it in part because they didn't know animals weren't smart and clever like our species is (or we think we are)?
- Why did Neanderthals survive for so long despite their constant migrations, small group size, and lack of the advanced innovations used by *Homo sapiens*?
- What inventions were part of Neanderthal heritage, such as cooking, sewing clothing, glue, medical treatments, and creation of fire (not just the use of fire)?
- Did it surprise you to learn that Neanderthals treated their kindred empathetically, as humans do? That they cared for those chronically ill?
- Neanderthals are believed to have left geometric symbols in caves throughout Europe that could indicate an effort at communication. What are your thoughts on that?
- We know Neanderthals were replaced by the more-advanced *Homo sapiens*. What characteristics and traits in this story help explain why?

Character Realism

- The Neanderthal are presented with many characteristics identifiable in today's hunter-gatherers. Your thoughts on that?
- Neanderthals were nomadic, unlike most hunter-gatherer tribes today. If you are familiar with nomadic civilizations, what similarities/differences do you see between them?
- The start of spiritualism in man is oft-discussed. Shamanism is believed to have begun around 100,000 years ago. What do you

think of the spiritual behavior found in this story? How about what isn't found?

- There is mixed evidence of religion, art, and music in artifacts from Neanderthals and early *Homo sapiens*. Do you think they appreciated these?

Character Choices

- What moral/ethical choices did the characters in this book make regarding animals and their treatment?
- Discuss how Yu'ung's and Fierce's kind raised children. Do other of today's primitive tribes handle families this way?
- Discuss the Neanderthal attitude toward ownership of belongings?

Construction

- Discuss the different approaches to managing a tribe evidenced by Neanderthals and the Tall Ones (*Homo sapiens*). One followed authoritarian leadership, the other groupthink. What other animals display either? Do you see them in other geopolitical cultures around the world?
- Scientists disagree over how or whether Neanderthals could speak, or whether they relied primarily on body language, gestures, facial expressions, as well as the rare vocalization. What are your thoughts on this?
- Discuss how Neanderthals described quantities (such as "Sun traveled a hand" or "as many as fit under the tree by homebase").
- How did Neanderthals explain the moon disappearing and reappearing time and again? Do their observations make sense to you?

Reactions to the Book

- Did the book lead you to a new awareness of how man evolved into who we are today? Did it help you understand something in your life that you didn't before, maybe seemed a "gut feeling" or instinctual?
- Did the book fulfill your expectations?

Other Questions

- What do you think will happen to the characters? Would you like to see a sequel to this trilogy?
- Discuss books you've read with a similar theme or set in a prehistoric time.